Another Precious Minute

J.D. GUICE

Another Precious Minute
Copyright © 2024 by J.D. Guice

Cover design by Keith Robinson

Dragonfire Press

Print ISBN: 978-1-958354-58-2

First Edition: 2024

DEDICATION

To my granddaughter, Marlee.

Your initial challenge brought me to the result–this book!

To my friend, Kathy. The first to read my final draft.

To everyone who reads this book whether you liked it or not, I'm honored that you read it. Thank you.

ACKNOWLEDGMENTS

First, to my beautiful granddaughter, Marlee:

Without you, and your initial challenge to write a book, this one would not have been written. Thank you for your encouragement and reassurance that I could do it. Thank you for all our late-night discussions, your insight, and your patience as I read part after part to you just to 'See if it sounds okay.'

Second, to my friend Kathy:

Thank you, my friend, for being the first person to read my final draft from beginning to end. For you to take the time to read my book simply because I asked you to means the world to me. Thank you for your praises, honest critique, and suggestions on how to improve the story. You're a true romantic!

Finally, to my publisher:

A huge thank you to Richard Fierce and Dragonfire Press for offering to mentor me in self-publishing and, ultimately, taking me on as a client. This book, most likely, would not have been published without you, Richard. I am forever grateful for the opportunity you have given me. Never would I have dreamed of working with an established author like you. I can never thank you enough.

PROLOGUE

15 Hours 2 Minutes

Wednesday, November 30
1:34 a.m.

My mind skips from thought to thought, replaying each moment of the day. I can't stop the images from creeping into my head when I close my eyes. Every detail of her face is vivid, reflecting each emotion she experienced during those moments. I see the fear in her eyes when he placed the rag over her nose and mouth, and she realized what was happening. From the moment she lost consciousness until the second he slammed the trunk, her body twisted on the carpeted floor—I see it all.

In my mind's eye, her face becomes his, their features twisting, merging into a nightmarish ripple. As he lifted her limp body into the trunk, fear and sadness filled his icy blue eyes, not hate and anger.

I tried to stop him from taking her, but he was too strong. I still feel the pressure of his hands on my shoulders, shoving me backward. In my dreamlike memory, I watch myself fall in slow motion, my head smashing a frozen mixture of sleet and snow on the pavement. I hear the ice pop and a hard pain explodes through my skull. Slowly losing consciousness, everything fades to black.

Since I witnessed the kidnapping yesterday morning, the two faces haunt my thoughts. The images won't leave me alone, not for a second.

Sitting on the window seat, I stretch out my legs. A shiver weaves through my body, so I wrap the blanket next to me around my arms and tuck my legs underneath.

Gazing into the dark, dreary Boston sky, I'm mesmerized by the soothing sounds surrounding me. The enchanting violin solo, *Ashokan Farewell,* one of my favorite pieces, is playing low. The rhythmic clink of the frozen rain battering the windowpane accompanies the violinist.

Seeming to get louder and louder, the clock above the mantel in the adjoining room drowns out the sound of the clinking rain.

The clock is ticking, *tick,* ticking, and with each *tick,* another precious minute goes by.

I've always heard the first forty-eight hours are the most critical. If it's true—she's running out of time.

CHAPTER 1

24 Hours 17 Minutes

Wednesday 10:39 a.m.

Like most interrogation rooms, this one is small, furnished with only a simple wooden desk and three somewhat padded chairs. A computer screen stares at me as I sit at the desk. It's hard to imagine how many others have been in this room doing the same thing I'm doing—searching for one particular face in an ocean of thousands.

With the push of a button, a photo flips past, then another, until the faces become a blur, a sea of images on a screen. So far this morning, I've viewed several hundred photos, and none resemble the kidnapper or victim.

Did I even see the man's face as clearly as I thought? Even though we were within inches of each other, am I sure what he looked like? Is it possible that I misinterpreted what was happening? I know he put a cloth over the woman's nose and mouth and dumped her crumpled body into the trunk of the old blue car.

So, how does anyone misunderstand something like that? I laugh and dismiss the idea. Yes, I *know* what he looks like. I remember every dimple, every pimple, and every hair on his face. I'll never forget what he looks like, perhaps never.

Weary, I slide the chair back and stand. I'm exhausted from spending hours scanning faces. My body is sore from sitting so long, and I'm disgusted with the tediousness of my task. I'm tired of looking at mugshots of thieves, murderers, and other criminals. It's a waste of time. I want to *do* something—something that will help find her! But what?

Thankfully, the sketch artist, Holly Sampler, captured the kidnapper's primary characteristics—his curly, dirty-blonde hair, scraggly beard, thin lips, and the small mole on his left cheek, with speed and accuracy. However, his eyes posed a problem. And no matter what shape we tried, something was off about them, so we never achieved the desired result.

Ms. Sampler compiled the sketch of the woman with little input from me. She drew the victim's long, smooth, chestnut-colored hair and sculpted facial features in a single attempt. I hope my description is accurate. I had a hard time seeing the woman when she was lying unconscious or, God forbid, dead in the trunk.

Still, it's difficult to describe one person, much less two. I only saw them for a few minutes in a tense situation. Sadly, nothing more can come from a second meeting with Ms. Sampler, but that's what I'm supposed to do this afternoon. I roll my eyes at the mere thought of discussing facial details again.

As I move around the desk, I can't suppress my yawn. After sitting so long, I stretch my arms and jiggle them to get the blood flowing. As I walk past the large window next to the door, I spot Detective Tomas Benson coming down the hall. He looks much more rested and less strained than when I met him at the hospital yesterday. The dark circles under his eyes are gone, and his face looks refreshed, no longer drawn and tired.

I didn't make a perfect first impression on him, either. At least today, I'm not lying on a hospital bed getting stitches in my head. And I'm not soaking wet from falling in a puddle of icy water, blood oozing down my head, and moaning in pain. That wasn't my finest moment. At least he'll see me cleaned up and dry in a fresh setting today. As I straighten my top, I move away from the window and wait to see if he comes in.

The detective cracks the door just wide enough to poke his head around. His lips curl to one side in a half smile as he greets me.

With several fine creases etched into the corners of his gentle light brown eyes, I'd guess the detective is in his late forties to mid-fifties. He stands about five-eleven to six feet tall and towers over my petite frame. He's a handsome man with a kind of magnetic appeal. The transition of his short, well-trimmed, dark mustache into his gray-flecked beard softens his facial features. His collar-length, salt-and-pepper hair lies in soft waves, giving him a younger, more stylish look than most men his age.

The black Patagonia winter jacket he's wearing is a perfect fit over his simple brown knit henley, defining his athletic build. I can see myself being attracted to him—if he were a little younger. I blush at the idea and grin.

"Morning, Miss Preston. You've been at it for quite a while. After this long, I bet you need a break. Why don't we get some fresh air."

Before I can object, Detective Benson picks up my dark blue wool coat from the back of the chair, guides my arms through the sleeves, and then leads me from the room.

Using his hand on my back to direct me, the detective leads me through the narrow corridor past several detectives who nod. He continues to the central area of the police station where most officers work. Directing my attention to specific officers, Detective Benson calls them by name and tells me about their areas of expertise. Now and then, some officers stop what they're doing, raise their heads, and acknowledge us as we walk past.

At one point, I spot the two officers who came to the hospital yesterday, the pricks who all but mocked me. They nod at Detective Benson, Cheshire cat smiles plastered on their faces. The detective tips his head in response, his eyes unblinking, his jaw rigid.

After we pass, the detective mumbles to himself, "Pricks."

I look up at him and smile, thankful he's the one working on this case.

As we walk through the central area, I feel self-conscious, like everyone is looking at me, so I avoid eye contact with most of the officers. I can't help but wonder if they presume I'm leading them down a blind alley the way the first two I spoke with yesterday did. But no matter what they think, I can't let my speculation about their thoughts intimidate me.

So, I hold my head high and plop my warm, fur-lined bucket hat atop my honey-brown hair. I wrap my burgundy wool scarf around my neck and tuck the ends inside my coat as we near the exit. My feet scurry, working to keep pace with the detective's long stride.

"There's a cafe down the block, on the corner. It's a nice little place to sit and relax for a bit. It's just a short walk if you're up to it," he suggests. He pulls a wool scally cap from an inside pocket and places it on his head before we step onto the snow-shoveled sidewalk.

The detective's accent is apparent but not overpowering, and I can't help but grin. Although I've lived in Boston for almost three years, I'm still intrigued by an authentic Bostonian dialect.

Detective Benson was the first officer to accept what I said to be true yesterday. He sat down with me and listened to my account of the kidnapping. He doesn't seem to see me as some strange, neurotic person making up a wild story for attention.

Even though I've just met him, Detective Benson appears to be an excellent detective. He's been helpful and kind. I feel comfortable—safe—when I'm around him. Despite being direct and assertive, he doesn't come across as intimidating.

The first officers I spoke with yesterday, Detective Brandy and Detective Gallion, are the detectives I spotted at the station house. They suggested I got the gash on my head from an accidental slip on the icy pavement—accidental, meaning I was in a hurry and ignorant of the weather hazards. When I told them a man kidnapping a woman shoved me backward, they shook their heads and grinned at each other. They treated me like some hysterical woman with a giant imagination.

All cocky and condescending, those officers were so full of

themselves. What made them assume I imagined the whole thing while I was unconscious? Both tried to conceal their giggles, but their rudeness was apparent. The detectives said a woman my size, in her right mind, wouldn't try to stop a big man from abducting someone. They made it plain they didn't buy my story, and having to make out a police report annoyed them even more. They even made me sound deranged in the written document. No wonder people don't report crimes. Who wants to deal with assholes like them?

When I recall the kidnapping, I realize how dangerous my actions were. Confronting that guy wasn't the most brilliant move I've ever made, that's for sure. But I've always been the one to defend the underdog, even when I was a kid. I can't count the number of times in grammar school I got my butt kicked by bullies when I tried to stop them from picking on other kids. Despite being small, like the ones they bullied, I didn't just stand by and watch.

And again yesterday, I tried to help the underdog—the woman. Since no one was around but me, I had to help. My only regret is not getting the tag number, but I couldn't do that lying unconscious on the ground. If I had thought about it, I could have gotten it before I rushed in the way I did. When I saw the man behind the woman, his hand over her mouth and her struggling to get it off, my reactions kicked in. I didn't think about what might be the best thing to do. I had no time to think, only act. It all happened so fast!

Detective Benson said I was lucky the man didn't take me too, that he just slung me to the ground instead of pushing me into the trunk. As I swipe my hand across the back of my head and touch the line of stitches through the bandage, a twinge of pain shoots through my scalp. It seems the detective was right. I was lucky that my only injuries were a small gash and a sore head. If the man had thrown me in with that woman, I'd be wherever she is, if not dead.

Even now, the fear I saw on the woman's face haunts me. I sense her fate lies in *my* hands, my finding the one person I've spent hours searching for. The one image I can't erase from my mind.

The kidnapper's face.

CHAPTER 2

24 Hours 32 Minutes

Wednesday 10:54 a.m.

When we arrive at B. J.'s Corner Brew, I notice the cafe has a distinct coffeehouse vibe with a free-spirited, boho-style decor. Lots of booths and tables are available for patrons to sit at. The bright patterned tablecloths draping the tables mix well with the gold, earth-tone sofas and soft chairs scattered about. Macrame wall hangings and art of different cultures add decorative character to the walls.

The fragrant aroma of brewed coffee and fresh-baked pastries drifting through the air arouses my senses. A subtle hint of incense mixes with the other aromatic fragrances, likely lingering from the evening crowd. It's the sort of place you'd expect to find in South Boston, not downtown.

Detective Benson selects a booth in the back, away from the crowd. After he takes my coat and drapes it over the back of the seat, he scoots into the booth opposite me as I remove my hat and gloves.

I have to say he chose well. This cafe is perfect for unwinding after a tough day. The atmosphere is very relaxed and cozy. Maybe I'll bring Nick one evening. It might be fun to listen to some singers and poets while sipping a warm drink with him. We've had little time together since he travels so much. We didn't even get Thanksgiving Day together, just a fifteen-minute video call.

Nick's gone a lot now that he's the project manager of excavation sites. All his assignments are for extended periods in other states or other countries. It's hard dating an archeologist since they're constantly moving from one dig to another. At least, that's been my experience. Our only contact in the past eight months has been phone calls and a rare visit home.

We were very close when we first started seeing each other. Nick wasn't gone as much, and we reveled in each other's company. Sighing, I fiddle with the bracelet he gave me. I know I have to accept that things have changed. Even though I wish he were here with me, that may not be what he wants now. Nick's job is important to him, and I understand. It just seems like I'm not anymore.

"Any special coffee you'd like, Miss Preston?" The detective slips off his jacket and lays his hat on his gloves next to him.

Lost in my thoughts, I only hear part of the detective's question. I'm surprised to see the server, a dark-haired, attractive woman in her thirties sporting tight jeans and a lavender turtleneck, standing beside the table. I didn't notice her when she walked up.

"Um, I'll have a latte—extra espresso, please."

"And you, detective?" Gazing into Detective Benson's eyes, she moistens her lips, licking them with her tongue. Acting as though she can't hear over the noise, she inches a little closer to him, leans down, and all but kisses him as she takes his order.

Judging by the way he's squirming, there's no doubt the server, Lisa, by her name tag, made an indelible impression on the detective. Enthralled by the flirtatious behavior, I watch for his response, and, as I expect, he grins and gives her a wink. This silver-haired gentleman is turning out to be quite the lady's man.

"I'll just have black coffee today, Lisa. No frills."

I wonder if this is a regular flirtation or a concealed romance. Not my business, though. Exhausted and depressed, I look down at my hands folded on the table and get lost in the intricate pattern on the tablecloth.

Detective Benson notices the solemn look on my face. "I bet you haven't had a bite to eat today. Would you like a sandwich or a cup of chowder?"

Searching the menu, I find nothing appetizing. I shake my head and mumble, "No, thank you. I don't think I could eat a bite."

Ignoring what I say, the detective glances at Lisa. "How 'bout bringing us two of your lunch chowders?"

"You got it." Lisa jots the order on the pad. "Be right back." She smiles and walks away, hips swaying.

As she moves out of view, the detective looks at me across the table. His face softens as though he's gazing at a wounded kitten. Compassionately, he lays a single hand on mine, pats it, and smiles.

"It'll be alright, ya know." His voice is soft and low, almost a whisper.

Although I want to cry, I force a tight-lipped smile and hold my tears inside. I'm an emotional wreck. Maybe it's because I banged my head on the ice or the trauma of the kidnapper overpowering me yesterday. It's made me feel weak. Perhaps it's because I'm also a victim, just not in the same way as the woman. I'm not a 'needy' person. Most of the time, I can handle anything thrown at me. But right now, I feel so fragile, so alone. And I am—except for the detective.

My parents are planning to fly up from Jacksonville on Saturday. They're concerned about my well-being. I'm hoping the police will find the woman before they get on the plane, so maybe they won't come. I'm just not up to the whole family thing right now. As much as I love them, it'll make it harder on me if they come. All the crying and pressure to act like I'm fine in front of them is more than I'm up for. I can get through these feelings, even if I do it alone—it'll just take me a little time.

My friends would be there for me, but I don't want them to worry, so I haven't called or returned their calls. Divorced with two children, Mickie has her hands full, and I wouldn't want to burden her with my problems. Alana and I have been friends since we started working together two years ago. I could call her, but I don't want anyone at work involved in my private business. She's trustworthy, but you never know when something might slip, not that the people at work won't find out eventually.

And there's Galvin—my very best friend. Last year, he became the concertmaster when he moved to the first violinist chair with the symphony. He's such a skilled musician and a wonderful person. He brings beautiful music to my life, not only with the music he plays but with his gentle soul. We've known each other since college and have shared many fun times and long conversations over the years. Right now, he spends most of his time at the symphony. I don't want to get him involved in something like this.

I always assume the role of comforter and protector, especially with my family and friends. And, judging by my reaction to the kidnapping, with strangers on the street, too. Sometimes, I just want someone to care for me and be my protector, but I'm not sure I can let my guard down long enough for that to happen.

If only I were more like Nick. He's an adventurer, out to see the world. His focus is on himself, his wants, and his needs. Having fun and being spontaneous can be exciting, but I can't just think about what I want all the time. Nick's selfish and not as compassionate as I would like. He's fun to be with, but I wouldn't want to spend my life with someone like him.

I don't want to see other countries the way Nick does. Dad was in the military and was stationed all over the world. We moved a lot when I was growing up, about every couple of years. The longest we stayed in one spot was four years in Hawaii. I loved it there. Maybe I should go back to Honolulu and set up my practice. I'm not sure I want to stay in Boston anymore, not after this.

Detective Benson sits, arms folded on the table, watching me, studying me, not saying a word. Lost in my thoughts, I notice the detective seems lost in his, too. However, judging by his intense gaze, I'm his subject. I wonder what he's thinking? We're both drawn back to the present as Lisa places our order on the table.

"Just let me know if you need anything else," she says, smiling at the detective.

"This is perfect, Lisa. Thanks," the detective replies. When she walks away, his eyes follow her across the room until she disappears into the kitchen.

Only then does he return his attention to me.

Detective Benson prepares his chowder, filling it with crackers and pepper, glancing up at me every few minutes. He blows on his chowder to cool it, then, eyeing me, takes his first bite.

"How you feelin' today, Miss Preston? How's your head?" he asks between spoonfuls.

"It's a little sore. Guess I'm not as hard-headed as people think." I chuckle, knowing how cliche it sounds. After stirring my chowder, I take a small bite. My brows squinch as I think about the kidnapping I witnessed. "I'm just afraid for that woman. I don't think I've been much help in finding her."

Pushing the chowder out of his way, the detective leans forward in his seat and props his folded arms on the table. "Miss Preston… Ivy, it's been over twenty-four hours, and so far, no one has reported a woman missing. Normally, someone would have discovered the person was gone by now and contacted the police."

My mind races, jumping from thought to thought, trying to grasp his implication. Does he doubt me, too? The one person I thought was on my side.

Shaking my head, confused, I ask, "What does that mean? That the woman's just hanging out somewhere with the guy who took her? That she's not missing? I know what I saw!"

"No, no, not at all! I don't doubt you saw someone kidnapped." Detective Benson takes a deep breath, leans back in his seat, and presses his lips together. Hesitating, he chooses his words carefully. "It's just that… without a victim, we can't put someone's face on the news and call him a suspected kidnapper. Not yet, anyway," he says, shrugging his shoulders.

What the detective says makes sense. He sounds like he still believes me, but I'm not sure. I breathe through pursed lips and try to calm my thoughts. I have so many questions flying through my mind.

"So, what happens now? The FBI gets involved in kidnapping cases, right? What do they think? Are they working on the case yet? Why haven't they interviewed me?" Launching an avalanche of questions, I give the detective no time to answer.

Despite all my quizzing, Detective Benson remains calm and unshaken. He takes his last bite of chowder and leans back. "Well," he replies, dabbing his napkin to his mouth. "I spoke with the FBI, but with no report of a missing person yet, that makes it a little more complicated." He squints his eyes and uses his hand, demonstrating 'a little' with his fingers.

My shoulders drop as my spirit falls, and I stare at the pattern on the table. I'm so disheartened and frustrated, almost to the point of giving up. But I can't give up, and I know it. A woman's life is at stake, and as far as I know, I'm the only one who saw her get taken.

Noticing how upset I am, the detective leans over the table. "Finding missing people is my area of expertise, you know. I'm no rookie." He smiles. "But the FBI is available to us should we need them."

Detective Benson pauses, allowing me time to process all he's saying. He relaxes, resting his arms on the table, and tilts his head. "I thought we might go back to the alley where you saw the kidnapping, just to see if something else might come to you." The detective leans back against the booth, watching me closely.

The thought of returning to that place and reliving the event makes my stomach flip. I toss the idea around in my head for a few minutes while I finish my coffee.

"When did you want to go? I have an appointment with Holly Sampler at two."

The detective rubs his chin, mulling over the options. "I'll let Holly know you'll be late. I think it's more important that we get back to the scene before much more time goes by while things are still kinda fresh in your mind."

Hesitating, I agree. "Okay, we can go back there, but I'm not sure it'll help. I told you everything I saw. I don't know what good it'll do." I push the half-eaten bowl of chowder away. Eating is the last thing on my mind.

"Well," he says, getting up from the booth. "You just never know what little detail might pop into your head when you return to the crime scene."

Detective Benson smiles as he downs his last bit of coffee and places a twenty on the table for the meal and another ten for Lisa.

CHAPTER 3

26 Hours 16 Minutes

Wednesday 12:38 p.m.

As we leave the coffee shop, a gust of harsh wind stings my face, sending a tingling sensation through my body. The feeling unnerves me for a second. I have a vague sense that something unpleasant is about to happen.

The detective changes his position, using his body to help block the wind off me. It's comforting to know he's trying to protect me, even if it's just from the wind.

We take the detective's black Dodge Charger to the Crestview Shopping Center in Monroe, a few miles southwest of Boston. He pulls the unmarked car into a parking space to the far side of Raymond's Shoes and Geordies, a high-end women's fashion shop.

Yellow crime scene tape outlines the investigation area in the alley between the two buildings. Two uniformed officers and one other man walk about inside the taped area, talking and pointing at different things. The snow and ice remain frozen in large patches on the pavement. The scene makes me uneasy.

Detective Benson unlatches his seat belt and looks around. "So, is this about where you parked yesterday?"

"I was where the green car is," I state, pointing to a spot two lanes to the left. "I picked up a birthday gift at Geordies for one of my friends, then cut across the parking lot in front of the alley, heading back to my car."

"Let's head that way. We should recreate your exact steps as best we can to jog any memory hiding in that pretty little head." He smiles, opens his door, and gets out. The hard ice crunches under his boots with every step he takes. It reminds me of the sound the kidnapper's boots made as he walked away before I lost consciousness.

As the detective opens my car door, I lift myself from the seat. Standing beside the car, all the sounds around me blend with the roar in my ears. My stomach rolls like an ocean tide, and I feel lightheaded. The detective grabs my arm to help steady me, and I sink back into the seat to keep from falling.

"Are you okay, Ivy?" he asks, easing me back into the car. He squats beside the open door. "Do you need something to drink?"

The sick feeling in my head fades as quickly as it came. "I'm okay now," I say. "I think I stood up too fast, but I feel better. Give me a few minutes to sit here, and I'll be fine."

"Has this happened before? Have you ever fainted or fallen without warning or anything like that?"

Baffled, I cock my head to one side, glaring at the detective. Oh, I see where his mind is going. He's wondering if I could have had a spell like this yesterday when I fell and hit my head. Damn, that makes me mad! Is anyone going to believe me and start looking for that woman? The *police* are wasting time.

Taking a few deep breaths, I ignore Detective Benson's question and lift myself out of the car. "I'm good now," I state. "It may have been the coffee I had—a caffeine rush. I got extra espresso." Flipping my scarf around my neck, I stare at the detective. "I'm ready. Let's go."

I sprint toward Geordies with the detective trailing behind. He knows he ticked me off, even if he doesn't know how.

"Okay, okay, slow down a sec!" he yells, hustling to catch up. "I didn't know short legs could move so fast!" He's joking, but I ignore him.

"If we're going to solve this crime, Ivy, we have to talk to each other." Catching up with me, he shoves his hands in his pockets and lowers his head like a meek puppy. "I'm sorry if I upset you. I was only concerned about your health."

He didn't intend to offend me, and I realize it, so I slow down. "It's okay. I'm a little sensitive today." I brush my hand across my forehead, push a loose strand of hair out of my eyes, and huff.

"Honestly, I saw a woman getting abducted, and I got shoved to the ground the way I said. I didn't just fall because I got dizzy."

Detective Benson leaps in front of me and places both hands on my shoulders to stop my forward motion. His brows arch, and he tilts his head, looking deep into my eyes. "Wait a sec. You need to understand one thing. I'm *not* your enemy, Ivy. I'm on your side."

I shift my eyes from his and look at the ground to break his deep gaze, but he moves his head to maintain eye contact. "Ya gotta understand," he insists, lifting my chin. "I believe everything you said happened. What you saw, you saw. I need your help to find that woman," he pleads. "Are ya with me on this or not?" His eyes, unblinking, are locked on mine.

Realizing he only wants to help, I see now that I made assumptions about what the detective was thinking when I didn't know his intent. That's not something I normally do. I'm off my game today. This kidnapping is getting to me.

"I'm so sorry, Detective Benson." I look down at the ground. "I'm just…"

"It's okay, Ivy," he interrupts. "I can't imagine how stressed you are. I understand, and it's okay." Detective Benson eases his grip on my shoulders. "You're not alone in this. I'm here with you. I'm going to get you through this, and I'm not gonna stop trying to find the woman you saw."

Taking a deep breath, I lift my shoulders and shake my head. "I'm truly sorry," I say once more.

"It's okay." He smiles. "I swear, it's okay." He scans the parking lot and then looks toward the alley. "Ok, so which way did you go?" he asks, directing our attention back to our purpose for being here.

"I left the store and was going back to my car." I point toward the parking spaces just beyond the alley. The alley is a small driveway between the buildings, barely wide enough for delivery trucks to drive through when they unload merchandise and supplies on the docks behind the shops.

The detective and I walk toward the officers standing inside the yellow tape. "Tell me at what point you first noticed the man and woman or the car," he says.

We reach the edge of Geordies, where the sidewalk slopes down. I stop and look toward the alley.

"Here, this is where I was." I point to a spot about halfway down the area. "I noticed some commotion from the corner of my eye, turned to look, and saw two people: a man, and a woman." I pause, gazing down the alley. "The man was behind the woman, and he reached up and held a piece of cloth or rag over her face. She struggled as he pushed her toward the car." Tears cloud my vision.

"It's okay, Ivy. Take your time." Detective Benson hands me a white handkerchief.

Dabbing my eyes with the soft cloth, I notice it smells just like the detective, fresh, not perfumy. I didn't know people still carried handkerchiefs. Hmm… interesting. He's quite a gentleman.

I picked up on that trait at the police station and again at the cafe when he helped me with my coat and held the doors for me to exit. He even opened the car door for me. You don't find men like that anymore. I guess chivalry isn't dead after all, at least in his generation.

"What'd you do next?"

"I yelled at the man and asked what he was doing. Then I dropped my bags and started running toward them, yelling and screaming at him. There wasn't much else I could do." I turn toward the detective. "She was clearly in trouble. He shoved her into the trunk and slammed it shut. The car was blue and… it was an old Plymouth. I don't know the model. He was blonde…"

My thoughts jumble. Everything is so vivid in my mind. It's as if it's happening all over again.

"Ivy?" Detective Benson touches my arm gently, pulling me from my thoughts. "What happened then?"

Regaining my composure, I wipe my gloved hand across my face, attempting to clear the dampness from my eyes.

"I got there just before the man closed the trunk. I saw the woman lying inside, just shoved in, sprawled out and not moving." Moving my hands, I describe how she looked. "Her body was twisted, stretching her neck into an odd position." I shake my head, grimacing. "I couldn't tell if she was even breathing."

My voice cracks. More tears puddle in my eyes. "The man was right in front of me. We were face to face!" I exclaim, placing my hand in front of my nose.

My breathing becomes more rapid. My throat tightens, and I struggle for air. Every moment of yesterday rushes into my mind like a tidal wave. Even now, my screams echo in my ears. The image of the woman in the trunk, the man's face, and every detail, every microsecond of my falling—all of it—replays in my mind.

"He grabbed me by the shoulders and pushed me backward." I take a moment and close my eyes, trying to control my emotions.

"I grabbed the kidnapper, trying to keep from falling. He grabbed the front of my jacket, pulled me up against him, and… said something, then pushed me off. That's when I fell, and my head hit the ground."

My chin quivers, and the tears moistening my eyes flow down my face with each blink.

"My mind is blank after that," I mumble.

Looking up at the detective, I realize it's not just tears wetting my face. Snow is peppering down, coating everything around us with another thin sheet of white, a sheet that will thicken and eventually turn to ice. It's been a hard, cold month, and winter is just beginning.

A gust of wind blows hard against us, forcing our bodies to stiffen and shift to keep our balance. The detective reaches out to help steady me, then glances around the shopping center. The tiny white flakes pour down like rain, and the wind gathers debris from the parking lot, swirling it through the air.

"That's enough for now." Detective Benson guides me toward the side of the building, hoping to block most of the wind whipping in from the northeast.

"I don't know why I'm so emotional. I defend people for crimes like this, many even more horrific, and I've never gotten this upset," I tell him as we walk.

"You've never been a witness to a crime before, Ivy, never directly involved." He looks down at me, his arm around my shoulder to brace me from the powerful gusts of wind. "It's a lot easier when you're on the outside looking in than when you're actively involved in a crime taking place. Trust me, I know."

It sounds like the detective has been in a similar position. Given his line of work, I'm sure he's been in many dangerous situations.

"We'll talk more about what else you remember later. Right now, you stay here. I'm gonna talk to the investigation team for a minute to see if they've found anything. I'll be right back, and we'll get out of this nasty weather."

I nod, my teeth chattering as the frigid wind whips the tiny snowflakes across the alley. I'm so ready to go. I stand, leaning against the wall with my hands in my pockets, somewhat protected from the snow by the building and the roof's overhang.

Detective Benson adjusts his jacket collar to cover his neck and shoves his gloved hands in his pockets. He walks toward a tall, dark-haired man holding a small bag, and they begin to talk.

Unable to hear what they're saying, I review the kidnapping in my mind, trying to recall every detail I can, anything unusual about the man, what the woman was wearing. Any piece of information I can remember, but it's no use. My mind's as frozen as the snow on the ground, so I give up and wait for the detective to return.

I glance around the parking lot. Dozens of people are moving about, some leaving their cars, others putting bags in their trunks, and several entering and exiting the various stores. Most take notice of the yellow taped area and the officers walking about, watch for a moment, and go on about their business.

My eyes wander from the people and their routine activities to the cars in the parking lot. Some are pulled into the parking spaces at funky angles, not lining up in the margins. A dark gold Honda takes up two parking spots, and some SUVs are sitting sideways under the trees near the road. A dark gray Ford Explorer is backed into a space under a tree near the road, directly facing the alley. The driver is sitting behind the steering wheel, wipers flapping. He must be waiting for someone. Since I can't see him very well through the heavy snow, I look back at the agents investigating the scene.

Leaning against the side of the wall, I wonder why the woman was this far down in the alley. There are no doors on the sides of the buildings; no reason anyone would park behind the stores that I can think of. The man could have lured her into the alley, called to her, or attracted her somehow. I don't know. It's strange.

As I glance back at the detective, I hear a loud cracking noise above me. It sounds like the overhang is breaking, so I take a few steps away from the building and look up. Almost instantly, my feet fly off the ground without warning, and I feel weightless, suspended above the icy, snow-covered pavement.

The moment is surreal as crystal white snowflakes slowly dance around my head, brushing my face as they drift by. I feel like I'm floating, frozen in time. If only this moment could last forever! I feel light as a feather, so free, so peaceful—but only for a moment.

BAM!

My body crashes like a boulder onto the hard, cold ground. My head bounces twice before resting in a frozen puddle of sleet and snow. I hear the ice crack beneath my skull, and a dull pain shoots through my head. As hard as I try, I cannot keep my eyes from closing. All sounds fade away.

I lie alone—cold and still, on the hard snow-covered pavement for the second time in two days.

CHAPTER 4

28 Hours 52 Minutes

Wednesday 3:14 p.m.

"Ivy! Ivy!" A faint voice pierces the quietness. "Ivy! Can you hear me? Wake up!"

The voice grows a little more defined, a little closer. There's a high-pitched, shrill sound far away. It's getting louder. My eyes are closed, but I sense someone near my face. Distant voices are becoming more distinct.

"Ivy, wake up. Please, wake up," the voice begs. I know his voice. "Ivy, open your eyes, please, open your eyes."

Someone's stroking my forehead. I open my eyes just a sliver, then press them closed. The light is so bright. I squint and blink multiple times. A few minutes pass, and I open my eyes again, just long enough to see an image near my face. It's a person, but their face is blurry.

"Open your eyes, Ivy. Look at me. It's Detective Benson. Please open your eyes."

My lids feel so heavy, but I force them open again. Through small slits, I see brown eyes close to my face, gazing at me. The man's silver hair falls forward, the waves framing his face. He smiles.

Magically, the face morphs into the image of a man with curly blonde hair; his eyes are no longer soft and brown but small and icy blue. Tears encircle the blue, but he holds them back, drops his chin, and looks away.

A second later, lifting his head, he stares into my eyes, leans forward, and whispers next to my ear. What? What is he saying? The words make no sense.

"It's not what you think," he mutters quickly. "She made me."

I feel like I know this person, but… who is he? I don't understand. His voice is raspy, quavering; his breathing rapid and shallow. The blue-eyed man vanishes as quickly as he appeared, vaporizing into the white-powdered sky.

"Ivy," the soft voice says again. "I'm right here. The ambulance is here. We're going to the hospital."

Opening my eyes a little more, I see Detective Benson kneeling beside me and realize I'm lying flat on the ground, cold and wet. The detective's jacket lies over me, its color changing from black to white as the falling snowflakes collect on it. A man with a green hat moves closer, and the white haze of the sky changes to bright blue when he places his umbrella above my upper body, shielding me from the cold snow showering down from the sky.

Faces gather all around, each one looking down at me. Some are fuzzy and contorted, moving in and out. The people close to me look huge, and the ones far away are tiny, like cartoon characters. Am I in a fun house or on some kind of drug? Nothing seems real.

I notice a man at the back of the crowd. He looks familiar—the man with icy blue eyes and a scraggly beard. His eyes dart around like he's uncomfortable, his movements nervous, jumpy. He's the same guy who was talking to me a minute ago, whispering in my ear.

Raising my arm, I tell the detective, "Look," and point to the man, but I can't get my words out fast enough. The man glances around as he backs up and disappears into the crowd.

"Are we at the carnival?" I ask, confused by the illusions and my impaired perception.

The detective smiles a sigh of relief that I'm awake. "No, kid, we're not at the carnival. You fell and hit your head again. The ambulance is here. We're going to the hospital."

I'm unsure what he's talking about, but I know he's caring for me. My attempt to smile at the detective is more of a wince in response to the pain in my head. I hope the detective understands. He's so sweet; it's a shame he's so old.

The EMTs place me on the stretcher and lift me into the ambulance. The detective climbs in with me. My eyes open just enough to see the commotion all around, then close as I focus on Detective Benson's comforting words, "I'm here, kid. You'll be okay. I'm here with you. I'm not going anywhere."

CHAPTER 5

29 Hours 20 Minutes

Wednesday 3:42 p.m.

Strapped down on my back, everything around me moves quickly. The lights flash like I'm on a train looking out the window. My head is spinning, and my eyes won't stay open for more than a second or two. Leaning my head to the right, my stomach spasms, and I vomit all over myself and the floor. A few minutes later, I drift off once more into nothingness.

* * *

The rhythmic pounding around me is terrifying. I open my eyes and see gray, curved walls inches from my face. What is that noise? It sounds like I'm in a jet engine. I try to turn my head, but it won't move. I try to raise my arms, but they won't move either. It feels like everything is pressing in on me. My head feels like it will explode, and my breathing becomes rapid and shallow. Attempting to scream, I open my mouth, but nothing comes out. My eyelids are so heavy they won't stay open.

* * *

The same soft voice calls again. "Ivy, wake up. It's time to wake up."

Squinching my eyes, I force them open. Detective Benson is sitting next to me, holding my hand. My vision is still blurry, but I can see it's him. The jet noise is gone. The room is silent except for the intermittent sounds from the surrounding machines. I shift just a little. I can move my head and arms now. A bag of liquid hangs from an infusion pump and drips through an IV tube leading to my hand. The IV line hinders my movement. I know I'm in a hospital, but I don't know why.

I look at the detective. "Hey." My words seep out just above a whisper.

"Hey there, I've been worried about you." Detective Benson emphasizes his concern by squeezing my hand and smiling. "The doctor says you'll be fine, good as new, in a couple of days."

Squirming, I try to push myself up to get out of bed.

"Whoa there, missy! Not so fast," he cautions, gently guiding my shoulders back down onto the pillows. "You're not quite ready to take off just yet, kid. The ice you fell on was a little harder than your head." He chuckles. "Let's slow down a bit before we have another bashed head to deal with."

Following the detective's directions, I lay back. My head throbs as though it has a heartbeat of its own. A loud roaring is in my ears like I'm standing under a waterfall. I close my eyes and hope the sounds go away.

"What happened? I don't remember."

"What do you remember, Ivy?"

"The memories I have are just fragments, pieces of a picture I can't quite put together," I mumble. "I'm not sure… I remember… it hurts too bad to think." My thoughts are all mixed up, out of order, incomplete.

The detective's forehead wrinkles as he inches closer to me. "Do you remember me, Ivy? Do you know who I am?"

Everything's out of focus, so I blink a few times and look hard at his face. Feeling giddy, I smile weakly and cup his cheek in my hand.

As I speak, my hand travels over his face, touching his mustache, pinching his cheek, and tousling his hair. "Yes, Detective Tomas Benson, I remember you. You and your cute little mustache, handsome face, and silver locks. Who could forget you?" I run my fingers through his hair and giggle like a silly schoolgirl.

The detective looks down for a second, his cheeks reddening with embarrassment. A tiny smile sneaks across his face, and his posture becomes more relaxed. I don't know why he's here with me, but I sense he's feeling better now.

"Do you remember who you are?" he asks while he adjusts my covers.

After pausing a second, I answer, "Yes, I'm Ivy Preston, Esquire, SJD, blah blah blah, at your service." I tip my head forward and lay my arm across my waist, trying to mimic a bow, then snicker.

"I see you haven't forgotten your sense of humor." A broad grin covers the detective's face. "Can you remember anything at all about today?"

My mind is empty, and my thoughts are misfiring. Why can't I remember? I try harder, and a couple of faint images fall together. It seems like something important is missing, though.

"I remember you and me in a nice little cafe. Maybe we had lunch or dinner? The smell was like cookies and incense?" I cock my head sideways and scrunch my nose. That's such a strange combination of odors. I search his face for any clue that I'm right.

He nods approval, and his eyes sparkle, reflecting the soft light above the bed. "Yes, that's right. We had lunch together today at *BJ's Corner Brew.* Do you remember what we did after that?"

Feeling like I'm in school taking a pop quiz, I clasp my hands, having got that answer right. Unfortunately, I have no other memories of lunch, but there's no way I'm telling him that. He seems pleased that I remember him and the cafe. I take my time answering his next question, reaching deep into my mind and trying to pull the memories to the top, but the answer just won't come.

"No," I say, discouraged. "I can't remember anything except waking up here with you."

"Do you remember slipping on the ice and hitting your head?"

"No... I don't remember that." I reach up to my head and feel a large bandage wrapped around it. The throbbing ache filling my head still lingers, refusing to ease.

"What about yesterday? Anything you remember about it?"

The tone of his voice has changed. It's like there's something special about yesterday. I try to remember, but the day is a blank screen, dark and empty, wiped out, as though it never happened. The rest of the week is foggy but not blank. I recall bits and pieces here and there, like talking on the phone with my mom and sitting in a boring meeting on Monday. I can't remember any details, just scattered moments in time. I struggle to piece them together, but I can't.

"I don't have any memory of yesterday, not a clue what I did. It's just a blank."

As I tell the detective my memories, my bottom lip trembles. "Everything is foggy. It's horrifying not being able to remember things, even little things like what you did, who you talked to, even what you ate," I confide. Unaware of my actions, I pick at the thumbnail on my right hand, a nervous habit I picked up in college.

The detective nods and takes my right hand between both of his. "Remember this, Ivy. I'm not gonna leave you. No, sir. Your memories will return when you can handle them, not a minute sooner. You're more important than your memories. Getting you well is the most important thing."

He pauses for a moment and looks down. I can almost swear he has a tear in his eye. "Close your eyes and rest for a few minutes. I'm gonna walk outside for a second and talk to the nurse. I'll be right back."

Detective Benson leaves, closing the exam room door behind him. I want to go home. I close my eyes and doze off to the soothing rhythm of the IV pump next to me.

After what seems like only a few minutes, I open my eyes. The detective rests in the chair next to the bed with his head propped on his hand and his eyes closed. He has to be tired if he can sleep in that position. Struggling, I get myself to a sitting position and swing my legs around so I'm on the bed's edge. The room spins a little.

In a flash, the detective appears at my bedside, scolding me. "No, no. You can't get up. The doctor will be here in a few minutes. Now, lay back down, Ivy."

Slapping my hands on the covers, I poke out my lips, tilt my head, and whine like a pouting child. "I just wanna go home."

Trying to keep from smiling, the detective seems amused at my regressed behavior. "We will. Be patient just a little longer. The nurse is getting your discharge papers ready."

The detective sits on the bed with me and explains my condition while we wait for the doctor. "You have a mild concussion. The stitches from your previous fall came loose, so the doctor restitched them. She ordered an MRI of your head to check for any structural damage to the skull, and all was clear. Dr. Sparta said it's not too serious, but you'll have to rest for a few days."

Standing, the detective adjusts the covers over me and fluffs my pillows. I can see the exhaustion in his eyes. Dark circles have formed under them, and his eyelids are puffy.

"No working or strenuous activity. The doctor said your memory might not be at a hundred percent for a while." He pauses, running his hand through his hair. "You need to do what she said so you get better. That's all that matters right now."

"Okay." I nod. "But what do you mean the second injury to my head? I thought you said I fell today?"

Sitting on the edge of the bed, Detective Benson is careful about his words. "You had a fall today," he begins, "but you also fell yesterday. That's when you first injured your head and had to have stitches. You struck your head on ice both times but didn't have a concussion until this fall. I first met you here at this hospital yesterday." He stops and waits for my response.

"That's strange. How could I fall twice like that?"

Before he can answer, the door opens, and a tall, attractive woman with blonde hair walks in. A white lab coat sits atop her green turtleneck knitted dress. Detective Benson stands and greets her, then introduces us.

"Ivy, this is Dr. Sparta. She's the doctor who's been taking care of you."

"I was the doctor working yesterday when you came in, too. You've had quite an eventful few days, Miss Preston." A tiny smile crosses her lips. Dr. Sparta moves close to the bed, holding a clipboard with some papers. "I can't say I've ever treated the same patient for the same type of injury two days in a row. You hold the record!"

She seems nice, with a pleasant bedside manner. "I'm sorry, but I don't remember you, Dr. Sparta. There's not much I can remember about yesterday or today. Would someone please explain how I fell twice like that? I'm not normally a clumsy person."

The detective looks at the doctor, and their eyes meet. They both have a funny tell on their face like there's a secret I'm unaware of.

After a moment or two, Dr. Sparta looks back at me. "We'll get to that, but first, tell me how you feel. How's your head? Do you have any dizziness or anything like that going on?"

It frustrates me that no one answered my question. Shifting so I'm sitting straight up in the bed, I touch the large bandage on my head and move my hand as I reference each area of pain.

"I have an awful headache and a roar in my ears, plus my eyes are hypersensitive to the light. I have this huge bandage on my head and, oh, yeah," I swing my hands out, palms up, "I can't remember anything that's happened in the last two days. Got some pills for any of that?" I slap my hand down on my lap and cock my head, glaring at her.

Why am I acting like this? I'm not a smartass. I'm known for having the patience of Job and the temperament of a monk! What's wrong with me?

My sarcastic attitude doesn't affect the doctor. She remains calm and composed, not taking offense. "Hmm. I'll add irritability to your list." She grins as she glances at Detective Benson, then makes a note on the papers.

"It's one of several symptoms that may occur with a concussion, along with the others you listed. You could also experience mood swings, fatigue, and getting agitated more easily. It's all in the discharge instructions in your packet. But all of this will go away over the next few weeks. The symptoms can last longer than that, but they will subside," the doctor assures me, nodding.

My behavior is not reflecting my usual self, so I tone it down and be more polite. "What about my memory?"

"It should return. You have post-traumatic amnesia caused by the stress and trauma you've experienced the past few days. There could be small pieces you might not recall, but most of your memory will return with time. I want you to follow up with your private physician in a couple of days and again in two weeks. Understand?" She looks at me above the bifocals perched on her nose.

Glancing at Detective Benson, he nods, so I nod, too.

"Return to the emergency room if you get worse or have new symptoms. I've discussed how to care for your head wound with Detective Benson. Your discharge papers include information on wound care. And I'm giving you a couple of prescriptions, one for your headache and swelling, along with something to help you relax."

"So I can go home now?"

"Yes, but with some restrictions. No driving or exercise for two weeks; you'll be out of work for a week or more. Stay in bed as much as you can for three to four days, and then only up as tolerated. Someone needs to stay with you at all times for the next week. Oh, and no alcohol or unprescribed medications unless it's acetaminophen for your headache."

Her directions are pretty straightforward. I'm unsure how to handle my scheduled college lectures or court cases for two weeks, but I guess I'll figure that out.

"You didn't list a contact person yesterday or today," the doctor continues. "Detective Benson said he is the one taking care of you. Is there anyone else you'd like us to contact?"

I can call one of my friends or my brother, but I don't want to impose on them. My family lives in other states, so that's not an option. I sure don't want to burden the detective with my problems. He can't be my twenty-four-hour caretaker for the next week. Maybe if he just takes me home, I can stay alone. That's a thought. I'm going with that option.

"No, no one I can think of right now. But I don't want to burden Detective Benson." Looking at the detective, I try to understand his thoughts about his role in my care. He has been attentive, but I don't remember him. I only met him yesterday.

"It's no bother at all, Ivy. Dr. Sparta and I talked about all this. I want to help any way I can."

The corners of his eyes crinkle when he smiles. He's a very kind person. I wonder why he was at the hospital with me yesterday. Was I mugged or something? That could be it. But why am I here today? How did I fall?

I nod my approval to the doctor and Detective Benson. I'm at a loss for who to rely on at the moment. I hope I'm not placing my life in danger by trusting him. Stop it! He's nice. He's just trying to help. Don't get paranoid.

"I've given Detective Benson all your discharge information." Dr. Sparta motions toward the blue folder the detective is holding. "There's information in the concussion packet, and I've called in your prescriptions to the pharmacy downstairs. Detective Benson can pick them up while the nurse helps you get dressed. Do you have any more questions, Miss Preston?" Dr. Sparta closes the file she's been referencing.

"No. I'm good. Thank you, doctor."

"I'll have the nurse help you, and she'll wheel you out while the detective gets your meds and brings his car around." She turns to Detective Benson. "Do you have questions, Tomas, um, detective?"

"No, I'm clear on everything." He reaches down and squeezes my hand. "I'll go get the car and see you downstairs." He opens the door for the doctor, and they both leave.

I caught that little slip by Dr. Sparta. She and the detective are on a first-name basis. Knowing that helps me feel better and less paranoid about my safety. A few minutes later, a nurse comes, assists me in dressing, and wheels me down the hall and into the elevator. Detective Benson is waiting in the patient pickup area just as he said he would be.

In the distance, the streetlamps lining the road brighten the night sky. The pure white snowflakes sparkle in the halo light as they drift to the ground. The wind calms for a moment, creating a peaceful and soothing scene. I'm not sure what's happened today, but I need some restful solitude for a while.

The detective and the nurse assist me as I get in the front seat and strap in. The detective buckles his seatbelt. "Well," he says. "Ready to go home?"

"Yes, I'm ready." I stare out the window at the snow again, then ask, "Which way's home?"

CHAPTER 6

34 Hours 16 Minutes

Wednesday 8:38 p.m.

It's beginning to get late. The clock on the dash shows 8:38 p.m. Today has flown by, especially since I don't remember it. Thankfully, it's only a short drive from the hospital to my home. At least, that's what Detective Benson told me. Since I recognize the names of the streets as we pass, I'm sure only parts of my memory are gone.

Detective Benson drives straight to my brownstone in Evanston, a small, affluent neighborhood a few miles away from Allston. When I moved to Boston three years ago, I wanted to live in a section with features similar to Boston, such as cobblestone streets and vintage lamp posts. Evanston gave me that, along with my renovated brownstone home, upscale shops, fine restaurants, and plenty of green space added to the charm. It's a perfect match for what I was looking for.

After the detective parks the car, he assists me up the steps and into the house. Snow and ice cover the sidewalk and stoop, leaving a narrow, salted path to walk on. He holds my hand and supports me with an arm around my waist to ensure I don't fall again. Wouldn't that be a hoot!

I recognize my home and can recall what's in my refrigerator, but not much else. The detective's help may jog my memory; that's what I hope.

"I'll just sit for a bit," I remark as I walk to the cream-colored sofa facing the fireplace. "It's a little early for bed."

"That's fine, just no getting up without me, understand?" Pointing his finger, he raises his brows and gives me my orders.

"Yes, sir, Mr. Detective." Putting on my most stern face, I salute him. As I laugh, my lips vibrate, making a bubbling noise. Whatever medication they gave me in the hospital has not worn off yet. I'm still giddy like I've had too much wine after dinner.

He shakes his head. "You're one tough lady, Miss Preston. Everything that's happened, and you can still laugh. I'm amazed at how resilient you are."

As I touch the bandage on my head, my lips spread into a half-hearted smile. "Thanks, detective. I sure don't feel very resilient today. I feel more beaten down than anything."

Detective Benson nods. "I understand how you could feel that way," he states. "You've had a long day. Get comfortable. I'm sure you're tired after all you've gone through."

He helps me remove my coat and boots and places a couple of throw pillows behind my back for support. He then lays a soft green throw he finds folded in a chair over me.

After starting a fire in the fireplace, Detective Benson remembers it's been hours since we ate. "You've gotta be hungry. We've had nothing to eat since lunch. I can whip us up something."

"There's no need to do that. I've caused you enough trouble. I can order delivery for us from the deli down the street."

Waving his hands, the detective shakes his head. "No, that's unnecessary. I'll scrounge through your kitchen and whip up something. This way, I can show off my culinary skills. Won't take but a minute." And, without further discussion, off he goes into the kitchen.

Considering how bare my pantry is, I doubt this will be the finest meal of the century. Immersing myself in the flickering flames of the fire, I try not to think, but more questions continue to rattle through my mind. I need to know more about Detective Benson and what brought us together yesterday. And how on earth did I bang my head on the ice two days in a row?

Maybe he knows me through work. He is more knowledgeable

about me than I am about him. That's likely it. Usually, Jamie gathers the records from the police department, but we could have met in court. He might have been a witness I've cross-examined in the past.

Is it possible that the detective has taken a course or independent class I teach at the college? My classes meet the criteria for law enforcement to receive job-required continuing education credit. A person doesn't have to be enrolled in college to get credit for the classes. It's part of Bainsbridge College's community outreach program.

All my thoughts and concerns drift from my mind as I get lost in the flicking flames, and I relax under the warm blanket. My head isn't throbbing as much. It feels good to be home. Gradually, my eyes shut, and I rest.

Not long after I wake up, the detective brings us two plates of food, a soda for me, and a lager for him. I guess I had his kind of beer in the fridge. After the day we've had, we could both use a drink. Shame I can't have one. He places all the food on the table in front of the sofa.

Astonished by the plate of corn beef and cabbage, yellow corn, and potato soup, my mouth falls open. "This looks incredible, detective, and it smells delicious. How did you ever put this together with my stock of groceries?"

"I think you're just hungrier than you thought." The detective cocks his head toward the kitchen. "We gotta get some groceries in there, or we'll starve!" He takes another bite. "But at least you have the best beer." He raises it to toast my soda. "Here's to you, Ivy. May tomorrow be injury-free." As we clink our bottles, a smile stretches across his face. He chugs his beer while I sip my soda, imagining it as a fine wine.

While we eat, we talk about a variety of subjects. We talk about Boston, how we like it here, a little about my job and his, and general stuff. After we finish our meal, the detective clears the table and even washes the dishes while I doze for a few minutes. It seems I need a lot of cat naps.

When he finishes, Detective Benson sits on the sofa beside me and sips his beer, gazing into the fire's glowing embers. Turning toward the detective, I tip his chin toward me.

"It's time we talk. There's a lot I don't remember. I can't wait weeks for my memory to return. I don't remember how I know you, how we met, or much else. How on earth could I fall two days in a row? I need to know." The stress is getting to me. As I reach for a tissue from a side table, I try to hold back the tears threatening to fall.

The detective slides around on the sofa so we are facing each other. He holds my hands between his and looks down at them. "I know," he whispers. "I've been thinking about what I should tell you and how. What's taken place the last two days is important." He raises his hand and touches the bandage on my head with his fingers. "I just don't want to set you back or throw too much at you at one time."

He stops for a moment, then squeezes my hands. "Truthfully, Ivy, there's an important matter that only you can..." The detective stops mid-sentence when his phone rings. Raising his hand to pause the conversation, Detective Benson becomes all business. "Just a sec, Ivy. I have to take this." He stands and walks away, far enough that I can only hear mumbles.

Damn it, I feel like I'm being left out of this whole day. First my memory gone, and now, I'm excluded from the phone conversation. I want to go to bed and pretend yesterday and today never happened. My eyes grow heavy, so I lean back on the soft, cuddly pillows. The headache and roaring in my ears have returned.

About ten minutes later, Detective Benson comes back with another lager. He twists the top off and sits down next to me, leans his head back, and relaxes on the sofa. I see the tiredness and stress on his face. He's no longer smiling. His eyes look weak and puffy, dark shadows circling underneath. Ashamed that my only concern has been me, I slide beside him and place half the blanket over him. He turns his head toward me and smiles. I lay my head on his shoulder. The phone call drained the last bit of energy from him.

"What's happened now?" I ask.

"Just making some adjustments in the case." He breathes out, squeezes the bridge of his nose, and takes another drink of his beer. Leaning his head on mine, his voice low, he says, "I think we need to call it a night and start again tomorrow."

Stifling a yawn, I cover my mouth and stretch out my arms. The physical and emotional exhaustion of the day has caught up with me, too. "I think you're right."

"I'll get you your meds, then get you settled into bed."

"Sounds good." I won't argue about him staying with me. He seems too tired to drive, and besides, I think I'll feel better with him here.

After taking the medication, the detective helps me up the stairs.

"This is a four-bedroom brownstone. I've turned one room into a study with a small library, but the others are still usable bedrooms. You're welcome to sleep in any of them you'd like."

When we get to the second floor, I show him the bedroom on the left side of the hall. "My friends usually stay in this one. It has an adjoining bath. Fresh towels and linen are in the closet in the bath. Extra toothbrushes and personal supplies are there, too. Everyone who's stayed says the bed is very comfortable."

"Thank you, Ivy. This one's fine. I didn't know my accommodations would be so wicked. It'll be much more comfortable than the chair I planned to sleep on."

"Whatever made you think I'd stick you in a chair?" I laugh. "Silly boy. Good night, detective." Smiling, I walk toward my room a few feet down the hall. The detective follows close behind. "Where are you going?" I ask, scrunching my forehead.

"To get you to bed," he replies as though I should have known. "That's what I said I would do, and that's what I'm gonna do. When I get you securely tucked in, I'll go to bed, but not a minute sooner, missy."

Arguing makes no sense because he's determined to do what he said. He's made it very clear, so I give in.

Without his assisting me, I change into my pajamas in my bathroom. At least he allowed me that. After I find a pair of Nick's winter pajamas for him to use and get my orders about not getting up without calling him, Detective Benson makes sure I'm comfortable, says goodnight, and goes to his room. I check the clock on my nightstand. It shows 11:55 p.m. It's been one hell of a day. At least the parts I can remember.

I only hope tomorrow brings back the things I've lost.

CHAPTER 7

44 Hours 52 Minutes

Thursday, December 1
7:14 a.m.

Waiting for my alarm to go off, I glance at the clock and realize I should have been up an hour ago. I'm supposed to be in court at nine for an arraignment. Taking no time to throw the covers off, I swing my legs around and spring out of bed.

Damn it! I plunge face-first to the floor, arms spread eagle like a squashed frog. My chin rests on the carpet.

"Not again," I mumble to myself. How many freaking times can one person fall in three days?

Hearing the thud of my not-so-graceful decline to the floor, Detective Benson rushes in. "Ivy! Are you okay?" He scoops me up and sits me on the bed. "What are you doing?" he exclaims, his face twisted into a scowl.

A little dazed, I squeeze my eyes tight and shake my head, trying to stop the dizziness. "Yes, I'm okay, detective. I just need to get my bearings. Guess I should have called you to help me out of bed, or at the least, eased myself up rather than jumping out like lightning struck me." Forcing a giggle, I laugh it off.

"Are you sure you're okay?"

"Yes, I'm sure. The only thing that got hurt this time was my ego." My face feels hot, and I blush with embarrassment at falling yet again.

Remembering why I was in such a hurry, I ramble, making little to no sense. I motion with my hands and move my head in every direction as I explain to the detective why I've got to leave.

"No one even knows I will be out at work," I state, throwing my hands out. Scanning the top of my nightstand, I fumble through the items lying on it. "Where's my phone?"

Unaffected by my ranting, the detective remains calm and rational. "The first thing I did this morning was call your office and speak with your assistant, Jamie. I asked him to handle anything you had scheduled for the day and told him you would call him later. I didn't give any details since I thought you'd like to be the one to explain that you'd have to be out of work for a few weeks."

He rubs his eyes with his thumb and finger and sighs. Sitting beside me on the bed, the detective massages his temple and then looks at me. It's obvious he's stressed.

"You and I have to talk, Ivy. How 'bout I help you to the bathroom to clean up a little. Then we can get you settled downstairs, or you can spend the day resting in bed. I can bring you some breakfast, meds, and phone," he offers.

Embarrassed at my outburst, I look down and fidget with the covers on the bed. "I'd rather clean up and go downstairs. It feels more normal that way."

He nods his head. "I get that. It's important to feel normal."

There's something off about Detective Benson. He doesn't seem the same as he was last night. His words are short and direct. He clears his throat and continues. "You left your phone downstairs on the table last night. I noticed it this morning when I went down to make coffee." He pauses and looks down. "I didn't use your phone to find your assistant's number if that's what you're thinking. As I told you, I called your office and asked to speak to your assistant. I didn't even know his name was Jamie when I called." He raises his head. "Look at me, Ivy," he says firmly.

I look up. The detective's eyes lock on mine. His eyebrows arch, and the muscles in his face bulge as he clenches his jaw. I can tell he's frustrated with me.

"At some point, you're going to have to trust me. I'm only trying to help you."

This man is so thoughtful and self-sacrificing, and here he is explaining his actions to me because he thinks I don't trust him. I'm so ashamed. I don't deserve to have his help. As bitchy and emotional as I've been, he's taken care of me, stayed calm, and been so patient with me.

I've been just awful to him. He didn't have to remain with me last night, but he did. There's no way I can repay him for all his help. I don't know how I can show him how thankful I am for all he's done and is still doing for me. And the thing is, he's under no obligation to do any of it.

My head drops, breaking eye contact with him. "Thank you for calling Jamie and taking care of things for me. That was a very thoughtful thing to do. I appreciate it more than you know." I look up at his face, and he nods, his lips pushed into a small, tight smile.

The detective assists me as I head toward the bathroom, his hand on my arm. Stopping, I turn and face him. "There's no way I can ever say thank you enough, Detective Benson. I don't know what I would've done without your help."

A tear tumbles from my eye, then another, and the flood begins. Losing all control, I sob. "I don't mean to be so emotional. I've been such a… a bitch!" I blubber out loud, cupping my face in my hands. "I don't know what's happening to me, why I'm acting this way!"

The detective wraps his arms around me and holds me, rubbing and patting my back while I fall apart. He pushes my hair off my face, tucking it behind my ears.

"Shush, it's alright, Ivy. I understand. You've been through so much. The concussion has your emotions all over the place. You'll feel normal soon."

When I'm all cried out, my shoulders heave as I suck breath after breath, trying to regain control. Detective Benson gives me one last rub and leans back. He looks at me, his face no longer stern, tilts my chin up toward him, and dabs the tears from my face with a tissue.

"Dry those tears," he whispers. "Let's get you cleaned up, and you'll feel better. We've got lots to do today, lots for you to get caught up on if we're going to solve this thing."

Solve this thing? I wonder what that means.

CHAPTER 8

46 Hours 26 Minutes

Thursday 8:48 a.m.

Despite only a few eggs in my fridge, the detective prepares a breakfast casserole that's out of this world. He's an unbelievable cook. I could get used to this. My typical meals are simple and quick: cereal or a breakfast bar, bags of chips or nuts on the run, and a can of soup or takeout for supper.

"Where'd you learn to cook like this?" I shove another forkful in my mouth. "It's wonderful. I didn't know the ingredients for something this good were even in my kitchen." I snicker.

"I'm glad you like it. It's easy to make. Judging by the lack of groceries in your pantry, you don't cook often. I may have to give you cooking lessons." He laughs as he scoops his last bite of casserole onto his fork. He pushes away from the table and sips his coffee.

"My grandmother taught me to cook. She always said if you wanna eat, learn to cook. So I did." He chuckles and continues talking about his grandmother and their adventures. "She raised me from the age of seven." He pauses and looks away for a moment. "I miss her."

Becoming emotional, the detective clears his throat and takes our plates to the kitchen. After refilling our cups, he reclaims his seat at the table. His facial expression has changed from relaxed to tense, his jaw clenched tight, and his lips pinched together. He sets his cup down and then interlocks his fingers, resting his hands on the table.

"We need to talk about what happened to you, Ivy. The parts you don't remember."

Shifting around in my chair, I feel apprehensive. I want to know what my mind has hidden from me, but I'm afraid to hear things about myself I don't remember. When I'm comfortable, I take a few sips of coffee. Still anxious, I rub my finger over my right thumbnail to reduce my stress.

"Okay, I'm ready. I think."

"You're gonna be uncomfortable with what I say, but we'll get through this. You're in no danger. Remember that," Detective Benson assures me. "You witnessed a kidnapping on Tuesday morning and tried to stop it but couldn't. The kidnapper shoved you to the ground. That was the first fall, the fall that cut your head."

The detective continues, telling me the details about everything that has happened the past two days. He tells me all I reported to the police about the kidnapping, the descriptions of the kidnapper and victim, and my attempt to stop it. We talk more about how I fell the first time and the cut on my head. Then, he explains how we returned to the crime scene and my second fall.

"With no report of a woman missing, no other witnesses that we've found yet, and now your memory loss, we're kinda at a standstill." His voice is low, and his shoulders slump as he looks at his half-empty cup. Then, running his palms over his face, the detective gazes at me and drops his head. He pushes the last of his cold coffee to the side. His expression, brows furrowed and muscles tense, reveals his anguish. Stone-faced, I stare unblinking at the detective. I can't believe what he's told me, and I'm unsure how to respond.

"Hold on," I utter. Taking a moment, I try to find my words. "I can't remember any of this. You're saying I witnessed a kidnapping and stuck my nose in the middle?" I snort. "There's no way."

I move my head in disbelief and stand up a little too fast. The room spins, and I become queasy. Sliding back into my seat, I lay my head on my folded arms. Detective Benson jumps to my aid. A minute or two after assuring him I'm okay, the nausea subsides, and the dizziness passes.

"How can this be real?" I mutter, trying to convince myself it's not. But the evidence is clear by looking at my head, the multiple stitches, a large white bandage, not to mention the two days of absent memories. My reporting of the kidnapping would also account for how I met the detective.

"So you and I first met at the hospital on Tuesday?"

"That's right. When the kidnapper pushed you, you hit your head on the ice. You were getting the gash in your head stitched up." The detective leans forward. "You were fearless. You didn't flinch, even when the doc injected the lidocaine in your head." Half smiling, he adds, "That's always been the most painful part to me, but you didn't seem to feel it."

"That doesn't sound like me at all. I hate needles." Grinning, I touch my head but can't feel the stitches through the bandage.

As I think back on what the detective said about the woman, I wonder if it's my fault they've not found her. "Are you saying something in my missing memory could be the key to finding the kidnapped woman?"

"No, that's not what I'm saying." The detective leans back, shaking his head. "Don't be upset, Ivy. You're not responsible for what happens to the woman."

Detective Benson remains calm and reassuring. "You've given us lots of information to go on. Because of you, Ivy, we know the color and make of the car the kidnapper was driving and have accurate sketches of both the suspect and the victim. Those are things we wouldn't know without you."

A faint memory of describing the kidnapper and victim to the sketch artist flashes in my mind when he mentions them. The images aren't clear, but I know the woman was tall with chestnut hair, and the man had long, curly blonde hair. Encouraged that I remember something about the past two days, I believe all my memories will return sooner than expected. When I share my fresh memory with the detective, he leans toward me, and a broad smile flashes across his now glowing face.

"That's amazing, Ivy! You remembered that quickly." Drumming the table with his fingers, the detective continues. "I have some thoughts on how we might jog your memory, but we'll get to that in a few minutes."

"We should move to the living room, where the atmosphere is more relaxed," I suggest.

Sitting on the sofa, I turn to face the detective, urging him to continue. "It's important that I know everything."

Detective Benson turns toward me so we can see each other face to face. He rests one arm on the sofa and leans closer to me. Arching his brows, the soft lines in his forehead deepen. His tone is professional and factual as he tells me everything about the case.

"When you and I returned to the scene yesterday, the team found some lipstick near where you said the blue Plymouth parked. We hoped to get some information from it. Forensics found some smudged fingerprints, but they were unusable. We've sent the lipstick for DNA testing, but it'll take a day or two to get the results back.

"The phone call I got last night was from my partner, Marc Phischer. I told him to release both sketches, the two people drawn by Holly as you described them, to the media as missing persons. Maybe we'll get a hit."

"This is a lot to take in," I state. "How can I help?"

"I need to check out a couple of things. I have an appointment to interview Dr. Marshall Winsloe, the gentleman who found you unconscious Tuesday, to see what else he might remember." His tone changes to one more personal and compassionate. "You were lucky he found you, Ivy. He's a heart surgeon who moved here from England a few months ago. And it's possible there is another witness we've not located yet, so I want to follow up on that, too."

The possibility of finding a new lead is exciting. Meeting the man who found me on Tuesday would be an honor. I want to express my gratitude for all he did, but I've got to word my request to the detective exactly right. Maybe I'm overstepping my bounds as a witness, so I try to squelch some of my excitement and appear calm. Shifting on the sofa, I fiddle with the sleeves of my sweatshirt, pulling them lower on my hands.

"Those sound like some promising possibilities, detective. You know, it might jog my memory if I'm with you when you speak with Dr. Winsloe," I suggest, casting my eyes upward, acting all demure and nonchalant.

The frown on the detective's face tells me I'm not winning him over, so I resort to my next best tactic—begging.

My hands clasped, and my brows squished together, I put on my best pouty lips and scoot closer to the detective. "I know I'm not a police officer or detective, but please let me come with you! I want to meet the man that found me, please."

Pressing his lips together tight, Detective Benson gives me a stern look and begins shaking his head.

"I don't think that's the way to go, Ivy. It wouldn't be proper for one witness to be present while interviewing another witness. You, of all people, know that."

Unfortunately, he is right from a legal standpoint. Reluctantly, I agree. "But there's got to be something I can do to help," I implore.

"I thought we could go over some more things later today, depending on how you feel. But, at the moment, you can do one important thing—for me," the detective adds. "I know you don't want to worry your family or friends, Ivy, but I don't want to leave you here alone. You'd be doing me a big favor if you'd call someone to stay with you until I return."

I know I can't keep relying on the detective to stay with me. He's been more than kind and gone way beyond his job requirements to take care of me. I'm just a witness to a crime, and he has no personal obligation to me. I wonder why he has been so compassionate and attentive. He's treating me like we've known each other for years. It feels more like we're friends than acquaintances. Oddly, I feel close to him, drawn to him. It's bizarre.

Either I stay alone or call someone to stay with me. I'm not sure why I want the detective's permission to stay in my home alone. Yet, he's asked nothing of me and has done so much for me. I kind of feel obligated to do as he asks.

"Truly, detective, I appreciate your concern, but I just don't see any sense in calling someone to babysit me when I can care for myself." I try to sound confident. "I'll just sit right here, and I'll be fine."

The look on Detective Benson's face tells me he's not happy with my suggestion. Trying to ease his mind, I continue, "I'd call someone just for you, but my family lives in another state, and all my friends are at work." I shrug my shoulders and hold my hands palm-side up. "I promise, I won't move off this sofa any more than is necessary."

He takes my hands in his and looks straight into my eyes. "I don't feel good about it, Ivy. I know I don't have any right to tell you what to do, but I'm asking that you do this one thing for me. Just call someone to come for a few hours. I'm gonna run some errands when I finish my investigation, but I should be back by four." His tone is pleading.

No one has ever worried about me like this except my family; no man I've ever been in a relationship with, and not Nick, it seems. I'm unsure if the detective's concern is because he cares about me or thinks I could be in danger since I'm a witness to a crime. Whatever the reason, I know his concern is genuine.

With his hands still enveloping mine, I squeeze Detective

Benson's fingers. "Okay, just for you, I'll call my friend Galvin. He doesn't go to work until late, so he may be home. He might stay with me awhile. Still, I refuse to tell him anything except that I fell and have a mild concussion."

Detective Benson sighs, and a smile eases across his worried face. He grips my hands a little tighter, then lets them go. "You call him," the detective says, handing me my phone. He heads to the kitchen, saying he needs to tidy up, but I know he's leaving so I can talk with Galvin alone.

Taking the phone, I make the call. Galvin agrees to come with no hesitation and no questions. The detective returns from the kitchen as I'm hanging up the phone.

"Galvin lives in Allston, so it won't take him long to get here. You could leave now if you want to. It's almost ten thirty. What time are you supposed to meet with Dr. Winsloe?"

"We're meeting at my office around twelve, so I've got a little time. I'd like to meet Galvin. Didn't you say that he's a musician with the symphony? He sounds like an interesting guy."

"Yes, he's the concertmaster," I reply. "Galvin's very talented." I continue bragging as if he was my child. My thoughts turn to the problem I am about to face. I look at the detective, puzzled. "I don't know how I'm going to explain a detective being at my house."

With a grin, the detective leans over and whispers in my ear, "You could just say I'm your new boyfriend."

CHAPTER 9

49 Hours 40 Minutes

Thursday 12:02 p.m.

After arriving at my office, I pull out the file on the kidnapping case and review the report prepared by my partner from his interview with Dr. Marshall Winsloe. Locating a copy of the sketches of the suspect and victim, I lay them face down on the desk a few seconds before the door opens. Detective Phischer escorts Dr. Winsloe, a tall, dignified gentleman with a stylish short beard, inside the room. The small amount of gray at his temples blends with his dark hair, making him appear older than his given age of forty-two.

Marc introduces us, and we shake hands.

"Thank you for coming, Dr. Winsloe," I begin. "Please, have a seat." I motion to the chair in front of my desk.

Dr. Winsloe says, "I'm happy to help in any way I can, but I gave Detective Phischer all the information I could remember Tuesday after I found the young lady unconscious. I believe her name is Ivy, yes, Ivy Preston, if I'm not mistaken. Do you know how she's doing?"

"She's doing well," I reply, "aside from a second head injury and some memory loss."

"Oh, I'm so sorry to hear that. I hope she'll be okay. How on earth did she get a second head injury?"

Knowing Dr. Winsloe is a physician, I feel comfortable telling him about Ivy. "She slipped on some ice and hit her head again. She has a mild concussion and, unfortunately, has lost her memory of the kidnapping."

"Oh, my," Dr. Winsloe exclaims. "That poor girl! She's gone through a lot the past few days. Please let me know if there is anything I can do to help."

"That's one reason I want to talk with you. Not that I don't trust my partner here," I jest, winking at Marc, "but do you mind if I go over what happened from your perspective again?"

"Certainly." Dr. Winsloe leans forward in his chair, propping an elbow on the chair arm, his hand stroking his beard. "I had just pulled into the shopping center and was about to park when I saw a woman lying in the alley between the two buildings. I pulled my car into the alley, jumped out, and ran to her."

He pauses, scratches his chin, and shifts in his seat. "I didn't know if she was alive or dead, so I checked for a pulse and had someone call 911 for an ambulance. That's the extent of my involvement. I stayed with her until the ambulance got there. When the police arrived, I spoke with your partner here," he gestures to Marc, "and told him what I'm telling you."

I nod my head. "I see. That's pretty clear cut, alright." Leaning forward in my chair, I rest my arms on the desk, hands folded, and ask, "Do you remember what time you pulled into the shopping center and the time you found the woman lying in the alley?"

The doctor replies without hesitation. "I know the exact time. It was ten twenty-eight. I had just looked at my watch because I had an appointment at eleven fifteen and knew I only had a few minutes to complete my shopping."

"When you were pulling in or at any point after that, did you notice any cars speeding or acting erratic?"

The doctor takes a moment before responding, then leans back in his chair, becoming more comfortable. "You know," he says thoughtfully, "there was an older blue car speeding toward me just before I turned into the shopping center. His tires spun on the icy road when he slammed his brakes and did a U-turn. He looked like he was heading toward I-90 West, though I can't be sure."

Marc and I look at each other, acknowledging the new information. Marc takes the lead. "You referred to the driver as 'he' several times. Was it a man driving the blue car?"

"It was indeed," the doctor replies. "He had curly hair, maybe chin level, blonde. I thought he was going to hit me when his car spun around. The roads were icy, and I remember mumbling a chain of profanities regarding crazy Boston drivers!" he chuckles.

Marc snickers, and I join in at the thought of this dignified gentleman releasing a string of obscenities.

"Can't say I haven't used a foul word, now and then, when I'm in traffic," I admit, smiling. "What you've remembered is a great help to the case, Dr. Winsloe." Flipping the sketch of the man over, I show it to him. "Is this the man driving the blue car?"

The doctor takes the drawing and examines every detail. "It looks a lot like him. I can't say for sure, but that could be him. It was snowing, and I was trying to avoid a collision, so I didn't pay that much attention to the driver." He hands the sketch back to me.

"Let's go back to the parking lot for a moment, Dr. Winsloe, when you approached the woman on the ground. You told Detective Phischer you saw a woman standing near Miss Preston, but she ran toward the back of the building. Is that right?"

"Let me see…" Dr. Winsloe pauses for a moment before speaking. "Yes, that is correct. She was standing over the unconscious woman. As I approached, I yelled, and she backed up, then ran, disappearing behind the building. I didn't get very close to her. She was almost at the back of the building when I got to Miss Preston."

"Her behavior was odd, as I recall." He scrunches his face and mimics the woman's behavior. "After disappearing behind the building, she would ease her head around the corner and then pop back behind it." He looks at Marc and then at me. "It was so strange. I remember she did that several times, but my mind was on the girl lying on the pavement, so I didn't pay her much attention."

Marc comments as I nod my head, "That is weird."

"You're doing well, sir," I continue. "We're almost done, just a couple of more questions."

Dr. Winsloe nods.

"In your original interview, you stated the woman was sharp-looking. Tell me something about her appearance."

The doctor shakes his head. "I glimpsed her, only for a few seconds." He pauses, raking his hand through his hair. "She may have been wearing a sweater or knit top with a high neck, like a cowl neck. It was a dark color. Yes, dark blue, perhaps. Oh, and she wore high heels. She stumbled once when she was backing away." Dr. Winsloe rubs his forehead and looks up at me. "That's all I can recall."

With the interview coming to a close, I jump in with one more question. "You also said the woman's hair was blonde, right?"

Without hesitation, the doctor states, "Yes, I believe that is what I said, but actually, her hair was more of a reddish color. I think it was short, a bob, maybe about mid-length. I remember because she had the same hair color as my wife, not blonde but more of a light red. I believe I gave Detective Phischer an inaccurate description of her hair color." The doctor turns toward Marc. "I apologize, detective. With all that was happening, it was difficult to concentrate on minor details when I first spoke with you. I hope it didn't impede your investigation."

"Not at all, sir. Thank you for clearing it up," Marc says. "Would you say her hair color was natural?"

"I didn't see her that well, but it was natural. It suited her well. She was young, perhaps in her twenties or early thirties, and her hair gave her a very stylish, distinct look."

Resuming my questioning, I inquire, "You also said she was standing behind the building. Which building, Geordies or Raymond's Shoes?"

"It was... the building to my right as I faced the alley.

Geordies."

"One more question, and we're done for today. Could you tell if the woman went in the back door of the building or if she might have been walking to her car?"

"No, I couldn't tell," Dr. Winsloe replies. "She was standing close to the building so she could have gone inside. I didn't see her in the crowd, only behind the building. I didn't see a car leave from that direction."

I nod and close the interview, believing we've gotten all the information we can from Dr. Winsloe, at least for today. "You've been a great help, sir. I think that'll do it for now. We may have other questions later." I rise from my chair and extend my hand. "We appreciate you coming in, Dr. Winsloe."

The doctor stands and shakes my hand. "I have to admit," he says. "I never realized, until now, how vital trivial information can be in an investigation or how difficult it can be to recall it. I can't imagine how difficult your job is. Please let me know if I can be of further help."

Marc escorts the doctor to the door. "I'll see you out, sir."

When they reach the door, Dr. Winsloe turns to speak to me one last time. "Memory loss is not my specialty, but I have some colleagues who might be helpful in situations such as Miss Preston's. They may help her recall some recent events quicker than waiting for her memory to return. I know that can take weeks, even months, and you don't have that kind of time if she's your best witness. If she's interested in trying, just call me." He hands me his card.

"It's been a pleasure, gentlemen," he says as he steps into the hall. "No need to escort me out, detective," he tells Marc. "I won't have any problem finding my way. I know you both have a lot to discuss. Good luck with your case." He smiles as he leaves and closes the door behind him.

CHAPTER 10

50 Hours 53 Minutes

Thursday 1:15 p.m.

Marc ambles his six-foot frame back to his chair. Flopping down, he brushes his hands through his short, curly, blonde hair. It bounces back into the same position as before he touched it, just as it always does.

"Well, Tomas, it looks like we have some searching to do for the mysterious redhead behind the building," he says, leaning back in his chair.

"My thoughts exactly, and the sooner we get to it, the better." As quickly as possible, I place the documents from the case back into the folder. "We need to get to Geordies and see what we can find out."

"Officer Belmond and I interviewed the supervisor and several of the employees at Geordies right after the incident occurred, but we were searching for a blonde, not a woman with red hair."

Marc props his elbows on his knees, leans forward, and clasps his hands together. "I don't know if it would have made any difference what color her hair was. We didn't see anyone suspicious, and nobody in the shop remembered anything unusual happening or anyone acting out of the ordinary."

I know Marc well. I sense he feels like he might have missed something during Tuesday's investigation. I stop what I'm doing and turn toward him.

"Marc, you know it didn't make any difference in finding the woman. If you'd spotted anyone suspicious, you'd have followed up on it, regardless of hair color. Now we know the woman had reddish-blonde hair, so we need to keep our eyes open for a female fitting that description. She might have on high heels, something else we didn't know before. Lots of pertinent information can come out in the second interview with a witness. You know that."

"Right," he agrees. He stands, retrieves his black North Face parka from the hook rack by the door, and slips it on. "I'll be on the lookout for her. If she works there, she shouldn't be hard to spot."

Opening his mouth a small amount, almost forming a small oval with his lips, Marc runs his finger and thumb over his evenly trimmed mustache, following it down to his low, short, boxed beard. He's obsessed with making sure every hair is neat and in place. I've noticed him smoothing his mustache with his fingers often since he grew it a few months ago. It's becoming a habit—an annoying one.

Marc's a good-looking man, for sure. The ladies flock to him every time we go out together. It's not just his curly blonde hair and ocean-blue eyes that attract them, but a combination of that and his easy-going, quirky personality. No way a premature graying guy like me can compete with him. We joke he may have good looks and charm, but I'm the quiet, mysterious guy with sex appeal. I smile, thinking about it.

Marc doesn't know it, but I'm on a schedule today, and my time is short. Besides working on the case, I need to go by my apartment to get a few things for tonight, then pick up some groceries on my way to Ivy's house. I told her I would be there by four, and I don't want to be late.

In a rush to get to Geordies, I round my desk, reach to get my coat and drop the folder. Papers and notes scatter across the floor. Frustrated, I throw my briefcase down, mumbling several obscenities under my breath. Taking a step back, Marc's eyes bulge, surprised by my outburst. As I squat to retrieve the papers, he bends down and helps pick them up. Without even giving a thank you, I shove the documents into the briefcase, grab my coat, and head for the door, Marc close at my heels.

Rushing down the hall toward the elevator, Marc hustles to keep pace.

"You seem to be in a big hurry today, partner."

"Things to do, places to be," I reply curtly, not wanting to get into a long discussion about my plans for the evening. "The quicker we get to Geordies, the quicker we find that woman."

Nodding, Marc lets it pass.

As we wait for the elevator, my thoughts center on Ivy. Even though Galvin is with her, I shouldn't have left her today. Should I pull myself from the case and let Marc handle it so I can be there for Ivy? Sneaking a peek at Marc, I scratch my head and wonder, not about the quality of his work, but about me—how I'm handling this case.

Solving the crime should come first. It always has, but I can't get my mind off Ivy—and I don't know why. I know I can't let my concern for her interfere with my investigation, but I wonder if it's not. I want to believe that my only interest in her is professional. I have a case to solve. My gut keeps telling me I need to be with Ivy to protect her and keep her safe, but safe from what?

"Where the hell's the elevator!" I growl, pushing the call button multiple times.

The longer I look at the elevator floor indicator, the more my impatience grows. It hasn't moved from the fifth floor since we've been waiting.

Shifting my weight from side to side, I try to calm down, but that's not happening. My eyes dart around the hall, land on the elevator, and then flip to Marc.

"I want to get the footage reviewed from the street cams on Tuesday morning around the time of the crime. Dammit, Marc, didn't we ask for that already? A guy in a blue car bangin' a U-ey won't be hard to spot!" I all but shout as I pace the floor. "We might get a tag number from the footage if we *had* the footage!"

Knowing I'm snappy and irritable makes me aggravated with

myself and how I'm behaving. Maybe I'm just tired. A constant, dull ache begins behind my eyes. I press my forehead, hoping to make the pain go away.

My attention jumps back to the missing elevator, the one still not here, and I beat the button several times with the side of my fist. We'd be in the car by now if we had taken the stairs. My headache, no longer a silent ache behind my eyes, has become a pulsating pounding in my temples.

Looking at me as though I've lost my mind, Marc's eyes squinch, and he cocks his head. He steps back, his hands in his jacket pockets, and watches me repeatedly attack the elevator button.

"Alright, Tomas, I'm trying to be patient with you, but I just have to ask—what the hell is wrong with you?" He swings his hands out, still in his pockets, flapping his jacket open.

Stepping closer to me, Marc positions himself in my line of view so we're face to face. "Why are you being so bitchy? And why in hell are you suddenly in such a freakin' hurry? You need to settle down, you hear me?" He backs away a few feet and points his finger at me. "You're pumpin' out questions without giving me time to answer them and practically accusing me of not doing my job!"

Opening his arms wide, Marc points to the elevator. "And now you're assaulting an elevator button. What the hell's wrong with you?"

Realizing I'm taking my frustrations out on him and everything around me, I rub my eyes. Taking a deep breath, I nod, showing that I understand how I've been acting.

Patting Marc on the shoulder, I apologize. "I'm sorry, Marc. There's just so much that's been going on. I guess it's catching up with me. I don't mean to take it out on you. I'm just in a hurry to get this case solved, that's all."

"Apology accepted. You don't look too good, Tomas. You okay?"

"Yeah, I'm okay. I got a headache is all. I'm just ready to get there and find the woman from the alley."

The elevator finally arrives. Marc blocks my hand as I reach for the floor panel, grins, and using light pressure, pushes the first-floor button.

Rushing out the door of the station house and through the parking lot, we climb into my charger. The tires squeal as I make a rapid turn into the traffic.

"Shit, Tomas, slow down! Here you go again. What's your friggin' hurry, man? You act like we got a fire to go to!" Marc yells as he grabs the dash to steady himself in the seat, his eyes big as moon pies.

Chuckling at the bug-eyed look on his face, I ease off the gas and take a deep, calming breath. "I'm sorry, Marc." Without thinking, I blurt out, "I've got to get back to Ivy's by four, and I don't have time to waste."

Hoping Marc didn't hear me, I circle back to a previous topic. "We should've had the info on the car before now. You requested it like I told you, right?"

"Alright, that's enough. You've already asked me that," he replies. "You know I did." Marc pauses, glaring at me, his face fixed, frigid—but not from the cold. "What's got into you with this Ivy woman? And what do you mean you gotta get back to her house?"

I glance at him as I drive but don't say a word. How can I explain to Marc what I don't understand myself? What should be just a case has turned into so much more, but I'm not sure what 'the more' is.

Having met Marc when I was a kid and being his partner for twelve years, we know each other inside and out. We're more than partners; we're best friends—family. Marc has always been there for me. I remember our first meeting. I was seven. My mom had died three days before, and I was sitting on the curb down from my grandma's house. Marc saw me crying, sat beside me, and put his arm around me. He just sat there, holding me, not saying a word. I remember asking him why he was there, and he said, '*Because you need me.*' I love him like a brother.

I avoid looking at Marc, ignoring his questions. Unfortunately, it doesn't work.

"Look at me, Tom, I'm talking to you," he insists. "What's going on?" He shakes his head as his face melts into an 'aha' look. "Ooh no, no, no," he repeats several times. "No, uh-uh, no way! Are you insane?" He continues to shake his head while squirming in his seat. "What the hell's got into you?"

Still, I say nothing. I don't know what to say. I shrug my shoulders and focus on getting to Crestview.

"How involved with her are you, Tom? You know you could lose your job. You know the rules." He tilts his head, his jaw clenched.

How could Marc think I'd ever violate my ethics and move beyond a professional relationship with a witness? I can't deny there's something special about Ivy, but I'd never cross that line. My primary attention is always on finding the victim as quickly as possible. It's important to me.

Still, I say nothing as I enter the shopping center and park near the alley.

"You think I'm gonna shut up about this, but you're wrong," Marc assures me. "No, sir. This conversation's not over." He gets out of the car, slamming the door behind him.

"This ain't over," he mumbles.

CHAPTER 11

51 Hours 33 Minutes

Thursday 1:55 p.m.

Marc and I head down the alley to explore the back of the building where Dr. Winslow said the female witness had disappeared. When we round the corner of the back wall, I stop.

"This must be where the woman was standing." Poking my head around the building, I check out the view she would have had of the scene.

Marc wanders further back, maybe twenty yards away. "Look, Tomas!" he calls, motioning me over. Kicking the icy slush, he points at an area of half-frozen dirty water. "Those brown and white clumps are possibly cigarette butts and that other stuff, tobacco. It looks like this is the place where employees come out to smoke. It's close to the back door."

"Check it; see if it's locked."

Marc pulls on the handle, and it opens without a problem. The light is on, so we enter. The room is large, filled with boxes, display racks, extra clothing covered in plastic, and other storage supplies, all grouped in sections. We go through the maze of well-organized materials and stumble on another door leading to Geordie's back hall. The employee lounge, offices, and public restrooms are in this section. The first shopping area we come upon is the women's lingerie department.

Two women stand behind a checkout counter. One is tall and thin, maybe in her fifties, wearing bright red lipstick, fake eyelashes, and blue eyeshadow. Her cheeks are heavy with blush, the only thing adding color to her pasty skin. The other woman is younger and petite. Her smooth, light brown skin does not need makeup and her long, thick, dark hair swings down her back in a low braid.

The two women have a clear view of us as we emerge from the back of the building. They glare at us, then glance at each other, confused by our presence. They couldn't have missed us going to the back hall if we had entered from the front of the store. Whispering to each other, their eyes still on us, the older woman shrugs her shoulders and shakes her head. The petite lady's eyes follow our every move.

Marc and I have been partners for so long that we can almost read each other's minds. Marc nods, showing he's got this, and strolls up to the women.

"Excuse me, ladies," he says, his smile inviting and natural. He flips his badge open and continues. "I'm Detective Phischer, and this is my partner, Detective Benson. How're you two doing today?"

Marc always has a warm smile on his face. He's the 'good' cop, most of the time. I just sort of go with the flow, whatever the situation calls for. I can't help but grin at Marc's technique with the ladies, all sugar-sweet and turning on the charm. To conceal my smile, I cover my mouth as though I'm coughing. Trying to reclaim a straight face, I stand back and observe as Marc does his thing.

"Where did you two come from?" the younger woman addresses Marc. She crosses her arms and shifts her weight to one leg. "We didn't see you go to the back," she states, her words commanding, authoritative.

Marc is not a person to be intimidated. He assumes a more assertive stance with an all-business attitude but maintains a soft, clear voice as he continues his inquiry.

"We're investigating a crime that occurred right outside, in the alley, Tuesday. We came in the back door. Does the door remain unlocked during store hours?

"You should speak with our supervisor, Monique Madison." The young woman steps from behind the counter.

Blocking her path, I notice her name tag. "Penny, we just need to ask a few questions. My partner spoke with your supervisor and some other employees here on Tuesday. You're welcome to get Ms. Madison if you feel the need, but every minute lost places a woman's life in jeopardy."

Penny hesitates and gives Marc and me a quick once-over. "Ok," she says. "It's supposed to stay locked at all times, but sometimes employees go behind the building to smoke on breaks. Sometimes, they forget to lock it when they come back in. I always check it before we close."

"You have a good view of the storage area from here. Do you see everyone that goes to the back area?" I ask.

The taller woman's name tag has 'Mildred' etched on it. She's a more nervous lady, constantly fiddling with her hands, but seems eager to cooperate. "Oh, yes, detective," she jumps in. "No one goes to the back that we don't see unless we're on break. But one of us always stays here," she smiles. "This is a bustling department, you know." She motions around at all the customers browsing through ladies' undergarments.

Lowering her voice almost to a whisper, Mildred leans closer to me and grins. "Lingerie is a splendid gift for the special woman in a man's life."

Marc looks at me, rolls his lips in, pressing them tight, and tries not to laugh aloud while I blush at the thought of buying Ivy frilly underwear. Why do I think of Ivy and frilly underwear? I don't even know her, not in that way. And besides, she has a freaking boyfriend. What the hell's wrong with me?

Knowing I'm embarrassed, Marc jumps in. "Were you two ladies working Tuesday when the crime occurred?"

"We were both here." Penny's posture is no longer stiff and defensive. She turns toward Marc, and their eyes meet. "I spoke with the police. I believe it was you and another officer after the ambulance took the woman to the hospital." She looks at Mildred, who nods in agreement. "We knew nothing about it until some shoppers rushed out front to see what was happening."

Turning on the charm, Marc leans toward Penny, slightly opens his mouth, and smooths his mustache with his thumb and finger. "Yes, I remember you, Penny." He smiles coyly, his charm oozing. "You were very cooperative when I spoke with you. As I remember, you were very nice, an actual pleasure to talk to. Today, we're just following up on some leads."

Penny succumbs to Marc's charm. She casts her eyes down, embarrassed. Peering from under her brows, she catches Marc's gaze. A tiny, warm smile passes her lips, and her cheeks flush a rosy pink, barely noticeable beneath her gorgeous natural glow.

"Did either of you go outside to see what was happening?" Marc continues.

Both women shake their heads no.

I nod to Marc, motioning that we need to talk, and ask the ladies to excuse us for a minute. We walk to the back hall, just far enough to still see the two ladies.

"Something was off about Mildred when you asked about having gone outside. She glanced twice toward a different department, but I couldn't tell which one." As I talk with Marc, Mildred's eyes continue to jump around, eyeing department after department as though she's searching for someone. "I think she might know more than she's letting on. Maybe we should separate them."

Nodding, Marc looks toward the woman. "I noticed it, too. She seems taken with you, my friend, a little flirty. Do you want me to talk to her? I might shake her up some."

"Sounds like a good idea. Walk Mildred around the store near other employees and departments. See if you notice anything. I'll hang back a little and watch from a distance."

As we return to the lingerie counter, I whisper, "I'll tell Penny we're going to talk with some of the other employees, and you make up some excuse to get Mildred away with you. You know what to do." I grin, winking at Marc. We've done this a thousand times, so it's pretty routine.

"Sounds good, partner." And the plan goes into action.

The shoe section is the closest to lingerie, so Marc guides Mildred in that direction. I observe Mildred and her coworkers from a distance to avoid arousing suspicion. The farther she gets from the lingerie section, the more tense she becomes. Mildred steers Marc away from the perfume and jewelry counters, altogether avoiding that section of the shop. Marc notices her behavior and guides her closer to that area.

He stops to look at some of the jewelry, and Mildred turns two shades lighter. She fidgets with her necklace, pressing her lips tight together. Her eyes dart around the store, never glancing toward the sales clerks behind the jewelry counter.

The female sales clerk has light strawberry blonde hair, about shoulder length, cut in a bob, just as Dr. Winsloe described the woman in the alley. Her four-inch heels make her much taller than her five-foot-two frame. The clerk eases behind a tall jewelry display and is no longer visible to Mildred and Marc.

Marc notices her actions and signals me to approach. He moves on Mildred, confronting her regarding her involvement in concealing the witness's identity.

"You saw someone go out the back door Tuesday, didn't you, Mildred," he states, his face taut, his eyes gripping Mildred's. "I know you're trying to protect one of your friends, but you're interfering with a criminal investigation."

Relentless in his pursuit of the truth, he presses on. "A woman behind this building may have witnessed the entire kidnapping. If you know something and keep it secret, I can charge you for withholding evidence of a serious crime, Mildred. If I charge you, well, you could go to jail. You understand that, don't you?"

Rattled, poor Mildred is tearful by this point. With his tender heart, Marc eases up, giving her time to think.

"You'll feel better if you tell me, Mildred." Marc places his hand on her shoulder and bends down, looking more gently at her, face to face. "Your friend won't be in trouble. We just want to find the missing woman before it's too late for her," he pleads, his tone more mellow.

No matter how hard Mildred tries to stifle her tears, they plunge down her cheeks like Niagara Falls, leaving trails in her makeup. Marc places his arm around her shoulder and guides her to the employee lounge in the back hall.

Observing the entire interaction between Mildred and Marc, the jewelry clerk doesn't notice me as I approach. When they leave, she takes a deep breath, turns around, and is face to face with me. 'Francine' is inscribed on her employee name tag.

"Hello, there," she says, forcing a toothy smile. "Is there something in particular you would like to see?"

"Yes," I reply, pulling out my badge and showing it to her. "You."

CHAPTER 12

52 Hours 16 Minutes

Thursday 2:38 p.m.

Francine maintains her composure and turns to her coworker, who's gaping at my badge. "I'm going on break," she tells him bluntly. Francine then struts from behind the counter and tromps towards the back hall, about five steps ahead of me. I feel like I'm back in grammar school, getting escorted to the principal's office. She strikes me as a woman who's always in charge.

We get to the lounge as Marc completes his interview with Mildred. The two women stand, facing each other, and Mildred, regretful, begins apologizing to Francine.

"I'm so sorry, Francine. I had no choice. They knew I was hiding something." Mildred looks a mess from all her crying, mascara now smudged from her tears and one eyelash loosened from her lid, flopping when she blinks. Nervous, she twists and rubs her hands without ceasing. Although she did nothing wrong, Mildred apologizes to Francine, Marc, and everyone she sees.

Francine nods her head and forces a tight-lipped smile. "It's okay, Millie. It's okay. I should have come forward in the beginning. I never should have asked you to cover for me. That wasn't fair to you. I'm the one that's sorry.

"Go straighten your face, then tell Monique you need the rest of today off. I'm sure the detective can handle that for you." Francine hugs Mildred, pulls a couple of tissues from the box on a side table, and tips Mildred's chin up as she pats the tears from her face. Giving an 'it's okay' smile, she hands her off to Marc.

Assuming the role of guardian, Marc takes over. "Yes, ma'am, I'll take care of that. Don't you worry, Miss Mildred, I've got this." Marc places his arm around Mildred's shoulder and leads her to a separate area to tidy herself, leaving me alone with Francine to discuss what she saw Tuesday.

I motion to a blue sofa along a wall in the lounge. Francine stiffens her body, snarls her lip, and sits down, keeping her back straight and chin high. She crosses her legs and folds her hands in her lap, avoiding eye contact.

Sitting beside her at an angle, I begin by pulling out my notepad. "I'm Detective Benson. Francine, you were the woman at the back of the building Tuesday, and you saw something that scared you. Tell me what happened."

Francine's bottom lip quivers despite tightening her mouth, her frailty beginning to break through her tough gal exterior. "I know I should have told the police what I saw when they came Tuesday. But I was afraid, sort of in shock," she explains, looking down. "I didn't want to get involved." Francine looks at her hands lying in her lap and begins wringing them. "So I hid in the back room until they left."

A large teardrop falls from her eye, flows down her face, and drips off her chin. Another follows, and then another. I hand her the box of tissues sitting on the table. Even though I know she's upset, my compassion for her is thin, given her statement of not wanting to get involved. That's one thing I have little tolerance for unless there is a fantastic reason, like you'd get shot or stabbed or die, or something horrible might happen to someone.

"What did you see, Francine? Start at the beginning, when you first went outside."

She answers my questions in a matter-of-fact manner, emotionless. It's my impression that, since we've found her, she just wants to get this thing over with. She seems cold-hearted to me. Maybe I'm being too critical, but when I look at her response to the kidnapping and Ivy's, there's just no comparing the two reactions, one honorable and self-sacrificing, the other weak, self-protecting, self-absorbed.

"Well," she begins. "It was my break time, about ten-fifteen, so I walked out back to smoke a cigarette. Not long after I lit it, I heard a noise from the alley, like a car pulling in. I knew no trucks were delivering today, so I glanced around the corner to see what the noise was." Francine clears her throat and dabs her eyes with a tissue.

"A woman was yelling at a man standing near a dark blue car parked in the alley. She ran up to him and shoved him, screaming at him. She pushed him hard, and he almost fell, then he came back at her and knocked her to the ground." Her voice grows louder, and her eyes dart around the room as she motions with her hands.

"Go on, Francine," I encourage. "You're doing great. What happened then?"

"Well, the man bent over her, grabbed her purse, and jumped in the car. I thought he'd mugged her. He did a U-ey and took off fast out of the alley." She dries her eyes and blows her nose.

"There was no one else around… and the woman was just lying there, so I walked closer to see if she was alright. I didn't want to just leave her like that," she explains, taking another tissue from the now half-empty box.

"Did you call for help?" I inquire, already knowing the answer.

Francine drops her head and looks down at the shredded, damp tissue she's twisting in her hands. "No, I didn't," she whimpers, shaking her head.

"About that time, a man came running down the alley toward us, yelling, and I got scared. I thought he might think I had hurt the woman, so I backed away and went back behind the building. I looked around the corner twice to be sure the woman was being taken care of, and then I went back inside." Taking a deep breath, Francine composes herself. "I was terrified," she admits, her voice low, quivering.

Needing more clarification, I ask how Mildred became involved and what details she remembers about the kidnapper. Francine becomes agitated, shifting her position on the sofa several times, wincing as she readjusts her clothing, tugging at her sleeves, and pulling at her skirt.

"You could use a quick break," I surmise. "I'm sure I can find you some water or something to drink."

Francine nods her head. "I could use some water. I have some in my bag." She hastens to the line of lockers in the adjoining room. I follow close behind. Retrieving a bottle of water, she takes a few sips, leans against the lockers, and stares at a picture on the opposite wall.

After a few minutes, I interrupt the silence by resuming my questioning. "How did Mildred get involved?"

Much more relaxed, Francine takes a deep breath and sweeps a strand of her shiny red hair behind her ear. "Millie saw me in the back room when I came in. She knew something was wrong when I slammed the door shut and locked it."

She pauses, then explains, "I didn't go into details about anything with her. I just asked her not to say anything to anyone about my being out there. I told her I thought a woman got mugged but saw nothing. I know Millie is a woman of her word, a good woman." Francine stares at the floor. A few seconds later, she lifts her head, looks me straight in the eye, arches her brows, and adds, "So I made her promise."

It's difficult to gauge how much shame or guilt Francine feels for not coming forward after the kidnapping, involving Mildred in her cover-up, or leaving Ivy unconscious on the pavement. Francine never came forward of her own accord, but she did tell Mildred she was sorry for asking her to cover for her. Francine seemed sincere.

Dr. Winsloe also arrived to care for Ivy before Francine left, and she showed concern by looking to make sure Ivy was being cared for. I can understand how she could think we might accuse her of attacking Ivy. The man was gone by the time Dr. Winsloe arrived.

Regardless of what I believe about Francine and her not relating what she saw to the police, I'm not here to pass judgment on her or anyone else. I've heard many stories from witnesses over the years, and Francine's is not the most faint-hearted of them. Predicting how a person will react to a situation when scared is impossible. Most of the time, they don't handle difficult situations well, at least not how they imagined they would.

"Tell me about the man that threw the woman to the ground." I pull the suspect's face sketch from the folder and show it to her. "Is this him?"

She takes the drawing from my hand, stares at it for a minute or two, then hands it back. "I can't be sure. I couldn't see his face from so far away. I remember he was about medium height, with blondish hair. He wore a heavy brown coat with a dark-colored beanie or something like that on his head." She lowers her head and looks away as she hands the picture back to me.

She inches her way to the sofa and sits down. I remove the sketch of the woman from the folder. "Did you see this woman in the alley?" I ask, sitting down next to her.

Francine looks at the picture and thoughtfully inspects the image. "No, I'm sorry, detective. I didn't see any woman besides the one lying on the ground. I'm sorry. That's everything I saw."

"You've been helpful. We may have to contact you again if we have further questions." I stand, collecting my files, and add, "I want you to understand something, Francine." I take a deep breath. "If I choose to, I can charge you for withholding vital evidence. I understand the trauma of witnessing a crime, but as you said, you should have told the original officers what you saw."

Before I exit the door, I look back at her, still sitting on the sofa, looking down at her hands. I make one last statement. "Running away doesn't mean you escape the memory of what happened,

Francine. It just gives you one more thing you'll never forget."

Closing the door behind me, I leave Francine to deal with memories that will dwell in the corner of her mind—*forever.*

75

CHAPTER 13

53 Hours 26 Minutes

Thursday 3:48 p.m.

Having found the witness Dr. Winsloe told us about, we head for the car. Before Marc and I return to the office to review the case and decide our next steps, we opt for a quick bite from a fast-food joint since we have yet to have lunch. After we purchase our five-dollar meal deals, we find an empty booth, spread the luscious meals in front of us, and discuss the women we just interviewed.

"Did you get the last names of Mildred and Francine from the supervisor?"

"Yes sir, I wasn't gonna leave without 'em," Marc mumbles, chewing the bite of burger he just took. He glances at his notes and thumps the pad. "Francine Whittaker and Mildred Stone. I gotta say, I felt rather bad for Mildred. Her coworker put her in a hard place." His brows rise as he sips his soda and glances at me. "No telling what a friend will do to protect someone they care about. They'll keep all kinds of secrets, don't you think?"

I know what he's talking about, and it's not Mildred and Francine. He's telling me that if my relationship with Ivy has become more than professional, he won't say anything. It will be our secret. But most secrets don't stay hidden for long.

"You're right. A friend will do a lot for someone they work with, and even more for a genuine friend." Leaning back in my seat, I toss a few fries in my mouth, and half smile at Marc as a thought comes to mind. I reach across the table and, just for fun, poke his arm.

"Hell, Marc, I told you—I won't tell anybody about you and Ginger!"

Marc puffs up like a bullfrog when I mention Ginger. He finishes his meal and wads up the papers, tossing them on the tray. He knows

I'm joking, but it's still a sore spot.

Marc dated Ginger for several months a few years back. He bought her jewelry and all kinds of nice things. He thought she was the woman he could take home to Mama—until he saw her getting booked by the vice squad. Marc ducked down a hall so she wouldn't see him. He was so embarrassed, and he didn't want the guys at the station to know a hooker had hoodwinked him.

I laugh under my breath. Ginger had Marc snowed. I promised him I'd never tell the people at the station about his fling with Ginger—and I never have.

Still poking fun at Marc, I check my watch. Damn, it's almost four. I should be at Ivy's by now, but I'm still working on the case. I know I won't make it on time. I promised her, and she's depending on me.

I need to be there with her, but there's so much to do if we're going to find the kidnapped woman. It took too long to find Francine, and we learned nothing of real value. Nothing that will help us identify the suspect or the victim. We need to find out who they are. Time's running out.

"We gotta get going." I clench my jaw, grab both trays, and shove the trash in the can. Heading across the parking lot to the car, I pick up my pace, almost jogging.

"Whoa, slow down there, partner!" Marc hustles to keep up. "What's your hurry, Tomas?"

When we get in the car, I hit the start button, rev the engine, slam the charger into gear, and spin onto the road, tossing poor Marc around the front seat like popcorn bouncing in a popper. Yelling and cursing me with every breath, he grabs his seatbelt and tries to latch it, his body swaying from side to side as I weave in and out of traffic.

Although the road department brined the roads a few hours ago, the car skids to a stop when I slam on my brakes at a red light.

"What the hell, Tom! What's got into you?" His eyes bulge, his face is red, and his nostrils flare with every breath. "You're scaring the shit outta me. Slow the hell down, or I'm driving!"

Finally, adjusted in his seat with his safety belt latched, he clears his throat and shakes his head.

"I don't know what's wrong with you," he grumbles under his breath, ripping his hand through his hair. "I mean it, Tomas. I'm not putting up with this shit. I don't know what bee got in your ass, but I'm about to snatch it out!"

"Sorry, Marc. I know you're pissed, but I'm way behind schedule. I didn't know it was this late." I whip into a mini-mart parking lot. "How 'bout you get us a coffee while I make a quick call."

"What the hell… am I your errand boy now? What the shit? I know who you're calling." He shakes his gloved finger at my face. "We're gonna talk about this shit, I tell you, we are!"

Marc jerks the twenty from my hand and huffs off toward the store, still ranting and cursing.

In a microsecond, I hit the voice control button on the steering wheel. "Call Ivy."

"Calling," the automated voice responds.

Keeping my eye on the store for Marc's return, I whisper under my breath, "Please answer."

One ring.

"Please answer."

Two rings.

"Please answer."

Three rings.

"Hello, detective." Ivy's mellow voice greets me from the Bluetooth speaker.

My heart plays hopscotch in my chest for a second, and my mind goes blank. Not sure what to say, I blurt out, "I'm late."

"You're kidding!" she says, giggling. "I'm just joking. I didn't expect you to be here at precisely four." She sounds calm.

I feel better knowing she understands. "How about I pick up some supper when I head your way and grab groceries tomorrow? I still have to go by the office and review a few plans with my partner. It may be closer to six before I can get there. I'm so sorry, Ivy. Do you think Galvin will stay with you until then?"

"He and I talked earlier, and he's willing to stay as long as I need him to. We've had a perfect day. I've gotten a lot of rest. I told Galvin what happened, the kidnapping, and the clumsiness that caused my memory loss. How did your meeting with Dr. Winsloe go?"

"I'll tell you later. I gotta go," I utter, spotting Marc returning from the store. Before I finish the call, he reaches for the car door, climbs in, and hands me my coffee.

"I'll call you back in a bit, okay?" I hope Ivy says okay so Marc doesn't hear our conversation. But, of course, I'm not that lucky.

"Okay, no problem. There's no reason for you to stay again tonight, detective. Galvin is…"

"Wait a sec," I interrupt as quickly as possible. Juggling hot coffee in one hand, I perch a finger from my other hand on the end call button. "I've gotta go, but I'll call you in a bit, and we can talk. Bye now." Pushing the button, I end the call before Ivy can say anything else.

I don't want Marc to overhear more of the conversation than he already has. He already thinks something's going on between us. Judging by Marc's behavior after I hung up, I should've used my cell phone to call Ivy instead of the car's Bluetooth.

A few minutes pass, and everything is quiet except for the low hum of the engine. All other sounds, inside and out, seem frozen in time: no noise from the people crossing the parking lot or from the other cars, no conversation inside the Charger.

I fumble with my coffee and thank Marc for getting it for us, but he's having no part of me. He sits in silence, focused only on the scene in front of him. His brows squeeze inward, creating furrows in his forehead, and his lips press tight together with only a slit to sip his coffee.

"Talk to me, Marc. I know you're pissed at me, but I'm not sure why. What'd I do?"

Maintaining his rigid posture and unwavering gaze, Marc gives me the cold shoulder, ignoring me. He knows I can't handle the silent treatment. So, I decide to give him the cold shoulder treatment and stop the car engine, waiting for him to talk.

A few minutes later, a harsh wind blows, and the freezing temperature from outside seeps into the car, replacing the chilly atmosphere created by the silence with a physical coldness. And so we sit, becoming frostier by the minute, with only the heat from the coffee cups to warm our hands and the hot steam to brush the chill from our faces.

Fifteen minutes later, our coffee is gone, and we both still sit, staring out the snow-covered windshield, with only the occasional car horn disrupting the silence. Our bodies tremble to keep us warm, making me even more determined to break the icy silence between us.

Another twenty minutes pass. I've had all the frost-biting cold I can take. Marc turns and looks at me as my finger inches close to the ignition. His body quivers like a tambourine, and he rubs his arms with his gloved hands to warm them. His cheeks and the tip of his nose are rosy red from the plunging temperature in the car.

"D-damn, T-tom, are you p-p-p-laying freeze out? It's fr-friggin' c-c-cold in here! C-crank this b-baby up and get s-some heat going, or I'm ma-marching my ass in that st-st-store before it fr-freezes off!" His words stumble out, impaired by his jittering jaw.

"You g-got it, p-partner!" I bop him on the arm, then press the ignition button. The car starts.

Not remembering that it takes a few minutes for the heat to warm, I rev the gas twice, then turn the control on full blast. The rush of icy air from the dash smacks my face, making my cheeks sting with pain. My hands, numb from the cold, fumble to find the heat settings in the dim light. After removing a glove to feel the controls, I turn the airspeed down.

Waiting for the cold air trapped in the heater to warm, Marc and I hunch our shoulders as though we are doing sit-ups, bury our necks deeper into our coats, and hug ourselves even tighter with our arms, trying to guard ourselves against the plunging temperature inside the car.

Marc stares at me through squinched eyes, his teeth chattering, and his breath visible as white billows in the icy air. I'm not sure this was the best method for getting him to talk to me again, but it worked.

"I-I'm s-sorry," I say through chattering teeth. "W-we've b-been so b-b-busy with this c-case that I haven't had t-t-time to t-talk to you about anything," I blow warm air from my lungs through my frozen lips into my gloved hands.

Five minutes later, we're no longer shivering. Hot air flows from the heater vents. Our bodies relax as we warm, and our breath no longer hangs in the air.

Marc sits, staring out the windshield, his face drooping. I regret not telling him about my stay at Ivy's.

"I'm not hiding anything from you, Marc, and I never will. You're my family. I should've gone into more detail when I talked with you about Ivy's condition while I was at the hospital yesterday."

"What the hell were you thinking, turning off the car like that? It's freezing outside, with two feet of frozen snow on the ground and more falling. Not to mention the wind's blowin' like hell froze over!"

Marc doesn't do cold very well. I'm shocked he hasn't moved to a warmer climate. He's had plenty of offers, some that included promotions, but family is his tie to the area. He'd never leave his parents for a more comfortable environment. You wouldn't know it by his powerful appearance, but he's a real softy.

"Dammit, Tomas. You know better than to get involved with a witness. You gotta keep control of your emotions in cases like this."

I know I'm not involved with Ivy the way Marc thinks, but I am confused about my feelings for her. Concentrating on the swishing wipers struggling to remove the heavy snow collected on the windshield, I avoid glancing in Marc's direction.

"Look at me when I'm talking to you," he demands.

Marc's been protective of me since we met. He's only five months older than me, but he treats me like he's my big brother. I know I'm about to get a good lecture by his tone.

One thing you can say about Marc is that he commands attention, not only with his imposing six-foot stature and sculpted physique but also by the authoritative demeanor he can turn on and off like a light switch. He can be the jolly joker, as meek as a kitten, or as ferocious as a lion, depending on what the situation calls for.

When he knows he has my full attention, he continues his speech. "I know this kind of case is hard for you, a kidnapped woman. And I know you empathize with the witness, but you've got to stay objective, not get involved personally.

"I wish you'd get into a different department, Tomas, something besides kidnapping and murder cases. It's like you just want to torture and punish yourself for the rest of your life. No matter how many cases you solve, you can't change the past, Tom. You just keep bringing back old memories. Let 'em go." He reaches around my shoulder and gives me a firm one-arm hug.

Whenever we work cases like this, and I get too involved, Marc tells me the same thing: that I need to change departments and stop exposing myself to kidnappings and murders.

Every time, he ends up hugging me like this, too.

And, every time, I remember being hugged by him when I was seven, just after the most devastating event of my life.

Pushing the memories away, I try to ease Marc's concerns by clarifying my position with Ivy.

"I don't have a relationship with Ivy other than professionally, Marc. I'm just helping her out for a few days since she has a concussion and doesn't have anyone else to stay with her."

Squeezing his lips into a pucker like he just ate a sour lemon, he shakes his head. "You see what you're doing, right? You're justifying your actions. I know someone else can stay with her other than you. She had people in her life long before you came along. I heard her on the phone say somebody named Galvin would stay. He must be a friend or relative or something, so don't tell me you're the only one she can depend on. Got it?"

"I sort of feel responsible for her second head injury," I state in my defense, "since it was my fault she was at the crime scene when she fell. She wouldn't have a concussion if I hadn't taken her there. And now, with her memory loss, I thought if I was around her more, I could help her remember little details quicker, so maybe we can locate the missing woman."

Running my hands through my hair in frustration, I doubt myself. "Maybe I'm wrong," I murmur under my breath. "I just wanted to help Ivy out and solve the case."

Marc leans back in his seat, stretching his long legs as far as the car floor will allow. "I'm gonna run in and get some more coffee. My ass is still cold from that freeze-out shit you pulled." A wide smile sweeps across his face.

The clock on the dash reads five-fourteen. Marc and I still have to plan our next steps for solving the kidnapping case. We're used to putting in late-night hours when we have a lead, but I'd like to get to Ivy's if possible. I'll call her the minute we get back to the office. No matter how much Marc tells me I'm not responsible for Ivy's concussion, that's not how I feel. I don't want to risk him catching part of my conversation with her again if I can prevent it. It would just upset him further.

When Marc exits the mini-mart, I notice the bounce in his step has returned. I can tell we're good now, and he's over his anger.

"Here you go," he says as he hands me my coffee. "And I grabbed us a little snack, too." He passes me a couple of chocolate dunks wrapped in wax paper.

"Um, that smells good. I didn't realize I was still hungry. Thanks," I reply, shoving half a donut in my mouth. "Maybe we can talk about what we're gonna do with the case on our way back to the office and call it a night. A good night's sleep wouldn't hurt either of us. How's that sound?"

"I'd kinda like to finish our conversation about Ivy Preston before we move on to the case. We've gotta talk about her, Tomas. It's not just going away, not with you having stayed at her house last night. I just don't understand. That's not like you."

"I only stayed because she didn't want her family or friends to know she had gotten hurt. I went with her to the hospital from the crime scene and then drove her home. The doctor said she needed someone to stay with her for a few days. It was late, so I slept in a spare bedroom. That was it, period."

Finishing my second donut and half my coffee, I start the car, pull onto the road, and head for the office. Glancing at Marc as I drive, I add, "It's all innocent, Marc."

Marc gives me a doubting look and curls up one side of his mouth, shaking his head. "I can tell there's more to it," he insists.

I shrug my shoulders. "Okay, I'm attracted to her, and I might have even flirted with her a little, but that's all, nothing more than that."

Grinning, I nudge him and add, "It kinda boosts my ego to flirt with a young, beautiful woman like her. That's all it is. I've never crossed the line with a witness. After all the years we've known each other and worked together, you should know I'd never compromise my ethics. I never have, and I never will."

CHAPTER 14

55 Hours 35 Minutes

Thursday 5:57 p.m.

When I pull into the parking lot at the station, Marc and I are talking about the kidnapping case. I want to call Ivy since it's almost six, so I suggest we finish by reviewing the case in the small conference room just down from our offices.

"How about you get us set up, Marc. I need to take a quick break and stretch my legs for a few minutes. I think I'll grab another coffee, too. Want one?"

"That'd be great. I'll meet you in the small conference room."

When he's out of sight, I take out my phone and call Ivy. Marc's warning about not getting too involved flashes like a neon sign in my mind. Could he be right? Could Marc be sensing something I'm blind to? Ivy answers. I close my eyes and take a deep breath to clear my thoughts before I speak.

"Hey," I utter under my breath. "I'm so sorry I'm not there yet. Looks like I'm gonna be even later than I thought. It's been one of those days." My fingers travel through my hair, and I glance around to be sure no one can hear my conversation. "I'll be there soon, though. I promise."

The neon sign keeps flashing. I squeeze my forehead between my thumb and finger, trying to relieve the pressure in my head. The dull ache behind my eyes has returned.

In my mind, I know that if I'm hiding my conversation, it's unprofessional. But my instinct tells me I need to be with Ivy for her sake, to protect her.

"It's okay, detective. I understand. You have a job to do, and right now, finding that woman is the priority. Galvin plans to stay, so it's not a big deal. He's made us some supper, and I'm going to bed early. Maybe you can come over in the morning, and we can try to jog my memory. Would that work for you?"

Her voice breaks, and I can tell she's tired. She needs a good night's rest, and so do I. As long as someone is there with her, she should be fine. And going in the morning will also give Marc and me more time to work on the case without rushing.

"That's nice of Galvin to stay. It might be best I come in the morning since I don't know how long I'll be here. Did you take your medicine?" Shit. I wish I hadn't asked that. It makes me sound like a mother hen.

Ivy giggles, then answers, "Yes, sir, I'm doing everything the doctor said. I want to get back to normal as quickly as possible. There's no need to worry, detective—but I'm glad you do," she adds.

I can't quite figure out the meaning of her last comment, but it makes me feel good inside. A grin slips onto my face, and I squirm and shuffle my feet like a schoolboy.

"What time should I come in the morning? I want to be sure to get there before Galvin leaves."

"How does nine-thirty sound? That way, I can sleep late. Galvin doesn't go to work until one, so he'll still be here."

"That's good. I'll bring us all some breakfast. Just have coffee ready."

"I'll have it perked and waiting." Hesitating, her voice low, Ivy says, "May I ask you a question?"

"Sure, you can ask me anything."

"I've always heard that the first forty-eight hours are the most critical for solving a crime." She pauses and sniffs. "Forty-eight hours have passed. Does that mean you won't find the woman… alive?" Her voice cracks.

Through the phone, I hear Galvin asking her if she's okay. I know she's upset and beating herself up, thinking she could have done more to save the woman. I try to reassure her by answering as best I can without giving false hope.

"Ivy, stranger kidnappings are rare. The victim may know her kidnapper. We just have to find the link. Do you understand what I'm saying?"

"Yes, I understand," she replies, sniffling.

"To answer your question, the first forty-eight to seventy-two hours are ideal for gathering evidence and information because the leads are fresher, but evidence collecting and following leads doesn't stop there. Every moment is precious, especially in a missing person case. Most cases like this get solved within a few days to a week, not within two days. Sometimes, it's difficult to identify the suspect, like in this case. But that doesn't mean we won't find him."

There's only silence on the phone—no sound of breathing, no sniffling—just complete silence.

"Ivy, are you listening?"

"Uh-huh. I'm listening."

"You need to know one other thing," I emphasize. "I'm damn good at what I do."

Pausing, I take a deep breath. Having to say what I know Ivy doesn't want to hear, I temper my words as much as possible.

"I can't guarantee that we'll find her alive. No one can do that. But I can guarantee we *will* find her. Her family will not go through life not knowing what happened to her—I promise you that."

CHAPTER 15

56 Hours 11 Minutes

Thursday 6:33 p.m.

While waiting for the coffee to brew in my office, I check the evidence database to see if the DNA results are back on the lipstick. After printing the report, I pour two coffees and head down the hall to the conference room.

We've already posted the timeline on the bulletin board with the victim and suspect's sketches, along with the witness information. Marc is adding what we got today to the board. Sitting the coffee on the conference table, I read the DNA report while Marc completes his task.

"That's weird," I say, glancing at Marc. "The lab pulled DNA evidence from the lipstick sample, but it matches a deceased woman's DNA."

"That is weird." Marc rubs his bristled chin. "Think they made a mistake?"

"I dunno. I'll have to look into it further." Laying the report to the side for now, I sit down and eye the board as I sip my coffee.

Marc blows his coffee to cool it and scans the board before we start. "Okay, this is what we have, and I gotta say, partner, it's not a hell of a lot." He sits at the end of the table, turns his chair sideways to see the board, and begins.

"The timeline seems pretty accurate, given the three witness statements. All reports show the alleged kidnapping occurred on Tuesday, November 29th at 10:22 a.m." Marc pauses, then adds, "Let's speed this up, Tomas, don't you think?"

"I'm with you. I don't think there's much we can do tonight other than go over this and figure out our next steps."

"Okay, let's see." Marc directs my attention to the board. "There is a single witness, Ivy Preston, who states she saw a man, our suspect, place a cloth or rag over a woman's nose and mouth, our victim, and the woman went limp. He shoved the woman into the trunk of an old blue Plymouth. The witness struggled with the kidnapper, who subsequently shoved her to the ground, and Preston lost consciousness."

Sipping coffee, Marc points to the timetable.

"At 10:15, Francine Whittaker, an employee at Geordies, takes a break and goes out back to smoke. She heard a car in the alley and peered around the building."

Marc aims his laser pointer at the photo of the alley and the buildings specifying where everyone was during the crime and continues.

"Whittaker said she saw Preston arguing with a man beside a blue car and struggling with him. She verified Preston hit the ground and didn't get up."

Exhaling, he turns and faces me, tapping the laser on his palm. "Considering all times given by witnesses and the time it would have taken for the events described to have occurred, this likely happened between 10:20 and 10:25."

"That all seems to fit," I say. "Go on."

"Somewhere between 10:25 and 10:30, Whittaker approaches Preston, who is unconscious, then rushes away when Dr. Winsloe runs toward Preston to render help. Whittaker states she was afraid and returned to Geordies, staying out of sight when the police arrived a short time later."

Wasting no time, Marc wraps it up. "Dr. Winsloe is sure it was 10:28 when he arrived at the shopping center, spotted Preston almost immediately, got out to help her, and saw Whittaker leaving. He told a bystander, Kevin Hollister, to call 911. The center reports receiving the call at 10:32, and the ambulance and police arrived at 10:38. Hollister was not a witness to the events other than Preston unconscious and Dr. Winsloe assisting her.”

“That’s a good timeline of the events, Marc. We can present that to the captain tomorrow morning. Let me review the witness information, and we’ll decide what we will do next.”

Using my notes as a reference, I begin.

“The first witness, Ivy Preston, is the only one who saw the crime occur. Since her interview, she’s had a second fall that resulted in a concussion and now has no memory of the kidnapping. Her memory should return, but who knows how long that will take.” I pause and walk to the board.

“The only other person who witnessed any part of the crime,” I tap my finger on Francine Whittaker’s name, “did not see the kidnapping but can verify Preston was arguing with a man, struggled with him, and became unconscious. She also witnessed the suspect leaving the scene. Whittaker stated the suspect picked up a purse and tossed it into the car. Since Preston’s purse was not missing, we can assume it was the victim’s purse, and the lipstick taken for evidence was hers.”

Marc stands to stretch for a moment. “Need more coffee,” he demands as he hands me his cup, a sly smirk on his face.

“What am I now, your damn errand boy?” I smirk, picking at him.

Marc laughs, getting pleasure from the reversal of our roles. I shake my head and can’t help but chuckle as I take the cup and head down the hall to get us both more coffee. I’m used to drinking multiple cups daily, but I’ve overdosed on caffeine today. Much more, and I’ll be up all night.

Returning with the coffee and a couple of snacks I found in my desk drawer, I sit down at the conference table and continue my review.

“The next person on the scene is Dr. Marshall Winsloe, who has just pulled into the parking lot. He sees Preston unconscious on the ground with Whittaker standing over her. Whittaker runs away when Winsloe approaches, so the doc checks out Preston and tells a bystander to call 911, just like you said."

I flip through my interview notes with Dr. Winsloe.

"The doc did not witness any part of the crime itself but said that just before entering the parking lot, a blue car, driving too fast, banged a U-ey in front of him on the road. He thought the guy might've headed toward 90-West."

I wrap it up.

"So, all three witnesses said the kidnapper had curly blonde hair and drove an old dark blue Plymouth, unknown year and model. Only one witness saw the victim, a female in her thirties or early forties with long chestnut hair. We released sketches of the victim and suspect as missing persons."

Pausing, I stand and move around the room, stretching. It's been a long day, and I'm ready to go home. Unfortunately, Marc and I still have a lot to go over.

"So far," I continue, "over forty-eight hours later, no one has reported a missing woman that fits the victim's description, and we haven't identified who the suspect is, either. DNA results on the lipstick found at the scene, presumed to have belonged to the victim, link to a deceased woman in the database." I stop for a second and turn toward Marc. "So, partner, what now?"

Marc dons his most serious thinking face. Scrunching his brows, his hand stroking his beard, he contemplates our next move.

"We have the timeline but not an identified victim," Marc begins. "We've got all the camera footage from the parking lot, and McClusky's team is reviewing it and should have his report by tomorrow morning. I'll check to be sure the footage includes the location where Dr. Winsloe said the guy did the U-turn. I'm pretty sure it does, and I'll follow up on the camera footage on I-90, too."

I nod my head, signaling my agreement. "I'll follow up on the

DNA sample and its link to the deceased woman, talk to the lab, and do some research there."

"Something feels off about this entire case," I mumble, rubbing the back of my neck to ease the tightness in my shoulders. I stare at the investigation board.

"It doesn't feel right, Marc. My gut tells me the victim and kidnapper know each other, maybe a relationship gone bad, or professionally—I don't know. Surely someone would have reported a missing person by now unless they were covering it up." Leaning back in my chair, I interlock my fingers behind my head and rest my right ankle on my knee.

"I agree with you, Tomas. It feels off to me, too. I don't think it was a stranger kidnapping either."

Marc stands and walks around the corner of the table, studying the board. His eyes open a little wider, expressing that 'ah ha' look he gets when an idea pops into his head. He snaps his fingers and points at me.

"What if the victim wasn't from this area?" he proposes. "What if she was from some other town or state? There are always tourists here. We need to check with the local hotels and motels to see if an occupant might have left their belongings without checking out. What do you think, Tom?"

"Hell, Marc, we should have done that already!"

I realize my concern has been about Ivy. Typically, I would have had someone checking local motels before now. Because I spent so much time with Ivy yesterday, I haven't investigated the case from all perspectives as usual.

"It's my fault." I lean forward, prop my elbows on the table, and rest my chin in my hands as I think. "My game's off. Maybe you should take over this case, Marc. There's no excuse for me missing something like this. You must be right about my mind being more on Ivy than the case."

I've never even considered turning over the lead in an investigation to someone else. What's wrong with me? Am I more interested in Ivy than I think, and that's causing it? No, it can't be that. My feelings have never interfered with my investigations before. I don't think they are now either. I'm just off my game. Maybe it's because my mom and the victim share so many similarities. Could that be it?

"You couldn't have done anything before now that would change where we are on this case, Tomas. We've had very little to go on, and we're following all the leads we've found." Marc puts his hand on my shoulder, trying to reassure me.

"You did the right thing by taking Ivy back to the scene yesterday. I would have done the same thing," he insists. "Who would have thought she would fall again and end up at the hospital? I mean, what freakin' luck, right? We know what to do, so we'll start first thing in the morning."

"You're right. You handle the camera footage and make sure the sketches of the man and woman go nationwide. I'll get some guys to check the local hotels and follow up with the lab about the DNA results. It's too late to do anything tonight, so let's go home. My brain's exhausted. Maybe everything will fall together in the morning. I'm supposed to meet with Ivy at nine-thirty to see how her memory is coming along, but I'll get an early start."

"Sounds good, partner, and no more talk about stepping back and turning the lead over to me or anyone else, you hear me?"

To appease Marc, I nod. A short time later, we head home, plans in hand.

* * *

Having had only the burger since breakfast, I drop by *Milton's Cafe* to grab a good meal before going home. Cautiously, I pull into the snow-covered parking lot, leave the motor running, and remain in the car, staring out the windshield. The wipers swipe back and forth, their rhythmic movement hypnotizing me. Flipping the snow from side to side, the wipers never quite clear the collection of flakes from the glass.

That's how I feel—like my emotions are flipping back and forth, and nothing is becoming clear. I'm confused about my concerns for Ivy and wonder why I've not been as attentive to this case as usual.

Is my attachment to Ivy because she is an innocent bystander who got involved in a kidnapping? Because the kidnapper injured her? No, that can't be it. Most cases I've worked on involve innocent people as witnesses, and sometimes, they get hurt.

Could it be because the memories of my mom are resurfacing in my mind? Memories I've tried to suppress all these years. Memories returning because so many things are similar between the victim and my mom—both having long chestnut hair, and both…

Stop!

I refuse to let my mind go there. Fighting to keep the memory from taking control, I command it back into the recesses of my mind, imprisoning it once again. I won't allow the emotional pain and depression to consume me as they once did. Not again.

Could this be why I occupy myself more with Ivy? Because I'm trying to keep those memories buried?

The wipers fling themselves back and forth, still unable to keep up with the barrage of snow. And even though the motion of the wipers helps soothe my somber mood, I continue sitting in my car, warm and staring out the window, not wanting to move.

There's something special about Ivy that draws me to her. She's an attractive woman. I can't help but smile every time I see her beautiful tipped-up nose sprinkled with freckles and the luscious brown eyes I could get lost in. Her radiant smile brightens the gloomiest winter day, and the quirky look she sometimes gets on her face—who wouldn't find that alluring?

Ivy is compassionate and caring about people, particularly those in need. I've never worked on one of her cases, but I have observed her in court several times. I've watched how she interacts with her clients, witnesses, and others. She has an excellent reputation as an attorney, and everyone in the legal field respects her. I've wanted to get to know her better for a while now.

I'm fascinated by her, but that's not why I'm concerned about her. Although I can't pinpoint the reason, my instinct tells me she's unsafe. She's already gotten injured—two head injuries occurring in the same freakish way, falling on ice. But for some inexplicable reason, I sense she's in real danger, and I'm the only one who can protect her.

I don't know—none of it makes any sense. It's more than a hunch. It's the strangest feeling I've ever had.

My exhaustion is catching up with me, and I could sleep sitting here. The pressure behind my eyes is returning. Forcing myself to leave the warm comfort of the car, I step out into the harsh bite of the winter wind. Taking a deep, cleansing breath, I look at the night sky—no stars, no moon, only the dim light of the city reflecting into the emptiness. The snow isn't soft and white, floating like thin pieces of cotton from the sky like before. In seconds, it's transformed into hard ice pellets, plummeting to earth, bouncing on the pavement, and pelting my face like tiny rocks.

I have a feeling something terrible is about to happen.

CHAPTER 16

71 Hours 0 Minutes

Friday December 2
9:22 a.m.

Arriving at Ivy's, Galvin greets me at the door and takes the bags of breakfast foods to the kitchen. He seems like a nice guy, friendly, about average height with a lean body build.

Galvin's appearance reminds me more of a rock star than an expert violinist. His blonde-streaked hair is much longer than mine and hangs down his back in a low ponytail. Irregular length strands hang loose beside his face. His short, strappy beard suits him. Galvin's wearing the same clothes as yesterday—jeans, a plain blue long-sleeved tee shirt, socks, and sandals.

Following Galvin into the kitchen, I help him unload the items I bought.

"I didn't know what Ivy might have in her fridge, so I just picked up some quick-to-fix items: eggs, bacon, bread, and such. I'll whip it up in no time." I begin laying the items on the counter.

"Where's Ivy?" I ask. "I haven't heard a sound from her since I arrived."

Pulling out some skillets and butter, Galvin removes the remaining food from the bags and helps prepare breakfast.

"She's getting cleaned up," he replies, nibbling on some shredded cheese he took from a bag.

He stops what he's doing and stares at me. "Ivy said you were with her at the hospital both times when she fell and stayed with her all night on Wednesday so she wouldn't be alone. That was very kind of you. Most detectives wouldn't have assumed a responsibility like that." Galvin cocks his head like he's asking a question instead of making a statement.

Glancing at him, I shrug my shoulders and continue sorting the breakfast items. "I suppose they wouldn't," I acknowledge. "Fact is, she needed someone to stay, so I did. It was no big deal."

He seems to accept my answer.

"I told her she should have called me," he says, then shakes his head, frowning. "She's so stubborn. She lets no one help her do anything."

Galvin waves and swings the spoon he's holding to emphasize his words. "I'm surprised she let you stay," he says, pointing the spoon at me. "And I'm more surprised she finally called me." He points to himself with the spoon.

"Really?" I question. "I would have thought you'd have been more surprised she let me stay."

Galvin draws his head back, still nibbling at the cheese.

"Oh, no," he begins, waving the spoon. "Ivy's a very private person. She'd be more likely to let you stay since you already knew everything. She wouldn't want anyone she knows to see her vulnerable, needing help. Ivy's quick to help others but is very independent and doesn't like to rely on anyone for anything."

"Hmm, that's interesting." I take the bag of cheese from Galvin and nibble on it while I cook the bacon.

I've witnessed Ivy's stubborn and independent side several times since she and I met on Tuesday. She's very self-directed and determined, but I've also seen her most vulnerable side. I've seen her tender, scared, lonely side, the part of Ivy that longs for someone to depend on, to hold and comfort her. Judging by Galvin's description, she doesn't show that side often or to many people.

"Ivy's a military brat," he says, reaching to take the cheese from me, tossing more into his mouth. "She took some hard knocks growing up with moving around so much, which kept her from building close relationships, but it made her tough as nails and completely self-reliant."

"I see. I didn't know that, the military brat thing."

"Um-hm," Galvin cracks the eggs in a bowl. "Her dad's retired from the Air Force, a lieutenant general. She got her compassion for people from her mom. She was a defense attorney until a couple of years ago. Ivy followed in her footsteps, you know, becoming an attorney." He tosses the last eggshell in the trash. "They live in Jacksonville now."

I finish the first pan of bacon and begin a second while Galvin chops some veggies for the omelets.

"Ivy mentioned a couple of siblings the other night. I think one lived near here, but she wouldn't call him."

"She has two sisters, one in Georgia and one in Florida, and a brother, Ben. He lives in north Boston. Ivy sees him regularly and has dinner with him and his family every couple of weeks. He's a freelance writer and does well for himself. His wife teaches at one of the local schools. Ivy wouldn't want to bother Ben with her troubles. They're close and all, but, like I said, she's very independent."

I scoop the last bit of bacon onto a plate, place it on a warming rack in the oven, and then pull out the bread for toast.

Galvin's voice lowers, and his brows lift as he continues talking. He peeks around to check for Ivy. "I cleaned the wound on her head last night. There's a lot of swelling and a pretty big gash. What did the doctor say?"

"She said Ivy would be fine. Ivy took two hard blows to the head, and the second one caused her memory loss. It should be temporary, but nobody knows how long it will take to return. She has medicine to help with the swelling around the wound. We just have to be sure the wound is clean, and there's no sign of infection. The stitches will come out in about a week."

Galvin nods his head.

"She needs to have someone with her for several more days. Do you think you and her other friends might help?"

Galvin adds milk to the eggs and whips them with a whisk. "No problem. I'll contact Mickie and Alana, and we'll work it out between us. Ivy's parents were supposed to come on Saturday, but she called them last night, told them not to come, and that everything was okay. I caught her on the phone, and that's when she told me what was going on, the kidnapping, the concussion, and all."

He looks down, shaking his head. "Ivy's such a kind soul. I love her to death, and I'd do anything for her."

"Ivy said you had to be at work at one. Do you think one of her friends might stay with her this afternoon? She needs someone around at all times for the next few days. She could still have complications from the concussion. I'll stay as long as possible to see if I can help her recall some things, but I gotta work on the case."

Galvin takes a moment to think, then replies, "We may have to strong-arm her, but I'll make sure someone is with her twenty-four-seven as long as needed. I read the hospital discharge instructions and will give them to the ladies when they come."

Hearing Ivy coming down the stairs, we change the subject of our conversation. Ivy spies us in the kitchen and leans across the counter. Rested by a good night's sleep, she looks much less strained than the last two days. Her eyes are brighter, and her face has more color to it.

"I see you boys have this cooking thing down. It smells great! What can I do to help?"

"Nary a thing, m'lady," Galvin answers, giving his impression of a medieval servant, accent and all. "Let me help you to your seat, Madam, and Sir Tomas and I shall serve you your breakfast."

He sashays to Ivy, hooks his arm in hers, turns to me, and continues his antics. "If you'll excuse us, Sir Tomas, I shall escort the lady to the table and return shortly to help you finish." He half-bows and leads Ivy from the room. She giggles.

"Oh, thank you, Sir Galvin, and you too, Sir Detective," she laughs, waving her hand. She looks at me, smiling, her disposition light and springy.

I've never seen this side of Ivy before. Her face is fresh and filled with life, her cheeks are rosy pink, and her features are relaxed. Her brown eyes are bright, with no dark circles, no sad look, no worrying, just happy and enjoying the moment. This person is Ivy in her natural state. The Ivy that got pushed deep inside when she witnessed the kidnapping. This Ivy longs to be pulled to the surface and live again.

I was once the one forced deep inside. I know what it's like for your true self to hide, allowing fear, worry, and regret to take over your life. Once scarred by a tragic event, some people never return to who they once were but remain lost within themselves. Marc made sure that didn't happen to me, and I have to be sure it doesn't happen to Ivy.

Being around Galvin is good for her. She told me once that he brings beautiful music to her life, and I understand now what she meant. It's not just the music he plays but his attitude and personality. He seems to enjoy life and living, not let troubles weigh him down. He's a good guy. I like him.

I'm not sure I could compete with Galvin, but he's not her boyfriend. Why am I thinking this way? I'm not trying to compete with anyone, and Ivy has a boyfriend, Nick. My relationship with Ivy is just professional. I can't have anything distracting me. I have a case to solve, a woman to find. Stay focused.

When Galvin returns, I'm finishing the last omelet. He helps put everything on plates, places them on a tray, and carries it to the dining table. Meanwhile, I take the cups and saucers to the table, pour coffee for everyone, and take my seat.

Ivy gobbles down her food. "This is wonderful!" she exclaims. "I'm so not used to having a breakfast like this. I might just have to hire you two to be my regular chefs," she jokes, scooping a bite of her omelet onto her fork.

After finishing the last of my toast, I pour seconds of the coffee for everyone.

"Detective," Ivy begins, "how did the interview with Dr. Winsloe go yesterday? Have you found any new leads in the case?"

"Well," I raise an eyebrow, glancing at Galvin. I have to be careful what information I talk about since this is an active investigation. "It went well. We located another witness, and hopefully, with the doctor's information, we can solve the case soon."

"So, you got some good leads, then?" Galvin responds.

"Yes, I think so, but I want to talk with you a little more, Ivy, to see if anything new has come to your mind about the incident."

Galvin stands and begins clearing the breakfast dishes. "I'll take care of these and let the two of you talk. You might be more comfortable in the living room, or perhaps a short walk outside might do you both some good. Clean, crisp air refreshes the mind and body," he notes with zest as he gathers the dishes and heads to the kitchen.

"I would like a bit of air, if that's okay with you, detective. It seems like I haven't been out of this house in forever." Ivy stands and begins walking toward the foyer to get her coat.

OK, then—we're going for a walk.

CHAPTER 17

72 Hours 30 Minutes

Friday 10:52 a.m.

Days of snow and ice accumulation no longer coat the steps in front of Ivy's brownstone. The city has scraped the streets and shoveled the sidewalks as much as possible to allow safe passage for those who dare to venture out during the harsh winter weather. Dense gray clouds hang low in the sky, creating an oppressive, gloomy atmosphere. I'm accustomed to nor'easters in Boston.

Although this system is not a nor'easter, it's bringing a lot of stiff wind, heavy rain, snow, and ice early in the season. And it doesn't look to be moving out in the next few days.

Ivy links her arm to mine and snuggles close to me. "I don't want to take any chances of falling again, if you don't mind, detective," she smiles, clinging to my arm. She looks up at the clouds and scrunches her nose. "It's such a dreary day."

We turn to the right as we leave her house, away from the main road. It's an exquisite neighborhood; rows of well-maintained brownstones line the streets, and stylish lamp posts give off a soft glow in the haze. An extensive park sits at the back of the neighborhood, just a few blocks from Ivy's house.

We take shelter in a small pavilion near the front of the park. Several children are playing, some building snowmen, others running as they throw snowballs, and a few sledding down a small bank on one side of the park.

Ivy and I talk as we watch the children, not so much about the case but about thoughts and feelings, our likes and dislikes, and life in general.

"Do you have any children, detective?" Ivy asks, her voice low.

"No," I utter. A twinge of sadness surfaces in my voice. Not wanting Ivy to see the sorrow on my face, I scan the people in the park.

A few minutes later, she remarks, "I got the impression one time when we talked that you may have been a witness to a crime at some point. Were you?"

Feeling Ivy staring at me, the image of the terrified young boy creeps from the dark corners of my mind to haunt me again. The scared little boy was too young and weak to stop the man from punching the woman and too small to keep him from throwing her into the car's front seat and driving off.

The memories of that little boy are why I search for missing people, why I hunt down murderers, and why I am alone. I don't answer Ivy's question. I don't tell her about the seven-year-old boy. I only look deep into her eyes. The tears I suppress say more than I can put into words.

Ivy nods without pressuring me for an answer. "I understand. You don't have to answer." She looks back at the children. "If you ever want to talk, I'm here for you, just as you've been for me these past few days." Still clinging to my arm, she squeezes it and slides closer, letting me know she cares.

The neon sign flashes, reminding me of what Marc said earlier. I unplug it for now and shove it aside. Placing my hand over Ivy's, she leans her head on my shoulder. We sit for at least a half hour, not saying a word, just watching the children and taking comfort in each other's presence.

Disrupting our quiet solitude, two boys, about ten years old, start yelling at each other. Pushes follow, and they fall to the ground, punching each other as they roll in the snow. Both Ivy and I jump up and run to stop them.

"Hey, hey!" I pull the two boys apart, holding each by the jacket, one kid on either side of me. "What's going on here?" A third child, a little girl, stands to the side with her head down, not saying a word.

Ivy dusts the snow off the boy who was on the losing end of the battle. "He punched my snowman and tore his arms off!" he sobs, tears streaming down his cold red face. Ivy straightens his jacket and brushes the snow off his beanie.

"It's not what you think!" the bigger boy shouts. "It's not what you think! She made me!" he yells, pointing to the little girl. "She made me! Blaine said she would tell people I was a sissy if I didn't tear it down." Tears fill his eyes. "I didn't want to do it. We built it together. Kenny's my friend," he cries. Tracks of tears streak down his flushed face.

Walking over to the little girl, Ivy takes her by the hand, and they move a few feet away. Ivy squats down so she and the little girl are at eye level. She brushes the girl's blonde hair off her face as they talk. My hands are full, so I leave her to handle the female part of this battle.

"Okay, so what do we do now, guys? You have both lost on this one since you built the snowman together. Don't you think you should apologize for tearing it up?" I ask the bigger boy.

He sniffs and wipes his face with his snow-covered glove. "I'm sorry, Kenny. I wish I hadn't listened to Blaine. Maybe we can fix it."

Kenny pulls his knit hat down over his ears. "Okay, Clark, it's okay," he mumbles. Suddenly, a big smile lights up his face, his eyes widen twice their average size, and his brows disappear under his beanie. "Maybe we can make the snowman bigger!"

"Yeah," Clark chimes in, "we can make him bigger and get bigger sticks for his arms, too!" He jumps up and down in his excitement. "Mister, would you help us lift a bigger head on his body if we roll it up?"

"It's been a long time since I built a snowman, but let's see what we can do. Hey guys, you know what? I bet if we got those two girls over there to help us," I point to Ivy and the little girl, Blaine, "we could make an even bigger and better snowman." I summon all my enthusiasm to promote peace between the three children.

Clark looks at me and tips his head sideways, puzzled at my suggestion. "But Blaine made me do it."

"Did she, Clark? She may have *told* you to do it, but did she *make* you do it?"

He shuffles his feet and kicks the snow. "No, I guess I did it 'cause I didn't wanna be called a sissy. It was a stupid reason."

"I'm proud of you, Clark. It takes a brave man to take responsibility for something he did. I'm very proud of you." I turn and look at Kenny. "And I'm proud of you too, Kenny. You're a good friend. It takes a powerful man to forgive someone for what they did. I'm very proud of you, too."

Both boys grin and punch each other playfully.

"Now," I say, "how 'bout we see if those two girls want to help us build the best snowman ever?"

"Yeah," they yell as they run toward Ivy and the little girl. I can't hear what they're all saying, but the little girl grins, nodding. Ivy looks at me, a smile spreading across her face. The children run as fast as they can to the snowman, separating his body into three pieces.

Ivy waddles through the deep snow to me and takes my hands in hers. "So, we're building a snowman?" She bursts into unrestrained laughter, like a child herself, and pulls me toward the children.

The five of us roll three giant snowballs, heave them one on top of the other, and make the largest snowman I've seen. The boys find two large, crooked branches that work great as arms.

Together, Kenny, Clark, and Blaine use their combined strength to position the arms and push them into the body. Since I'm the biggest, tallest, and strongest, I lift Kenny high enough to place some stones and sticks on the snowman's face for the eyes, nose, and mouth. Using an old tin pot Clark found, I put it on the snowman's head for a hat. Ivy hands Blaine her blue striped scarf, and I lift her to add the final touch around the snowman's neck. We all step back a short distance to admire our work.

"He's big!" Kenny yells.

"He's the best!" Clark adds.

"He's beautiful!" Blaine exclaims. Looking at the two boys, she adds, "Thanks for letting me help build it. It was fun." Her eyes moisten just as the sky releases light snow. "I'm sorry I caused trouble earlier," she tells Clark and Kenny. "I really am." I hand her my handkerchief to dry her tears.

"If the first one hadn't got messed up, we never would have built this giant one!" Kenny raves, "So it's okay, Blaine. We should have let you help us before."

Clark nods and adds, "Maybe we can build a whole family of snowmen tomorrow!"

"Yeah! That'd be great!" Kenny yells. "What about you, Blaine? Can you play tomorrow?"

Excited to be invited by the boys, Blaine puts her hands on her mouth and nods, jumping up and down. "I'll see what I can find at home to put on the snowmen for eyes and stuff, and I'll bring it tomorrow!"

Both boys jump on board and start planning what they can bring.

"We've had fun," Ivy tells the children. She looks at me, and I nod my head.

"You guys should get home now. It's freezing out here, and you've been playing in the snow for a while. I'm sure your parents will expect you soon. There's no doubt that Mr. Pothead will still be here tomorrow." I laugh, patting the snowman on his huge, round belly. "This baby's not melting for a month."

"Oh, and one last thing before we go… snowball fight!" I shout as I run, balling up handfuls of snow and throwing them at the kids and Ivy.

Everyone scampers, grabs globs of snow, and molds snowballs, flinging them at each other. About ten minutes later, exhausted, we all fall onto the snow, spread our arms and legs, and make snow angels. Staying as long as they can, the children leave, and we wave goodbye as they head home.

Ivy takes my arm, and we walk from the park toward her house. Soft snowflakes float around us like down feathers dumped from the sky. Ivy looks up, sticks her tongue out to catch the white flakes, and her face breaks into a broad smile, causing her eyes to squinch and rosy red cheeks to rise.

CHAPTER 18

74 Hours 54 Minutes

Friday 1:16 p.m.

A few yards before we get to her house, I notice several cars parked on the street and a dark gray Ford Explorer, its engine still running.

"Ivy, whose cars are those, do you know?"

"Well, the silver BMW belongs to my neighbor over there," she points to a brownstone two houses down on the opposite side of the street. "The Lexis, pretty sure I've seen it here before. I think it belongs to a friend of Ralston, three houses down."

Pausing, Ivy gazes at the gray Ford parked two houses above the BMW.

"I don't know the Explorer, but I think I've seen it before," she hesitates, "but not here. Somewhere else, I think. It looks like there's someone in it."

"Yes, it does. It's the same one I saw at the park." Rushing, I lead Ivy up the steps to the stoop and open her unlocked front door. "Wait in here and don't come out. I'll be right back."

Before she can speak, I close the door, pull the collar on my jacket higher on my neck, and cross the road like I'm going to a neighbor's house. When I reach the front steps, I cut to the right and go to the back of the brownstone. Making my way behind the houses, I move toward the SUV.

Staying out of view, I peer around the corner of the house closest to it. I repeat the tag number several times, take out my cell phone, and call it in as a possible suspect sighting. I'd rather be wrong, and it is an innocent guy waiting on his girlfriend than let a kidnapper escape.

Removing the Glock 19 from my shoulder holster, I point it

toward the ground and maneuver to the back of the SUV. Knowing the driver will spot me immediately through his side mirror if I approach from the left, I stay on the right side of the vehicle, the passenger's side. Slowly, making my way toward the front of the Explorer, I get to the passenger's rear side window and ease my head up to look. The tinted windows make it difficult to see inside, but I can tell what's happening.

My position and the tall front seats hinder my view of the man behind the steering wheel. I can see his dirty-blond hair poking from the edges of the beanie he's pulled low on his face. Although I don't have a face-on view of him, I can tell he fits the description of the kidnapper. His focus is on the driver's outside mirror, angled out, giving him a better view of the houses on the opposite side of the road—the side where Ivy lives. The man appears nervous, constantly picking up and laying down the Smith & Wesson lying on the console between the seats. He doesn't notice me.

Leaping to the front side window. I aim at the man.

"Police! Hands on the wheel!"

The guy punches the gas and cuts the wheels toward me. I fire my weapon twice, the bullets shattering the passenger window and hitting the dash near the steering wheel. The SUV bolts forward and jerks to the right, striking my left side and knocking me to the ground. I roll to avoid being hit by the back wheel and get off two more rounds.

The Explorer jumps the curb, taking out several small bushes before it returns to the road. I'm pretty sure I missed the driver, but I know there's a hole in one of his tires. He won't get far.

Several police cars arrive with sirens blaring and blue lights flashing. Neighbors flock to their windows and yards to see what's going on. Ivy and an attractive, voluptuous woman with long black hair rush across the street to where I am. I don't know who the woman is, but I guess she's one of Ivy's friends, either Alana or

Mickie.

When Ivy reaches me, she grabs my face between her hands, positioning it so we are eye to eye.

"Are you okay?"

Not waiting for an answer, Ivy inches her hands over my face and head, inspecting each part, and continues down my arms, chest, and sides, squeezing and feeling each muscle and joint. Ivy pats me down like she's searching for a weapon on a criminal. Flipping me around, she examines my back in the same manner and slides her hands over my hips.

Not expecting such a comprehensive examination of my butt, I spin to face her and take her hands.

"Whoa Sally, gettin' a little frisky there," I joke. "What are ya doing?" I chuckle, confused by her intimate touch.

"I just want to make sure you're okay, that you don't have any injuries. I'm sorry," Ivy apologizes. "I was just concerned." She shies back, placing her hands in her pockets.

I flash Ivy a coy grin. "I'm just teasing. In fact," I lean close to Ivy's face and whisper seductively in her ear, "you can pat me down anytime you like. Maybe next time, though, it can be in a more private setting." I wink as I move back.

Blushing, Ivy tries to suppress a smile tickling the corners of her mouth. To sidestep her embarrassment, she falls back on her legal skills, bombarding me with questions about what happened.

Between the police and Ivy's inquisition, my head is spiraling. I look at Ivy to answer her, then to the officer in charge to respond to him. I imagine witnesses and criminals feel this way when two officers slam questions back and forth, not giving the person time to answer. It creates stress and doesn't allow the individual time to think. Law enforcement officials use this technique with interrogation. It sure feels different when you're on the receiving end.

Recognizing we're getting nowhere quickly, I take control of the situation since the officer doesn't. Before giving him a complete account of everything that happened, I remove Ivy from the scene. Taking her by the arm, I lead her and her friend across the street toward Ivy's house and explain that I must talk with the officer. I assure them I'll be right back.

They both express their understanding, nodding and apologizing for interfering.

"We'll go back to the house and wait for you," Ivy says. "You are okay, right?" she asks, her voice quivering.

Her face is pale, and her hands tremble, even with her gloves on. I can tell she's concerned about me, but more than that, she's frightened.

Although my shoulder and hip hurt from my run-in with the Explorer, I don't let on. "I'm good," I say confidently. "I'm a lot tougher than you'd think."

With Ivy and the woman heading to the brownstone, I locate the lead officer and give my report on the incident. He issues an all-points bulletin for the gray Ford Explorer and the blonde driver. Before heading to Ivy's, I call Marc to update him on the situation.

CHAPTER 19

75 Hours 48 Minutes

Friday 2:10 p.m.

While walking across the street to Ivy's house, I glance up and spy Ivy and the other woman peering from the cracked door. They remind me of a totem pole, like one you poke your head through while someone takes your picture on vacation. Ivy's head perches above the woman's, both staring, mouths gaping and eyes wide, at the scene. Occasionally, one looks up or down at the other and whispers.

As I climb the steps, I shake my head in amusement, covering my mouth with my hand to conceal my grin. When I reach the stoop, the door opens wide. Unexpectedly, Ivy reaches out, grabs my arm, and pulls me inside.

"Are you sure you're okay?" she asks, nervously brushing the snow from my jacket.

"Yes, I'm fine." I remove my hat, peel my gloves off, and place them in my pocket. "I don't believe I've met your friend. My guess is Alana?"

"Yes, yes. I'm so sorry," Ivy stumbles over her words as she introduces us. "This is my friend, Alana Kessler. Alana, this is the detective I told you about, Detective Tomas Benson."

"It's so nice to meet you, detective," Alana gushes. "I didn't know what was happening when Ivy first came in. I'm so glad you're alright. Galvin told me about some of what's happened, and I hope you and Ivy can fill in the blanks for me."

Alana brushes her long raven-black hair off her face as a tiny smile emerges from her sensual lips. As attracted as I am to Ivy, I can't help but appreciate the beauty of a gorgeous woman. I better keep Marc away from her.

Ivy giggles, "I have a lot of blanks that need filling in, too."

As we head to the living room, Alana offers us something hot to drink. She and Ivy choose hot tea. Although tea is not my go-to drink, I want something to warm me other than coffee, so I also have a cup.

"It'll just take a few minutes," Alana says, and she's off to the kitchen.

When Alana is out of sight, Ivy asks more about the incident with the man in the Explorer. "Was that the kidnapper, detective? Tell me." She motions to the sofa, and we sit down.

"I'm not sure," I begin. "It might have been. He had shaggy blonde hair, just like you and the other witnesses said, but we don't know yet. I know there's a bullet in one of his tires, and I'm pretty sure I hit the dash near the steering wheel, but I don't think I hit the driver. The police put out an APB," I state. "I'll need to get back to the station as soon as possible to see what develops." I pause, giving her time to process what I've said.

Alana reappears, holding a tray filled with three teacups, a small teapot, cream, sugar, honey, spoons, and napkins. She even brought some tea cookies.

"I told you it wouldn't take long." She smiles.

I take the tray from her and place it on the table near the sofa. Alana prepares and serves the tea for each of us.

"Thank you, Alana. This is just what I need." I allow the tea to cool a moment before sipping.

Realizing that all conversation ceased when she returned, Alana's eyes dart to Ivy, then me. "Have I interrupted something?" she asks. "Do I need to leave?"

"No, you don't need to leave," I reply. "We're just talking about what took place outside. I'm not sure how much Galvin told you about Ivy's situation, but I'm sure she will fill you in on all the details as soon as possible. Are you going to stay here tonight?"

Alana nods her head, sipping her tea. "Yes, I plan to stay through the weekend, longer if needed. Galvin and I can swap out staying if necessary. I know Mickie would be happy to stay too, but Galvin and I think it might be a bit too much for Ivy since Mickie has two children," she explains, looking at Ivy for confirmation. Ivy nods in agreement, and Alana continues, "We'll get her in the loop, maybe with some meals or errands or just staying a few hours. We don't want her to feel excluded. After all, Mickie's a close friend, too. She'd want to help. She'd never forgive us if we left her out."

Ivy smiles, her eyes locked on the flames in the fireplace. Her thoughts have drifted far away from our conversation.

"Are you okay?" I ask her. "You look like something's bothering you. Are you feeling alright?"

Pressing her lips together, Ivy squeezes her eyes to a half-closed position, turns to me, and asks, "Remember when I said I thought I'd seen the Explorer before, and you said it was in the park?"

"Yes, I remember. I saw it in the park. It pulled into the small parking area on the left just after we got there."

"Yes, I'm sure you did, but that's not where I saw it," she asserts. "I saw it in the Crestview Shopping Center parking lot when we were there on Wednesday. I saw it before I fell."

My eyes widen, and I can't stop the cheek-to-cheek smile from taking over my face. "You remember." I all but yell with excitement. "You remember Wednesday!" I hold her hands, squeezing them, then hug her. "I'm so thrilled, Ivy. Your memories are returning."

"Oh, Ivy, that's wonderful!" Alana exclaims, patting Ivy's leg. "I knew it wouldn't take long for your memory to return!"

"I don't know," Ivy replies, shaking her head. "I remember very little. Just a few things that don't make a lot of sense." She places her hand on her forehead, rubbing it with her fingers.

Glancing at me, she continues. "I remember seeing the Explorer parked near the road. It backed into the parking space with a direct view of the alley, where the kidnapping took place, where we were when you left me to talk to the tall, dark-haired guy with the investigation team. It looked like someone might have been in the SUV, but it was snowing, and I couldn't tell for sure."

"You're recalling a lot of detail, the alley and snow, and even knowing the man I talked to had dark hair," I say, shocked that so much of her memory has returned at once.

Waiting a few seconds, I ask, "Do you remember anything else about that day? Anything about the kidnapping itself?"

Ivy nods her head. "But this is the weird part that makes no sense." She stops, places her fingers on her chin, presses her lips together, and taps them with a finger.

"Ivy, tell me," I plead. "Maybe we can make sense of it together."

She nods. "Okay, but I don't know what it means. When the kidnapper and I struggled, he grabbed me by the shoulders and got right up to my face." Ivy places her palm close to her face. Tears pool in her eyes. She takes a deep breath and continues. "He shook me and said, *It's not what you think*' and then said, *She made me.*' He said it, just like that," she emphasizes, "one sentence behind the other." Tears trickle down her cheeks and her bottom lip quivers.

Alana places her arm around Ivy's shoulder. "It's okay," she whispers. "Shush, that's all over. It's just a memory." Alana wraps her arms around her weeping friend, consoling her.

"No, Ivy, no," I counter, "your memory is confused."

She lifts her head from Alana's shoulder, wiping her eyes. "What do you mean? How do you know that?" Her tone is defiant, and her face tightens.

Shifting my position to look into Ivy's eyes, I remind her of earlier adventures in the park. "Remember when we were in the park, and the two little boys fought?"

Ivy nods.

"Remember the little boy that started the fight, Clark, and how he said Blaine made him do it?"

"Yes, but…"

"Those are the same words Clark used. '*It's not what you think*' and '*She made me.*' Those exact words refer to Blaine making him tear down the snowman because she called him a sissy. Remember? You were standing right there beside me when he said it."

"I remember that," Ivy acknowledges as she nods her head. "But detective, that's what sparked my memory," she insists emphatically. "I didn't remember when Clark first said it, but seeing the Ford Explorer triggered several memories simultaneously. I swear to you; those are the words the kidnapper used just before pushing me backward."

Ivy stands and walks to the fireplace, her arms crossed. She turns, looks at Alana, then me.

"I know it makes no sense at all." Hesitating for a moment, she stares at the fire, then murmurs, "I can still hear his voice, low and pitiful. It was almost as though he was sorry for what he was doing—that he was sorry for kidnapping the woman."

Ivy tilts her head to one side and gazes deep into my eyes. It's as though she wants to impart her memory to my mind.

"I saw *sadness* in his face—*fear* and sadness."

The room is silent. I pause a moment and think about what Ivy just said. She stands quietly by the fire, waiting for my response. In my mind, I combine the evidence and facts of the case with Ivy's new recollection of the kidnapper.

Everything Ivy is saying can't possibly be true. She can't know exactly how the kidnapper was feeling. That's subjective, not factual. I'm sure she's projecting her feelings onto him. She wants him to feel the way she describes him. She can't accept that he could be just an evil person with evil intentions. After all, most of her legal cases involve some type of underprivileged or wronged victim or criminal. From my review of her history and my interactions with her, I am well aware of her compassion.

Still, I can't completely discount a victim or witness's impression of the criminal or their motives. Emotions experienced during the commission of a crime create lasting memories. Impressions can be just as important as facts sometimes. If the kidnapper had uttered those words to Ivy, they would have stuck in her memory. But the question would then be, what could his words have meant?

Ivy's impatience gets the better of her. "Well," she implores, "do you believe me, detective?" Her posture droops as though she carries the world's weight on her shoulders, her eyes swollen from the tears she's cried.

My heart grieves for Ivy losing the normalcy in her life. A once ordinary person doing usual things is now involved in a mysterious kidnapping case, suffered not one but two head injuries, and lost her memory. There's nothing ordinary about her life, at least not right now.

My thoughts revert to age seven, and I recall how suddenly normal disappears, sometimes never to return. I hope with all my heart that's not the case for Ivy.

Walking to where Ivy stands gazing into the fire, I take her hands in mine. "Do you know what the kidnapper might've meant when he said *'it's not what you think'*?"

"No," she sighs. "I don't. I know the man was kidnapping the woman. He put her in the trunk, so what else could it have been? I don't see how that could be fake or anything. It makes no sense," she admits. "And what could *'she made me'* possibly mean? How could the woman have made him kidnap her?"

Ivy looks at Alana sitting on the sofa. "That's why I said it all seems so mixed up. Maybe my memory isn't complete. Maybe I'm only remembering pieces."

She searches Alana's face for support and then mine.

"Maybe I'm all wrong. Things are coming back randomly, in bits and pieces. I don't feel sure of anything," she says, doubting herself. Ivy puts her hands near her face and lets her head fall into them.

"Well, what I know for sure, Ivy, is that you need some rest," Alana insists as she rises from the sofa. "Don't you agree, Detective Benson?"

"Yes. It's been a long day, Ivy. I'm thrilled your memory is returning, but you can't push it. Things like this take time and rest. You still have a concussion, you know." I turn, preparing to leave. "I need to get to the office to see what's happening from the other angles we're working."

Ivy and Alana walk me to the entry, where I get my coat. As I put on my gloves and hat, I turn to Ivy. "I'll see if I can make some sense of what you said about the kidnapper. I'll go over it with my partner. He's got a good mind for figuring out puzzles and riddles."

Putting my hands on her shoulders, I say, "You did good, Ivy. My guess is you'll have even more memories returned by tomorrow. Get some rest, and let Alana take care of you, okay?" I want to hug her but resist. I know it wouldn't be proper, not now. "Alana can see me out but call if you need me."

"I am tired. I think I'll lie down for a while," Ivy sighs. "Will you keep me updated?"

"Of course."

"Good afternoon, detective. I'm glad you didn't get hurt earlier. Please be careful."

Ivy turns and walks up the stairs. She takes a few steps and stops, looks at me, and raises her brows.

"Oh, there's one other thing I remember," she begins. "When we returned to the shopping center Wednesday and I started to wake up from hitting my head on the ice, I could see the people standing around me. The kidnapper was there, in the back of the crowd. I saw him clearly. He was there, then he left."

Thinking she must be confused, I move toward her and place my hand on the railing. "I didn't see anyone fitting that description, Ivy. Are you sure he was there?"

"Yes, I'm sure," she states with certainty. "Remember, I told you I saw a Ford Explorer in the shopping center parking lot facing the alley? I thought someone was in it, but I couldn't tell what the person looked like because of the snow. It had to be the kidnapper, and when he saw me fall, he must have walked over to see what was going on. I saw him when I was waking up. I know I saw him."

"Why didn't you tell me this before?"

She arches her eyebrows and flashes a sideways smile. "I've just remembered it." Ivy drops her head and stares at the floor, an emptiness in her eyes. "I think he must be watching me. He was there that day and parked across the street today."

"It's only a matter of time before we find him, Ivy. There's damage to his car, and the police are looking for him as we speak."

She nods her head without looking up. I can tell I haven't eased her mind. "There's no way he could have known you would be at the shopping center Wednesday. His being there was a coincidence. That's all. It's not uncommon for a suspect to return to the crime scene. He probably saw you fall and was just curious. Nothing more than that."

Ivy maintains her posture, her gaze frozen on the steps, so I move my head to make eye contact. Locking eyes, I assure her she's safe, although I'm not sure that's true.

"Besides, even if he is watching you, Ivy, you're protected. Someone is with you all the time. Alana is here with you tonight, but I can always stay. I don't mind."

"No," she stretches her lips into a strained, tired smile. "Thank you, detective, but you've done all you can to help me. I won't impose on you like that again. Besides, you're right," she admits, trying to be more positive. "The police are looking for him, and Alana's here with me. I'm sure everything will be fine. You need to work on finding him and that woman. That's the most important thing," she insists.

"It's all going to be okay," I say, knowing my words are empty.

"I'm going to rest now. Please take care of yourself, detective." She turns and continues up the stairs.

Alana accompanies me to the front door and opens it. When I'm sure Ivy is out of earshot, I express my concerns to Alana.

"Just between you and me, and I don't want to frighten you, Alana, but I'm not sure why the Explorer parked near Ivy's house today, or if it even was the kidnapper Ivy saw." I walk onto the stoop exiting the house and add, "I'd feel a lot better having a patrol car watch the neighborhood for a few days, just 'till we get this thing settled."

"I think that's a great idea, detective. I'm worried about that man being in the neighborhood, too. Ivy and I would feel better knowing officers are around."

As I walk down the first step, I pause. "Let's keep this between us for now. No need to say anything to Ivy about it. You can tell her about the patrol watching her house, but don't let on that I'm concerned. Tell her it's just for her peace of mind. If she thought I was concerned," I stop, carefully choosing my words so Alana doesn't become frightened. "Let's just say she doesn't need more to worry about."

Nodding her head, she agrees to keep it quiet. Leaving her my cell phone number, we say goodbye, and Alana closes the door. Hearing the click of the deadbolt locking, I continue down the steps to my car. The wind is picking up, swirling the snow through the air. Opening the car door, I peek back at Ivy's brownstone, its architectural lines blurred by the heavy snow blanketing the air.

I don't think I'm going to say anything to Ivy, but my main concern is if the man in the Explorer was the kidnapper, and I believe he was, what was the real reason he approached her in the alley after she fell at the crime scene, and why was he parked outside of her house?

He must know Ivy was the key witness and tracked down where she lives. But what are his intentions? His showing up at the shopping center Wednesday was a coincidence, but being in her neighborhood today wasn't. What is he planning?

CHAPTER 20

78 Hours 10 Minutes

Friday 4:32 p.m.

Arriving at the station, I head to the captain's office to report today's events. Marc spies me as I enter the building. Motioning for him to join me, we hop on the elevator, and I push the third-floor button. On the ride up, I ask him about the patrol assigned to watch Ivy's house and neighborhood.

"We've got one car assigned to her house and a second to patrol the neighborhood and the road into it. Both cars are in place now. She should be safe, Tomas," Marc assures me, placing his hand on my shoulder.

"I can't believe the suspect would show up outside her house like that. Man, is he dumb or what?" he snorts, laughing as he turns the sympathetic shoulder squeeze into a playful shove.

Agreeing with his deduction of the guy's intelligence, I snicker, "You're right. That was a dumb move for sure."

Reaching the third floor, we exit the elevator and continue our conversation as we walk down the hall to the captain's office.

"What about the tag number or the Explorer itself? Is there any word on that?" I ask.

"Yep," he begins. We stop outside the captain's door. "It was stolen. We traced the license plate to a Dodge Ram belonging to Madison McCallum in Oxford, three counties over. So that doesn't help at all."

"Dammit," I murmur under my breath, barely audible. I shake my head, frustrated. "And the Explorer? Was it located? I'm sure I blew a tire out."

Marc shakes his head. "No, we didn't find the Explorer," he says, then adds with a bit more enthusiasm, "but we found the tire you shot in a nearby parking deck. It looks like he pulled in there and changed it to the spare. We put a tracer on the numbers to determine who purchased it and where, but it's a long shot. I'm not sure the information we get will be helpful, anyway. We've pulled the parking garage's camera footage. Hopefully, there's something worth seeing on it. It's being reviewed by Detective Carruthers' team, just like all the other camera footage we've got."

His enthusiasm wanes, then explodes again like a firecracker popped in his head. I'd swear Marc's bipolar if I didn't know better.

"We got the footage back on the street cams near Crestview, and, sure enough, the video shows a blue 1975 Plymouth Duster bangin' a U-ey right in front of Dr. Winsloe's silver Mercedes. Can you believe it? Right there on camera! We got the tag number, too, off a cam on I-90. He was heading west, just like the doc said."

I'm all pumped by the new leads until, once again, Marc's ecstatic mood turns sour, plummeting like a flailing rocket.

"What now?" I sigh, frustrated. I take a step back, and I throw my hands out to my sides.

I'm exhausted by the emotional roller coaster Marc's taking me on. For some reason, I think he's enjoying the ride. I'm definitely not.

Marc peers at me with his new favorite expression, eyebrows scrunched and mouth pinched tight.

"Well," he begins, "the license plate on the Plymouth was stolen, too, from a car registered in Texas, so it was no help either. And we didn't get a good view of the kidnapper on the road cameras." He pauses. Slowly, an immense grin creeps across his face, and his brows arch. His exuberance returns as he begins, "But one of them…"

The door to Captain Ottley's office jerks open. Marc stops speaking mid-sentence, leaving me in suspense, like a cliffhanger on a TV show's season finale. Lucy, the captain's secretary, stands in the doorway, her eyes wide behind the bright blue frames of her glasses, one hand on her hip.

She looks at us as though we are naughty school boys tardy for class, raises her hand, and points her finger, raving.

"Where the hell have you two been? Captain's been waiting for you!" She pulls us by the arms, hustling us to the captain's office. "Some of us would like to get off at a decent hour for once," she shrieks. "But that's never gonna happen," she continues, shaking her head and murmuring as much to herself as to us.

Tossing us into the captain's office, she announces, "Well, here they are, finally. The two misfits and," her laser eyes aim directly at me, "*missing* boy have arrived at last. Now," she brushes her hands together showing her work is done. "I'm going home. Do as you will, captain." She flips around and exits, leaving the door open.

Marc and I glance at each other, roll our eyes, and grin. Typical Lucy. Standing four feet eleven, about a hundred-forty, Lucy can come across with a roar, but everyone knows she's harmless. You can tell she was a natural beauty in her day. Her crystal blue eyes are a little less blue than in her younger years, and her wine-colored hair has streaks of gray. She's a little heavier now, but her curvy body would have knocked any man off his feet back then. I've seen pictures of Lucy when she was younger, and all I can say is: wow!

We watch as she gathers her large blue purse, tosses in a few items, then wraps up in her brown wool swing coat and bright blue hat with matching earmuffs. When she reaches the main office door, Lucy turns, a grin on her face, and flips a quick wave to signal her departure for the day.

Still smiling, Marc and I turn, only to find ourselves face to face with the captain. I can tell by the scowl on his face and the shifting of his almost white walrus mustache as he tightens his lips that he's had a bad day. And we're not making it any better. Erasing our grins and donning a straight face, Marc and I creep into the chairs facing the captain's desk and wait for him to speak.

His greeting is far less warm than Lucy's. "Where the hell have you been, Benson?" Captain Ottley scowls. His bushy white brows scrunch, causing the crevices in his forehead to deepen. "We haven't seen or heard from you all day until you called in the incident on Highlander Lane."

Before I can answer, the captain's gruff voice circles to the case. "And what's going on with this kidnapping case? Are we close to finding that woman yet?" He shakes the file he's holding and ambles behind his desk. His eyes dart from me to Marc.

"Well," he pauses, "I'm waiting." He tosses the file onto the desk, then plops his hefty frame down in the heavily worn desk chair, his body molding to the imprints on the padding created by years of use.

Marc is always jittery when he's around Captain Ottley. He takes several deep breaths, trying to calm himself, and smooths his mustache with his fingers several times.

While Marc fidgets with his hair, I try to ease his tension by lightening the atmosphere. "Have any coffee, captain? It sure is cold outside. I could use some warming," I begin casually. "I think this is gonna take a few minutes, sir." I brush my hair off my face and lean back in the chair, waiting for his response.

Captain Ottley leans back and pushes away from the desk. Pulling out a bottom drawer, he retrieves a pint of bourbon and three old-fashioned whiskey glasses. "This'll warm us up," the captain grunts, pouring a generous serving of the whiskey for each of us.

The captain reaches into another drawer and pulls out an elegant cigar case, a well-used ashtray, and a lighter.

"Care for one?" he asks, pushing the case toward us.

"No, no sir, Cap, haven't smoked in years," I answer, waving my hand back and forth.

"You, detective?" he says, offering a cigar to Marc.

Marc's nerves get the better of him, and he rambles. "Well, I would, sir, but the boys at the gym ever got wind of me smoking, let's just say, it wouldn't go over well with them, me being their role model and all. You know, sir." He chuckles as he squirms in his seat, repeatedly running his fingers over his mustache. It's obvious Marc's uncomfortable.

Captain Ottley nods his head, not once changing his expression. He takes a cigar from the case, sniffs its aroma, then gently rolls it between his fingers several times before lighting it. Blowing a perfect ring with the smoke as he exhales, the captain leans back in his chair to get comfortable, and his face relaxes.

"Any objection to the drink, Marc?" he asks, motioning to the bourbon with his cigar.

"Oh, no. No sir, none at all. I drink all the time," Marc replies confidently. Leaning back in his chair, he places his ankle across his knee.

The captain smiles. His gold tooth peeks beneath the large white mustache, its soft luster glistening against his dark brown skin. I roll my eyes and look away from Marc, covering my mouth with my hand to help silence my laughter.

Realizing what he said, Marc's face reddens. He shuffles in his seat, leans forward, and brushes a hand through his hair.

"Well, sir, I don't mean *all* the time, just sometimes, you know, now and then."

Eager to calm his nervousness, Marc downs the drink in two gulps and releases an 'ahh' sound as he exhales. His voice is raspy from the whiskey burn, and he slides his glass back to the captain. "I could use another one, captain, if you don't mind."

Grinning, Captain Ottley fills Marc's glass, then refreshes mine and his. "Okay, so, fellas, fill me in on what's happening with this case."

After clearing his throat, Marc gives the details of the timeline we reviewed last night, and I handle the witness information. I present our evidence, including the lipstick DNA matching a deceased woman and my findings from this morning, that the woman was a local college student murdered five years ago. Marc follows up with the latest results from the camera footage.

"As I told Detective Benson just before we came in, a camera in the shopping center parking lot caught the entire kidnapping on film, faces and all." Marc turns to me, grinning from ear to ear.

"We're running the picture of the kidnapper and the victim through the system to see if we get a facial match. None of the tag numbers led us anywhere since they were all stolen plates." Marc points toward me. "Tomas can give you an excellent account of what happened in the witness's neighborhood."

Sitting with my arms propped on my knees, I look up from the empty glass I hold and place it on the desk. The captain pours me another drink.

"Well, sir," I mumble, cautiously choosing my words. "After I followed up on the lipstick DNA this morning, I went to the witness's house to see if I could jog her memory about the kidnapping." I look up to see what reaction the captain has. His face is solemn as he takes in every word, puffing his cigar.

I take a few sips of the bourbon and continue. "Miss Preston wanted some fresh air, so we spent time together in the park at the back of her neighborhood. When we first got to the park, I noticed a gray Ford Explorer pulling into a small parking area. At first, I thought nothing about it, but when we returned home, I saw the same Explorer parked on the opposite side of her house, just down the street. The motor was still running, and someone was in the driver's seat, so I snuck up to check it out. I could see the driver fit the suspect's description. It looked like he was watching the witness's house through the outside mirror. He had his right hand on a gun lying on the console."

Shifting my weight in the chair, I lock eyes with Marc. Looking back at the captain, I continue. "He got away. We posted two patrol cars in the area in case the suspect returns for the witness's protection. He knows who she is, or he wouldn't have been there."

I gulp the last of my bourbon, place the glass on the desk, and wave my hand, signaling *no more* when the captain raises the bottle to pour me another.

The captain leans forward, placing his arms on the desk, and clears his throat. "Are we sure the guy was the suspect?"

"Pretty sure. The witness remembered seeing the Explorer in the Crestview parking lot on Wednesday before her second fall. Considering he had a gun, met the witness's description, and had a stolen license plate on the Explorer, he probably kidnapped the woman Tuesday."

As he nods, Captain Ottley pours himself one more drink and takes a sip, savoring the flavor. The captain likes to mull things over, so Marc and I sit, waiting for him to share his thoughts. After about ten minutes, the captain stands.

"Cases like this are tough," he declares.

Marc and I follow the captain's lead and stand.

"Sounds like you two have things pretty close to being wrapped up. Just find that missing woman as quickly as you can. Get back to me when you have more." He snuffs his cigar out and ambles from behind his desk. "Get on home and get some rest. I think you're going to need it before all this is over. Good work, detectives."

"There are a few more things we need to do before we go home," replies Marc, "but thank you, sir. Have a good night." He semi-salutes the captain and walks out ahead of me.

Captain Ottley watches Marc as he leaves. "Take care of him, Tomas. Don't let him drive if he's had too much. I'm not sure he can hold his liquor." He grins, his bushy brows arching high.

"I got it, sir. He'll be fine. You know he gets nervous around you."

The captain laughs, his dark eyes sparkling. Placing his hand on my shoulder, he walks me to the door. "I know he does. Marc tickles me. It's fun to watch him squirm and stammer." He shakes his head in amusement, still grinning. "Not too many pleasures in this job, Tomas. I like Marc and have a lot of respect for him. He's a mighty good detective, but I do like messing with him." Captain Ottley pats my shoulder. "Night, Tomas. Keep me updated."

Half smiling, I nod my head and say good night.

Marc and I have some things to discuss, but I'm ready to go home. I spot him waiting for me at the elevator and take a deep breath, exhausted from the day's events.

"How 'bout we call it for tonight, partner? I'm a little bruised and sore after my run-in with the SUV… could use some dinner, a bath, and bed. Why don't we call it a night, grab a bite to eat, and go home? We can get together first thing in the morning. I should feel better by then. The file on the college girl linked to the DNA should be back; hopefully, we will have an ID of the suspect. Maybe we'll get lucky and find out something about the victim."

Remembering what Ivy said the kidnapper told her before he pushed her down, I tell Marc.

"We can discuss it tomorrow. I just wanted to tell you before I forgot. Give it some thought to see if you can figure out what the kidnapper meant by it. I told Ivy you were good at riddles and puzzles," I joke.

"That's strange," Marc utters, tilting his head. "I'll think about it. Think he could have said something else, and she misunderstood?"

"Don't know. Could be, I guess."

"Hmm," Marc ponders for a moment. Without a logical explanation for the kidnapper's words, he concedes, "Alright, that's it for tonight. We'll meet in the morning first thing. Now, Tomas, how's The Barnacle Bay sound? I've been wanting one of their crab rolls." He licks his lips and pats his stomach. "But one condition. No more discussion about work. We're off for the night."

"Deal," I agree, thankful this day is almost over. It's been a long one.

CHAPTER 21

94 Hours 8 Minutes

Saturday December 3
8:30 a.m.

After arriving at the station, I head to the break room and pour my first coffee. The television mounted on the wall is always on. Chuck Drummond, the meteorologist on Channel 8, is talking about a powerful nor'easter expected to hit Boston Sunday night.

"This weather system will bring heavy rain, but mostly snow and ice; at least another fourteen inches of snow on top of the two feet already on the ground," he announces. Chuck continues, pointing to the weather data on the map behind him, painting a bleak picture of what's coming.

"Whatever is on the ground will freeze as the temperatures drop. We expect damaging winds at a sustained speed of forty-five miles per hour. Gusts may reach as high as sixty-five miles per hour or more."

Chuck encourages everyone to be prepared for power outages and blizzard conditions. The radar image displays an immense area of twisting white clouds extending far into the Atlantic Ocean and swooping over the northeast coast, covering Boston and the surrounding areas. The large white patch swirls, but there's no visible movement as the time ticks off the radar screen. Once here, this storm won't be leaving for several days.

"Travel will be hazardous, so we urge you, don't go out unless it's essential," Chuck stresses. "The effects of this system will linger for weeks, if not longer."

Walking up behind me, Marc exclaims, "Man, can you believe this weather?"

Catching a glimpse of him as he moves beside me, I stir the

creamer into my coffee. "Yeah, I think this one's gonna be bad. Remember the blizzard of 2015 when we got over twenty-four inches of snow in two days? With the snow and ice already on the ground, this storm will make that one look like a spring vacation."

As we walk to my office to work on the kidnapping case, we discuss our progress and leads. "Any matches to the photos of the suspect and victim from the camera in the parking lot?" I ask, pushing the door to my office open.

Marc pulls a chair close to the desk and swings the computer around so we can see the screen. He taps a few keys, and the rap sheet on Justin Clairy with his picture fills the screen.

"This is our suspect," he declares confidently, tapping the image with his pen.

Then, Marc presents the info about Clairy while doing his reporter's voice, enunciating each word and syllable to make a dramatic impact. Sometimes, his antics tickle me.

"Justin Clairy, five-ten, one-hundred fifty-five pounds, curly blond hair, blue eyes, a small mole on the left cheek," he begins, his head moving with his words. "Age twenty-seven from Milton, West Virginia. The last known address was Rockdale, Tennessee, but that was over a year ago. Parents live in Wainsburg, West Virginia, and own a small grocery store there. One brother." Marc loses his reporter's voice, snickers, and pokes me. "And get this," he continues, "his brother is a cop in New York."

"Nuh-uh," I mumble, glancing at Marc.

"Yes, sir, and he works homicide, too." Marc slaps me on the shoulder and rares back in his chair, snickering.

"What? I think these two apples fell from different trees."

Slipping on my drugstore reading glasses, I look closer at Clairy and his record. His boyish face glares at me from the computer. His curly, dirty-blonde hair lies in ringlets around his oval face, and the mole on his left cheek is barely noticeable. Clairy's thin lips form a small sideways smile, not in a cocky way, but more like he's posing for a family picture. Since the mugshot is from several years ago, I'm sure he's aged a little. Otherwise, Ivy's description was dead on, a hundred percent accurate, right down to the shape of the mole on his cheek.

The file doesn't have much in it. I examine Clairy's arrest record but see nothing significant, nothing I would've expected of someone bold enough to kidnap a woman in a busy upscale shopping center, especially in broad daylight.

"He's committed no crime that would make you think he'd try a kidnapping, Marc. Mostly petty crimes. Just one grocery store robbery when he was twenty-two, no weapon involved, and a couple of DUI arrests, parole violation, things like that," I state. "Not much of a rap sheet for a kidnapper."

Laying my glasses down, I push back from the desk, sip my coffee, and massage my neck, trying to ease the tightening in the muscles. The past few days are beginning to wear on me. With getting hit by the Explorer and my concerns about Ivy, not to mention our caseload, I'm feeling more tense than usual.

Our department is short-staffed, so Marc and I carry an extra load. Last week, we solved a child kidnapping case, and now, the little boy is back unharmed, safe and sound with his parents. We have ten homicides we're working on and at least seven ongoing missing person cases. For now, our focus must be on this kidnapping case if we're going to find the woman alive. The chances of that lessen every day.

"What about the victim, Marc? Did her pic show up in the database?"

Marc stands and shakes his head as he walks to the coffeepot. "No luck there yet. I'm gonna fill the pot and make some more coffee. I swear I'm getting you a twelve-cup pot for Christmas. I'll be back in a sec, and we'll talk about the missing woman. I have some thoughts, but I dunno," he mutters, then leaves to get the water.

I stand, yawning, and stretch my arms out wide, pushing them as far behind me as possible. The tightness in my neck has turned into a dull, aching pain in my left shoulder, radiating into my lower back and hip. Searching the desk drawers, I find a small bottle of acetaminophen. I pop two in my mouth, wash them down with my last gulp of coffee, and toss the bottle on my desk.

Opening the blinds on the window behind me, I survey the dismal winter day. It's no longer snowing, but the sky is a sheet of steel gray, not a pinch of light wiggling through. The flags across the street in the courtyard thrash about as the wind whips by. The harsh blowing wind is just a preview of what's coming.

My anxiety builds, knowing I've got to get to Ivy's before the nor'easter arrives. There's a high chance of being snowbound for a few days. I have to make sure she's safe.

My thoughts turn to the likely outcome of the case, but I force myself to be optimistic. Knowing Clairy is the kidnapper will help us figure out who the victim is and where he took her, preferably before the storm hits. That would be ideal.

Absorbed in my thoughts, I don't notice Marc has returned. As I turn from the window, I catch him pouring two cups of the coffee he just made.

"Looks like you were deep in thought, partner," Marc says, sneaking a look at me from under his brows. He hands me one of the filled cups. "Got anything more on that DNA?"

Somehow, I manage not to moan as I slowly lower myself into the chair behind my desk and pick up my reading glasses. "I did some more research on the lipstick DNA results and the college girl it matched. Her name was…" I rustle through my notes. "Hannah Bellstone. She was a student at Werthmore University, murdered five years ago after being kidnapped. Hunters discovered her body months after the kidnapper killed her. It was a horrible sight."

Looking up from the note, I eye Marc over my glasses. "We worked that case, remember? I just can't recall all the minor details about it."

I lay my glasses on the desk and rub my eyes. Forcing the image of the poor girl out of my mind, I try to concentrate only on the evidence. Not wanting to review the gruesome details of the Bellstone case again, I nudge my notes toward Marc.

"You can read it. No one caught the kidnapper, remember?" I hope Marc can recall some of the finer details escaping my memory.

Marc shakes his head and paces the floor. "I remember the case, but the details are fuzzy. It's been five years. We've had lots of cases since then." He sits down and leans back, holding his coffee between his hands. "Any link to the victim that you know of?" he asks.

"Not so far," I reply. "I'm still digging. I don't have the complete case file yet, but I've requested it. Should be here any time. Any ideas?"

He moves his head from side to side as he sets his coffee down. He places his arms on the desk and leans forward. "Well, Tom, let's just toss some things out there and see what we come up with," he suggests.

"Okay." I smile, leaning back and propping my feet on the desk. We often do our best work when we brainstorm, no matter how bizarre our ideas might be.

"You start."

"Hmm, well…" Marc pauses, looks around the room, then at the computer screen and the notes. "Wonder if our kidnapper, Justin Clairy, kidnapped the college girl," Marc proposes, pointing to Clairy's mug shot. "And he had the lipstick in the car, you know, kinda like a trophy. Maybe the kidnapper dropped it when he took our victim, and that's how it ended up at the crime scene. That could explain it."

Pressing my lips tight, I nod and then blow on my coffee. "Could be," I say. "That would explain how the lipstick with the college girl's DNA got there. Francine Whittaker said the kidnapper grabbed a purse and threw it in the car. Maybe the guy had the college girl's purse, and the lipstick fell out." I make a tumbling motion with my hand.

"Yep, that would explain the whole thing." Mark taps his finger on the note lying on the desk. "We didn't catch her kidnapper, so Clairy certainly could have done it. We need to get her complete file and review it to see if this idea fits." He sits back in his chair and props his feet on the desk, hands clasped behind his head.

"Pretty smug looking," I joke, "considering this is just a theory."

"Well, I'm going with it until we have proof otherwise." Marc's smile widens, all his pearly whites gleaming.

Leaning forward, close to the desk, I pick at Marc. "That's why I'm in charge. Never make assumptions until you have all the facts, partner." I playfully shove his feet off my desk.

I stand and walk across the room—my face twists, revealing the pinching pain in my back. I press my hands deep into the lower part of my spine, hoping to ease the pressure, working the massage over to my left hip. Even though it hasn't been that long since I took the acetaminophen, the pain has become more intense with my bending and sitting. When I move a certain way, a sudden surge of sharp pain shoots through every nerve woven into my shoulder, back, and hip like the tentacles of a jellyfish are stinging me.

Leaning over my desk, I think about Marc's explanation for the lipstick being present at the scene.

"The more I think about it, the more the lipstick and the kidnapper having it doesn't make much sense," I state.

Marc looks puzzled. "How come?"

"Why would a kidnapper take a previous victim's purse or even just a tube of lipstick with him to commit another crime? I can see him keeping it as a trophy, but hauling it around in his car all these years? I just can't picture that, not when I look at it from a criminal's perspective. It's not like a lock of hair or jewelry stowed in the glove compartment."

Nodding his head, Marc agrees. "Yeah, it doesn't make sense when you think about it. It's more likely that the purse Whittaker said the suspect tossed in the car belonged to the victim than the college girl. But I can't imagine why she would have a tube of lipstick that Hannah Bellstone had used."

We're both stumped, unable to determine the lipstick's connection. Shaking my head, I ease myself into my chair and shrug my shoulders, confused. I place my hands over my face and slowly drag them off my chin. This is a tough case.

I lean back and tell Marc, "Maybe when I get the full report on Hannah Bellstone's murder, the pieces will fall together. We're missing something. This entire case makes little sense. The pieces aren't connecting the way they should."

Taking a quick breath, Marc props his arms on the desk and stares at the image of Clairy on the computer screen.

Moving on, I add, "Anyway, that doesn't help us identify our missing victim in this case. So far, we have nothing except a witness's sketch and a video of the kidnapping that shows very little of her face."

"What about the idea that she was not from here? Anything on that?" Marc inquires.

"We've checked the hotels and motels near Crestview Shopping Center for missing guests. So far, nothing, not even a staff member recognizing her from the sketch. We're expanding the search area."

Sitting is so uncomfortable that I stand again, not realizing I'm groaning with every move. Leaning backward, hands on my lower back, I stretch again and moan low under my breath. My hand reaches for my left shoulder, and I massage the muscle to loosen the hard knot bulging under my shirt.

"Hold that thought, partner," Marc says as he throws his hand up.

Without saying where he's going, he leaves the room. Returning about ten minutes later, Marc's holding a small lumbar pillow and a heating pad. He places them both in my chair and motions for me to sit down.

When I'm comfortable, Marc puts one hand on the back of the chair, leans close to my face, and gives me a death stare, his eyes wide, locked on mine.

"If this doesn't help, you see a doctor first thing in the morning before that storm hits, you understand?" he insists firmly. "You might have broken some bones or have some nerve damage. If I have to, I'll take you myself." Marc's tone is commanding as he issues my ultimatum.

"Um-hm," I grunt. "Thanks for the pillow and pad." I nod, breaking my partner's intense gaze. "Now, back to the case."

Marc jumps right back to where he left off without missing a beat. "No one from Geordies or the other stores in the shopping center remembers the victim coming in, so she must have either just got there or was meeting someone in the alley, and it went bad," Marc continues, returning to his seat. "The cameras don't clearly show where she came from, just her walking into the alley, maybe from the parking lot. We never found an abandoned car, though, so that's weird, too."

I bang my fist on the desk in frustration. "The victim had to know the suspect. There's just no other way! Maybe she was with the guy. They argued in the car. She got out, went to the alley, the man followed her in the car, then took her," I speculate.

Leaning back against the heating pad, I cradle my coffee. "If that's not how it happened, someone either brought the woman there and dropped her off or took her car after the incident. Let's see..." a thought forms in my mind. "Could the kidnapper have had a partner?" My coffee is almost gone, so I place the near-empty cup on the desk.

"It's got to be one of these scenarios. There's no other explanation," I say, throwing my hands up in defeat.

Marc stands and paces the floor, rubbing his chin as he walks. In an instant, he pivots to face me and snaps his fingers. "I've got it!"

He takes a minute to organize his thoughts before speaking. "Okay," Marc begins. "If we bring in the words Ivy told you the man said to her before he shoved her to the ground and assume that the man knew the victim," his voice rises an octave, and his brows arch as his eyes widen, "it makes more sense."

"How so?"

"The guy first told her, 'It's not what you think,' right?"

"Yeah."

"So obviously then, it wasn't just a kidnapping. Maybe the kidnapper meant he wasn't kidnapping her. It's possible, in his mind," Marc points to his head, "it wasn't kidnapping because he knew her. Maybe they had fought like that before, and she would become so irrational and angry that he would forcefully remove her from wherever they were. A party. A street." He cocks his head and smiles smugly. "Or a shopping center."

Running the scenario through my mind, I nod. "I can picture that happening. It could even explain the kidnapper's second statement to Ivy, 'She made me.' He could have felt it was the victim's fault because *her* behavior made him take her to settle her down."

I stand, place my hands on my lower back, and lean forward, then back. Taking the bottle of pills from my desk, I toss two more in my mouth, swallowing them with a swig of the cold coffee remaining in my cup.

The light in the room flickers, and I wonder if we are about to lose power. I walk across the room to the window to check the weather. The sky has grown darker and bleaker. Judging by the flags in the courtyard, the wind is getting stronger. Snow is falling again. Only a few people remain on the street, bracing themselves against the powerful gusts as they walk. Shop owners who have delayed boarding their windows struggle against the wind's power to nail them up. Everything looks dismal from where I'm standing, including this case.

"That could explain everything," I say with vigor, my attempt at optimism. "One, why no one found the victim's car; two, why no one has reported a missing person; three, why someone took the victim; and four, what the man meant by the things he said to Ivy." I turn toward Marc, rubbing my brow. "But it doesn't explain why the man placed a cloth over the victim's nose and mouth and tossed her into the trunk. That makes it look more like a forced kidnapping to me."

Hesitating, Marc agrees. "You're right. Too many pieces of this puzzle are missing." He shakes his head. "We've gotta be missing something. There's one missing piece, and, as you said, Tomas, we still don't know who the victim is. None of the evidence seems to help us with that."

"Why don't we grab lunch and see if something turns up this afternoon? Maybe we'll get lucky, and Justin Clairy will make a stupid mistake and get arrested for some traffic violation," I laugh.

Mark snickers. "If we could be so lucky." He bows and motions to the door. "After you, sir," he says, and we head off for lunch.

As we're walking down the hall, the door to the elevator opens, and Lucy scurries out. She rushes down the hall yelling, her blue blouse billowing in the breeze she's creating with her rapid movement.

"Detective, detective!" Her eyes focus on me. "I was just coming to get you," she pants, winded from her sprint. "Captain needs to see you. Both of you, now. It's urgent!"

Taking her by the shoulders, I try to slow her down. "Calm

down, Lucy. Take a few breaths," I say. "Inhale through your nose, and exhale through your mouth." We do that several times until she looks calmer and her face has regained its rosy glow. "Now, let's go see what the captain wants."

"What's going on, Lucy?" Marc asks as we step onto the elevator.

"I really don't know. Captain just said to get you both, quick." Her eyes bounce from me to Marc. "I tried to call your office phone, but you didn't answer, so I jumped on the elevator and rushed down here to get you."

"We must have just left the office when you called," I explain. "You can always call my cell. Save yourself the trouble of trying to find me."

Lucy nods her head, a blank look on her face. "I didn't think of that."

When we reach Captain Ottley's office, Lucy escorts us in. The captain is sitting behind his desk with the phone held to his ear.

"Yep… uh-huh… okay. I got it. Thanks. Keep me updated," he orders, then hangs up.

"Detectives," the captain nods. "There's no easy way to put this." He looks at Marc and then maintains eye contact with me.

"Your witness, Ivy Preston, disappeared this morning. The evidence suggests a possible kidnapping."

CHAPTER 22

Saturday 12:46 p.m.

I think my eyes are open, but I see nothing. There's only black, suffocating darkness surrounding me. Not a sliver of light peeps from a window. No stars are sparkling in the night sky. No glow from a street lamp softly illuminating the misty air. No light of any kind. I can't tell if it's day or night.

I can't remember anything except being at home with Alana. What happened? And where am I?

"Alana!" I yell, my voice weak. "Alana!"

No one answers. The dark presses in on me, enclosing me in a tomb. The weight of the blackness surrounding me feels like it's crushing my chest. My heart echoes in my ears, beating faster and faster, louder and louder.

I'm scared. I don't know where I'm at or how I got here. I'm more than scared—I'm *terrified.*

I can't breathe. Struggling to bring air into and out of my lungs, I claw at my neck, peeling my robe away from my chest. What air I inhale is musty and stagnant, filled with fumes that smell like gasoline or oil. The spasms in my throat cause me to cough as I choke on the strong odors, the stench leaching the oxygen from the air—the oxygen my lungs yearn for. My mind is foggy, and I'm dizzy. The more I cough, the more confused I get.

My lips are numb from the cold and dampness surrounding me. My tongue feels gritty and dry, and there's some kind of weird taste in my mouth. Could it be medicine?

"Hello?" I yell as loudly as my parched throat will allow. "Have I been in an accident?"

With no response, I call out again.

"Hey! Is anyone there?"

The only sound I hear is a mechanical rumbling, like when I was in the MRI machine, but I sense I'm in a more frightful place than that.

Is there something covering my eyes, keeping me from seeing? I feel and find nothing. To clear my vision, I squeeze my eyes tight several times, then force them wide open, but everything around me stays black.

My body shakes, and my fingers and toes are numb from the cold. I snuggle deep into my robe, trying to ease the constant shaking. Tears hang in my eyes, but I refuse to cry.

Thud.

My entire body bounces up and down like a Yo-Yo, and my forehead slams into a hard object near my face just before my head whips back.

What the hell is happening?

It happens again, *thud—thud.* I feel like a bowling ball tossed down a lane, bouncing toward the gutter. The back of my head hits something hard, and my eyes squeeze together, my face twisting in agony.

"Shit," I mumble.

The painful blow makes the tears in my eyes drip down my face.

The bumping and bouncing continues for several minutes. Each unexpected bounce slings me from side to side or up and down.

I feel like I'm moving, but I can't tell. Music is playing, and someone is singing in the distance.

There's another thud. My body tosses like the pitch of a boat on the ocean waves. Bouncing high off the ground, I fall back with a hard thud. A sharp pain rolls through my hip and spreads down my leg.

As I reach my hands out to brace myself, I feel what seems like hard metal above me, encircling me like a shield. Removing my gloves, I trace the curve of the metal until it merges with the rough, prickly, flat surface I'm lying on, some kind of stiff, fuzzy rug or worn-down carpet.

Something tickles the skin beside my eye. Thinking it's a bug or a spider, I swipe at it with my hand, attempting to brush it away. My hand rakes across a warm liquid trickling down my face, and I realize it's fresh blood. Following the trail, I find a hard lump on my forehead, just above my left eye. The wound throbs a little, but it's more numb from the lick it took than painful.

The back of my head burns like hot knives are cutting into it. Tears puddle in my eyes once again, but I force them back, grit my teeth, and fight through the pain.

Now is *not* the time to cry.

Touching the back of my head, I can tell the old wound is open, oozing blood. Since I can't see anything, I feel around for something to hold against it to stop the bleeding. There's a rag lying under my leg, so I pull it out and press it to the open wound. The rag is just the right length to reach around my head. I wrap it from back to front, covering both injuries and tie the ends together, securing it in place. I pull my hat down over the homemade bandage to help keep the dressing in place.

The fogginess in my mind is clearing. I remember being in my backyard. A thick, icy snow covered everything. Yes, I remember— the poor birds couldn't find anything to eat. I walked into the backyard to put food in their feeders. A dog whimpered behind the gate. When I went to look, I heard something behind me. Before I could turn around to look, someone grabbed me and pressed something over my mouth and nose.

Then… nothing.

I can't remember anything else until I woke up alone in the dark.

All movement stops, and I'm hurled to my left, rolling until I strike the edge of… of something. I hear a noise, like a car door slamming and some people mumbling. There's a pungent smell. I sniff and know without a doubt that it's gasoline.

There's not much room to move around, so I can't get to a sitting position. Twisting and turning, I reposition myself enough to swipe my hands around. Finding a large, round, bumpy object near my feet, I discover it's a tire.

Now *is* the time to cry.

Blind in the dark, my tears mix with the blood dried on my face and drip off my chin. I no longer have a handkerchief that smells like the detective to catch my tears. Detective Benson did all he could to keep me safe, but it didn't work.

Someone—the man who took the woman—has now taken me, and, like the woman, he tossed me into the trunk of a car. Probably the same dark blue Plymouth he dumped her in.

Panic consumes me, and I can't focus on anything for more than a few seconds. Even though I'm freezing and trembling from the cold, my body sweats, and my skin is clammy. My hands shake nervously. Sliding my gloves back on is difficult because my hands are so damp. My stomach knots up, pushing into my throat. And I become dizzy and nauseous.

My instinct says to breathe to keep from passing out, so I do, taking slow, controlled breaths. The stench makes me even sicker, and I heave a deep hacking cough.

I have to get help. Since the car isn't moving, I feel sure we've stopped to get gas. Now is my chance to let someone know I'm locked in the trunk. It could be the last chance I'll have.

I try not to panic, but fear has robbed me of my voice. I open my mouth to yell, and all that comes out is a squeak, barely above a whisper. I can feel my heart racing. Desperate, knowing I have only a few moments to tell someone I'm here, I concentrate only on my voice. After several attempts to yell, my squeak becomes a scream.

The screams get louder and louder, and I pound on the trunk with all my might, hoping someone will hear me.

"Help! Help me! Please help me!"

There's some commotion from outside, and I hear raised voices. It sounds like two men are arguing. A resounding thud lands on top of me. Something, or someone, hit the car.

The car door slams again, the engine revs up, and the tires squeal as the car speeds off with me still in it. The music gets louder, drowning out my screams. My hope of someone hearing me fades away as the vehicle moves further down the road.

I'm no longer afraid—now I'm petrified. My heart's doing jumping jacks in my chest. What's going to happen now? Was that my last hope of being found? Am I going to… die?

I close my eyes and breathe, trying to calm myself. Think. Think! I have to be logical. I can't let the panic control my emotions. I've stood up to bullies and gone against formidable attorneys in court. I just have to think my way out of this situation. I have to be smarter than the person who took me. Just because he got me doesn't mean he'll keep me. I'm an intelligent person; I am a determined person; I can do anything I set my mind to. I *will* come out of this alive and okay.

"I am a *fighter*! I am a *winner*!" I scream at the driver. He can't hear me over the music blasting in the car, but I don't care.

Eventually, this person will stop and open the trunk, and I need to be ready to defend myself, so I feel around in the dark for something I can use as a weapon. Even though I can't see in the darkness, I open my eyes wide as a thought comes to me—if there's a tire, there must be a tire iron and a jack.

Usually, the jack is underneath the tire or in a side compartment, sometimes even under the carpet. Jammed in here with junk I can't see, I shove the useless items out of my way as I squirm around to face the tire. I feel inside the middle of the tire to see if the jack is lying there, but no luck. Hugging the tire, I reach over it and stretch my hand as far as possible to check behind it for a side compartment.

Yes! I feel the jack secured to the side wall of the trunk in a creviced area, but no matter how hard I tug, I can't pull it out. Refusing to give up, I strain, stretching my body across the tire to reach deeper into the crevice. My fingers fold around a long, hard, pipe-like object. Grimacing in pain, I struggle to get a full grip on it. I try to unclasp it from the wall and pull it straight up with all my might, but it won't budge. After several more attempts, the pipe pops free. Somehow, I keep ahold of it, successfully retrieving it. Exhausted, I slide off the tire and roll back on the floor, clinging to the tire iron, and close my eyes in relief.

"Thank you," I whisper. "Thank you."

CHAPTER 23

4 Days 4 Hours 7 Minutes
2 Hours 47 Minutes

Saturday 2:29 p.m.

The car jolts to a halt without warning, hurling me to the back of the trunk. A door slams hard enough to cause the vehicle to vibrate. Muffled voices penetrate the steel surrounding me, but I can't distinguish the words. The voices grow louder and angrier. At least two people are yelling and screaming at each other. One is the voice of a man. I'm sure he's the kidnapper. The different voice is louder and high-pitched. I think it's a woman.

The people move closer to the trunk, and I can hear their words more clearly. My heart beats like horses are galloping in my chest. I'm terrified. What's going to happen to me?

"Now we have a real mess," a woman rants. "I told you to leave it alone. She wasn't a threat, but now—just think about what you've done, Justin! You weren't supposed to bring her here."

"I didn't have a choice!" The man, Justin, yells. "It's my freakin' face all over the TV, not yours, and it's all because of *her*."

Bam!

Something hard hits the trunk from the outside. Startled by the sudden loud noise so close to me, my eyes pop wide, and I press my hands over my mouth. I can't make a sound, or they might hear me. The voices become a roar in my ears. I wish I could see. If only I had some light to strangle the darkness.

Instead, the darkness strangles me.

After a few moments of silence, the man continues. "I couldn't kill her there, not in her yard like that. I would've gotten caught. Besides, I don't wanna kill anybody. That wasn't the plan."

"*This* sure as hell wasn't the plan! What are we gonna do?"

"Dammit, Henlie," he whimpers, his voice lower. "I don't know. I didn't want to do this at all, any of it. You talked me into it. You made me do it. I knew it was a bad idea. I knew something would go wrong."

The thought of dying at the hands of the kidnapper paralyzes me. He was there at my house, standing right behind me. There's no telling how long he had been watching me. He could have done more than kidnap me, but he didn't.

Was it because he was afraid of getting caught? Does he plan on killing me here—wherever here is? What's going to happen to me when he opens the trunk?

I'm not just having a bad dream that I'll wake up from when my alarm goes off. This is real.

A wave of panic engulfs me, stealing my breath. My heart pounds harder, faster. Each breath I take comes quicker than the last, shallower and more labored. Salty sweat trickles down my face, stinging my eyes. Lying still and quiet, I sob and wonder if I will survive.

It's the woman's voice I hear next. She's calmer now. "It's okay. We'll figure this out. Let's get things set up in the barn. We'll just have to put her there until we decide what to do."

"What about that other woman? She's in there. They might talk, and we can get in a lot of trouble. Ahh, Henlie, all our plans are gonna have to change now. This ain't what I agreed to."

"We'll figure it out, Justin. It'll all work out. I promise, baby. Everything will be okay. Trust me. We've already got the money, so it don't matter what happens to either of 'em. Me and you'll be sittin' on a beach in Cancun before you know it."

Knowing I won't survive if I let my emotions guide my actions and terror consume my mind, I take three deep breaths and try to gain control of the fear consuming me. No matter what happens, I have to focus on making a solid attack when I have to.

My life depends on me alone—what I *choose* to do.

Gripping the tire iron with my shaking hands, I scrunch against the side of the trunk, pulling my knees up and curving my body into a ball. I hold my weapon close so it's not seen. That way, he won't be prepared for my strike. It's best if I kick hard, then come out stabbing with the sharp edge of the tire iron, not swinging it since I have very little room to maneuver. I'd never get enough momentum to do any damage that way. My first strike has to count, and I intend to make sure it does.

The voices become lower and softer, and I can't hear the words anymore. Then there's silence. Unaware of how much time has passed since the last sound I heard from the outside, I lie, anticipating what happens next. Sweat continues to drip from my forehead despite the intense cold surrounding me.

I know they're going to open the trunk.

What I don't know is when.

Did I hear the man say another woman is in the barn? It has to be the woman I saw getting kidnapped. If she's still in the barn, and he's afraid we might talk, she has to be alive. I hope I'll be able to save her, but for now, I have to think about my own survival. If I'm dead, I'm no help to her. Somehow, I've got to get out of this trunk and escape if I'm going to get help.

Trapped in this metallic cocoon, I scan the area and spot a tiny streak of light on the back wall of the trunk. Shifting my body, I move closer and trace the spot with my fingers. There's a split like the wall separates from the trunk. The light must come from the passenger area. I try to insert my fingers into the split, but it's too tight, so I push on the middle near the lighted area with all my might. The wall shifts about a quarter of an inch, and the slit enlarges.

Hearing the voices return, I freeze where I am and strain to understand what they are saying. There's some commotion around the trunk, but I can't tell what's happening. Then, all is silent once again as the voices move away.

Now is my chance. I turn my body so my feet are flat on the back of the trunk near the lighted area and kick with all my might, pounding the back wall. With each blow, the wall gives a little more. The streak of light becomes broader and longer. My excitement—my hope—grows with every kick.

I've been in total blackness for so long that my eyes are sensitive to the light, so I try squinting through the small opening. Still unable to focus, I blink multiple times to clear the blurriness. Frustrated, I lean back, close my eyes, and take a deep breath before I peer through the opening again.

It's hard to tell what I'm looking at, but I think it is the car's interior. I can see a little of a car door with vinyl upholstery and an older, pull-style lock poking up near the cracked side window. This wall has to be a fold-down rear seat. I must have broken the lock on it when I kicked it. If I have enough time, maybe I can force the back down and escape. Where did Henlie and Justin go? If I knew, I would feel better about what I'm doing. Since I can't hear them, I hope they don't hear me.

Once again, I place my feet flat against what has to be the back of the rear seat. My knees bent, I count to three and push with my legs as hard as possible. The seat moves another couple of inches. My legs shake; every muscle in my body is tense, quivering. It moves another four, five, six inches. Light flows into the trunk. Groaning as if I'm giving birth, I push as hard as I can one more time, using all the energy remaining in my body.

The seat falls forward with a thump. My heart flips and flutters as excitement and nervousness fill my mind. Escape is a real possibility. That's the motivation I need to keep going.

Poking my face through the opening, I scan the area outside. Snow is everywhere, covering the ground and crushing down on the trees like a heavy blanket, their limbs drooping from the weight.

A large, weathered building about a hundred yards to the right looks like an old, rundown barn. It has double doors on the front and a smaller door centered above them. Both of my kidnappers are there.

The male, Justin, sits on a crate, his elbows propped on his bent knees and his face between his hands. Henlie is squatting down and talking Justin, her hands on his knees. A tiny Yorkshire Terrier bounces around them and lies beside the man. The man smiles as he reaches for the dog, petting and playing with the small animal.

Glancing around, I look out the front windshield. The car faces a small, faded green shed, maybe a storage building for garden tools. I can't see inside, and the door has a padlock. There's no way I can get in without being heard and seen. I could use the shed for partial blockage but wouldn't get far before being spotted.

Looking further to the left, I see a maze of snow and ice-coated trees. Their limbs, covered in white, dip toward the ground. Some heavy branches have snapped and lie beneath the trees. Other limbs have broken but still cling to the trees by a thread, dancing in the wind. The further I look, the denser the trees become, eventually fusing into one solid mass of white.

If I leave the car without being seen and go for the trees, there's a good chance I'll die from the weather. There's supposed to be a nasty winter storm moving in tonight or tomorrow. I'm unsure when the storm will hit since I don't know how long I was in the trunk.

Crawling further into the car, I pop my head up a few times and spot a shabby old cabin about fifty yards away. It looks like no one has lived there for years. Some of the logs forming the walls have split, and several wooden shutters dangle on nails. All the windows have boards on them. The tin roof is sagging in spots from the weight of at least a foot or more of snow on top of it. Smoke billows from the cracked stone chimney. A dog food bowl sits near the door, and a large green tarp covers a pile of cut logs on the far side of the small porch.

If I can get to the side of the house, I could get inside and bolt the door. It's a risky idea since the cabin is in the direct view of my kidnappers.

The only other option is to get to the cabin and use it for cover. If I make it to the side, Justin and Henlie won't be able to see me from their position in the yard. Then I could run to the tree line behind the house. The big question is whether I can get there without being noticed. If they stay behind the barn, it would be easy. But should they start back this way at all, they would spot me in a heartbeat.

All I have to keep me warm is my hat, gloves, furry boots, and the long robe I threw on before I fed the birds. The loose gray sweatshirt and my pants underneath are my only real clothes. My skin's already icy cold to the touch, so I know I won't be able to survive in the woods. But maybe, just maybe, if I could find some shelter, I might make it. It's a possibility. Given my situation, I may not have another choice.

I took a survival course once, and Nick and I have gone hiking and camping several times. My dad taught me most of my survival skills; being military, he taught me well. Dad… thinking of him draws silent tears to my eyes. Will I ever see him again? Or Mom? A few tears slip past my lids. Rubbing my gloved hand over my face, I wipe the rest away. I don't have time to be emotional right now. I have to get out of here.

Crawling into the back seat, I pull my entire body from the confines of the trunk. It feels so good to lengthen my legs and stretch my back. My muscles are weak and achy. I still see Helie and Justin sitting and talking. But I know there's not much time before they come back.

Could I be lucky enough that Justin left his keys in the ignition or lying on the seat or dash? After maneuvering to get a better view,

I can see the ignition between the bucket seats.

"Shit," I whisper to myself. No keys. Why would he take them with him? It's not like there's anybody around that would steal his car.

My lips tighten and twist into a full pout. A strand of hair falls into my face. Blowing a puff of air out the side of my mouth, I hope to get it out of my eyes, but it flops back down, blocking my view. To avoid being seen. I lower my head to my hand and tuck the strand under the rag still wrapped around my head.

To help me concentrate, I close my eyes tightly for a few seconds. Think. Think! What should I do?

Squeezing between the front seats, I check the floors for any objects left there. A couple of rags and some papers lie on the passenger seat, and I spot a lighter on the dash. I grab the papers and rags, stuffing them in the pockets of my robe.

The lighter is tempting, but I risk getting seen if I reach for it. Deciding to leave it alone, I open the glove compartment and find a small flashlight, an adjustable wrench, and, lucky me, two lighters and a pack of cigarettes. A smile stretches across my face as I squeak out a "Yes" and grab everything, including about half the cigarettes, even though I don't smoke. Given my circumstances, this might be a good time to start.

I scoot myself back into the edge of the trunk and rake my hands around the floor until I find the tire iron. It's my only weapon other than the wrench. I can't lose them.

My decision is made: I'm going to make a run for the house and try to get to the woods. Checking one more time for my kidnappers, I pull on the passenger door handle on the driver's side and pray that it doesn't squeak when I open it. The door is open just wide enough to get one leg out when Justin and Henlie stand. I freeze in my crunched position and watch, waiting to see what happens. Do I run if they come this way, or do I fight?

Both are at the far side of the barn, talking and gesturing with their hands. It looks like Justin gave in to whatever Henlie wanted him to do. He walks to the other side of the barn, and she follows him. The two of them disappear beside the barn. I know this is my best chance to get away.

As I push the car door wider, both of them emerge, moving in my direction. I hurry back into the car and dive into the trunk, pulling the back seat up by its handle, but leaving it slightly open to make it easier to escape if I get a chance. As I crawl back into my original attack position, I feel my muscles tighten and I prepare to fight. My mind is hyperalert.

I hear the clunk of the lock releasing, and my heart thunders in my chest.

The trunk lid lifts. My breathing quickens.

I'm as ready as I can be.

CHAPTER 24

4 Days 5 Hours 2 Minutes
3 Hours 42 Minutes

Saturday 3:24 p.m.

The trunk starts to open, and despite the fear surging inside me, I remain steadfast in my position, poised to strike. I channel all my energy and emotions into my arms and legs to win this battle.

The looming terror inside wants to consume me, but rather than let it take over, I concentrate on my breathing, taking deep, controlled breaths, inhaling, and exhaling slowly. It reduces my anxiety and helps me stay focused, at least a little.

My first blows have to count, or it's over. What if Justin has a gun? I hadn't thought about that, but it doesn't matter. My only chance of survival is to fight with all I have in me, and that's what I'm going to do.

Justin will probably stand in the center of the trunk, so I fix my eyes there. Most likely, Henlie will be behind him or to his left side, close to me. Gripping the tire iron with both hands, I conceal it as much as possible with my robe. I pull my knees to my chest so my feet are close to the center of the trunk near the latch, braced to kick.

This is the moment—live or possibly die.

The opening to the outside widens, and the man peers in to see where I am.

Bam!

I kick as hard as possible, landing a solid hit to the front of his face. Henlie looks at him, stunned. She stands there, shifting from leg to leg, back and forth, then reaches out toward him. Her hands shake. She stares at Justin, her eyes glazed and mouth open. The woman's chin moves up and down as though she wants to speak, but no words come.

Justin grabs his face, cursing, blood pouring from his mouth and nose. Again, he leans his body into the trunk, reaching for me. Without thinking, I make a rapid, hard thrust with the tire iron. The cold steel penetrates his left lower abdomen and lodges there. He wails in agony, grabbing the metal rod. Quickly, I retract it before he can get a solid grip. Blood pours from the wound. His tan shirt becomes bright red as it soaks up the liquid seeping across his side.

Arms swinging wildly and pupils dilated, Henlie touches his side, then pulls her hands back, covering her mouth.

"Justin! Justin! Oh! Oh, no! Justin!" She screams. "Chapri for losca press doms ta pah mash pah!"

The woman's words make no sense and are difficult to understand. Her voice is flat, and even though she's screaming, her face is emotionless—no blinking or crying, no expression—just hysterical yelling, rambling, and spasmodic shaking. Backing away from Justin, Henlie utters the word 'no' several times, then trips and falls backward onto the snow. Struggling to get up, she turns and runs toward the cabin, still yelling, her arms flapping like a flag in the wind.

Eyes bulging, teeth clenched, Justin is obviously angry. He reaches for me again and grabs my right leg. Kicking him as hard as I can, I raise the tire iron above my head, thrust it down, and ram it into his left bicep. I feel the steel jerk as it rips through the tissue. The man's gut-wrenching howl echoes through the woods. He releases his grip on my leg, backs away, and slams the trunk down.

The black nothingness envelopes me again. I squeeze my eyes tight. The adrenaline rushing through my body keeps me alert, but my thoughts are disorganized. Anxiety explodes through every inch of me. I swallow hard and choke on the dryness in my mouth and throat. Breathing comes in short, rapid bursts, and my heart is doing backflips in my chest. I know I have little time. They'll be back any second.

What should I do? What *can* I do? My mind jumps from thought to thought.

"I hurt him real bad," I whisper, smiling grimly.

That might not be a good thing, though. It could make it worse for me. If Justin had thought about killing me before, I know he wouldn't hesitate now. Looking around the trunk, I spy light encircling the back seat's edges. Escape is the only option I have left. I can't lie here waiting for them to return. Even if I freeze in the woods, I've got to get out of here—now!

Determined to escape, I cling to the tire iron and shove the back seat down. Worming my way through the trunk onto the car's rear floor, I push on the open left passenger door and open it a little more. Methodically, I move out of the car, feet first. My boots sink deep into the snow on the ground. Gripping the tire iron in one hand, I inch my way out of the vehicle. I stay squatted, keeping low to the ground.

As I push the door closed, a black fur-lined boot appears beneath it. The door moves away from my hand. My eyes scroll up to the figure behind the door. Henlie stands fixed, a shotgun in her hands, the barrel inches from my temple. Her face is blank, her eyes cold and empty. Frozen in my crouched position, not a muscle twitching, I feel the pressure of the gun barrel against my head. Slowly, I shift my gaze to her face. I don't blink or speak and barely breathe. There's a roar in my ears, and everything around me, all sounds, all images, blend together.

My hope of escaping this nightmare is gone; the tears create tiny holes in the snow as they spill down my face, falling to the ground like rain. My shoulders rise and fall as I sob uncontrollably. Sinking to the snow-covered ground, I lie on my side, curl into a ball, my knees cradled in my arms, and weep uncontrollably. I give up. Despite my best effort, I've lost.

I heard somewhere you don't hear the bullet coming. It could have been a line from a movie, or it could be the truth. Since I don't know, I wait for the shotgun's trigger to click.

Without saying a word, the woman lowers the weapon and lunges at me. A forceful blow from her boot strikes the middle of my back, knocking the air out of my lungs. I arch my spine and gasp for air, unable to scream. As I lie on the ground, struggling for breath, she strikes a glancing blow to my face. My head jerks to one side, and my cheek feels like it's ripping off. Blood splatters the snow-covered ground.

The woman follows with a savage kick to my shoulder and another to my ribs. I can barely make a sound, not even as much as a groan. My mind screams from the excruciating pain surging through my body as I roll onto my stomach.

Defeated, I'm helpless and at the mercy of these people. The once-white snow beneath my face is scarlet from the blood pouring out my nose and mouth. Choking on the secretions flowing down my throat, I push myself up and onto my knees. Coughing up the metallic-tasting fluid, I spit it onto the ground and gasp for air.

Dazed from the blows, I raise my head and stare at the woman. Henlie takes two or three steps backward, then leans forward, glaring at me, her eyes dull and lifeless, her hair wild and untamed. The woman spreads her arms wide, and her entire body jerks like someone is shooting her with a taser. She throws her head back, looks up at the sky, and releases the loudest ear-piercing sound imaginable, more animalistic than human.

The woman rages at me, then races forward, fearless, like a lion attacking its prey. The ramblings coming from her mouth are like before when I stabbed Justin, more of a bizarre combination of sounds than actual words.

She swings her foot to kick me again, but my reflexes kick in, and I roll out of the way. She misses, and her other foot slips on the half-frozen snow. Falling with a hard thud, flat on her back, she lands a few feet from me. With a loud moan, the woman reaches her hand to the small of her back and rolls to her side.

The shotgun lies a few feet from her, waiting for me to grab it. Wasting no time, I scurry through the snow on all fours and grip the barrel, pulling the gun toward me as I roll to a sitting position.

Unexpectedly, my body moves past sitting, propelled by a blurred object crashing into the side of my upper arm and shoulder.

The red snow around me turns black as the darkness returns.

CHAPTER 25

4 Days 12 Hours 50 Minutes
11 Hours 30 Minutes

Saturday 11:12 p.m.

"Hey… hey," a distant voice calls softly. "Wake up… wake up before they come back. You awake? Wake up." The voice is a whisper.

My head rolls from side to side as I rouse from my oblivious state. I can hear the voice calling to me. It grows more distinct but remains low.

Pain ravages my body, no one part more agonizing than another. My left eye refuses to open because of the swelling, and my right eye only opens about halfway. Even though the room is dark, it seems to move in circles around me, like I'm riding a carousel on a moonless night. Waves of nausea strike without warning, and my stomach spasms. The sound of my retching floods the room.

Because of the swelling, I can't breathe through my nose, so I roll to my back and gulp air through my mouth. I feel like I have a horrible sinus infection, but the pain and pressure in my face tell me it's more than just a terrible cold.

The voice calls to me once more. "Are you okay? Hey, are you okay?"

The most I can squeeze out is a grunt, followed by a hoarse whisper.

"I don't know."

"I thought you were dead when they brought you in, but I heard moaning," the person, a woman, says slowly between sobs. "I'm so sorry. This is all my fault."

With my vision impaired, figuring out where I am is complicated. As I become more alert, I remember what happened—

being taken from my backyard, locked in the car's trunk, the strange woman, Henlie, and what she did to me.

"Where am I?" My voice is raspy with a pronounced nasal quality, my words strained. "I don't remember anything after I blacked out."

The woman sniffles. "We're in a barn, about two hours outside of Boston off I-90. Justin dragged you in here and tied you up hours ago. I could see daylight when he opened the barn door, but it's night now. Everything's dark." She pauses. "That's when it begins," she whimpers, her voice quivering.

Her broken, tearful words reveal her fear. She's terrified of something, something about the dark. Her fear and my inability to see cause my apprehension to grow; nevertheless, I feel lucky to be alive after the beating from Henlie and whatever Justin hit me with before I blacked out.

How does this woman know so much about where we are? What happens in the dark? So many questions race through my cloudy mind.

"Who are you? How did you get here?"

"Shush," her voice lowers. "I think I hear them."

Listening, I only hear silence. Looking, I only see darkness. I listen more intensely for any sound, any movement, a creak or rustle, anything that would signal someone approaching. There's nothing but the sound of the wind whirling through the trees and the squeak of the building attempting to resist the storm pressing in on it.

Recalling bits and pieces of seeing a woman getting kidnapped, along with what Detective Benson told me about it, I know this has to be the woman I saw.

"There's no one there," I say. "It's just the wind outside. There's supposed to be a storm coming. Who are you? How do you know where we…"

I stop mid-sentence when an artillery of bright spotlights

suddenly flashes from various areas in the room, all aimed in my direction. The lights stay on for only a few seconds, then go off. My eyes are so used to the darkness, and the lights are so bright.

Briefly blinded, I close my eyes and turn away. The bright lights flash randomly, on then off, fifteen to twenty times. A few minutes after they go off for the last time, I hear a loud commotion not far from me.

The woman yells at someone.

"No more! Please stop! I'm done! Take the money and let us go!" she pleads, weeping loudly.

A few seconds later, I hear a thud to my left and feel the wall vibrate when something, or someone, strikes it. A loud, painful moan that seems to go on forever follows. Then, the woman's frightening screams pierce my ears.

I scream, too, not in fear, but at whoever is in the room with us.

"Hey! Hey you! What are you doing?" I repeat the phrase several times, yelling as loudly as I can.

There's no response.

Then, I hear scuffling and scraping noises to the left of me, where the woman's voice came from. The noises begin moving away, like something or someone is being dragged. The woman's screams and moans become more distant and gradually disappear.

Then I hear nothing—nothing but the empty sound of deafening silence.

"Lady! Lady! Are you still there?"

No reply.

They took her—I know it—but where? And why?

Will I be next?

Terror consumes me, and my instinct is to run. I've got to get out of here before they come back. My legs, cold and stiff, will barely move. Each movement brings another groan as I force myself onto my hands and knees. Leaning against what feels like a wall for support, I finally stand.

Despite the frigid environment, I'm hot, and my skin is clammy. Raising my hands to wipe away the salty sweat burning my eyes, I realize I'm not running anywhere; a rope binds my wrists. Not ready to give up, I grip the rope and follow it to its end. I can tell it's looped through a ring mounted on the wall. Using all my weight and the little strength left in my body, I walk up the wall and place a foot on each side of the ring. I lean back and pull as hard as possible, but the ring holds firm.

My hope of escape fades. Tears fill my eyes, and I slip down the wall, slumping to the ground, forced to accept the reality of my situation. I'm scared and alone. I don't know what will happen next. I don't know where I am. Battered and bruised, I'm trapped here, unable to get free.

The darkness overwhelms me; its immenseness crushing me. My throat feels tight, and I struggle to breathe. My heart pounds harder, beating against my chest like it wants to escape. I prop myself against the wall and open the top of my robe, hoping to relieve the pressure.

Icy-cold air blows in from somewhere I can't see, and I shiver intensely. Exhausted and freezing, my ears roar from the pain in my head. My face feels like someone squeezed it in a vise, and a dull pain creeps through my body. Wanting to disappear and let the darkness take me, I scrunch into a fetal position, wrap my robe around me, and softly sob. Even crying hurts.

There is no sound within this place. There is no light—only dark, eternal night.

But there *is* the sweet smell of hay covering the dirt floor. I think only of that and drift into the memories of my life as it once was. I think of rolling in the hay with Paul Barkley when I was fifteen— the sweet smell when we dove into it and the terrible itching we dealt with after.

It was a beautiful summer day, now lost somewhere in the past, a shadow stored in a closet filled with my memories.

I close my eyes and sleep.

CHAPTER 26

4 Days 16 Hours 48 Minutes
15 Hours 28 Minutes

Saturday December 4
3:10 a.m.

Deep in a beautiful dream of warm sunshine and summer breezes, I wake instantly when a bucket of ice cold water hits my face. Gasping in shock, I open my eyes as wide as the swelling will allow and search the darkness for any sign of who doused me. My robe is the only thing protecting me from the frigid temperature; now it's soaking wet. The cold winter air penetrates deeper into my damp body, and I shiver uncontrollably.

"Bitch!" a woman shouts in my ear. "You stupid bitch!"

My mind is fuzzy and confused. The blackness is so thick that I can't see the person standing beside me.

"Who do you think you are, Miss Fancy Lawyer? Shoulda kept your nose where it belonged, and you wouldn't be here," the voice snaps as it moves away.

Suddenly, my cheek stings and my head whips to the right. The slap shocks me, but I know she's within arm's reach. I swipe the area with one of my legs, hoping to trip her and grab toward the voice.

Damn it, I missed.

"You hurt my Justin!" she snarls. "You're gonna pay for that. I promise you. You're gonna pay!"

Henlie, it's Henlie.

Trying to center on her voice, I can tell she's moved away and is no longer within reach. A rag of some sort hits me in the face. I can't see it, but it feels like a towel. Then, a larger fluffy object falls over me. A blanket.

"Dry yourself up, you rich bitch. I don't want you to die, not yet." Henlie's voice is gruff, cold, and callous. "There ain't no heat out here, and it's gonna get real cold. A bad nor'easter's gonna hit today, hard winds, another two feet of snow."

Henlie lets out an eerie giggle. "You'll be lucky if this barn's still standing after this one. The rafters are already sagging in spots."

Not sure how to respond, I decide to take the therapeutic approach.

"Thank you for the towel and blanket, Henlie. That was very thoughtful of you." I need to get her to see I am a person, not her enemy. If I can do that, I may stand a better chance of surviving this ordeal.

A grunt of disgust is her only response.

"We'll see if either of you live through this storm. Could just be that's how the police find you both, frozen stiff, half eaten by the wolves and in pieces. Just like that precious sister!"

Henlie's sharp, high-pitched cackle hurts my ears. It's as though she's excited at the thought of us freezing to death. As she leaves, her laughter mingles with the rambling, senseless words and weird sounds she's making. I imagine she looks just like she did before she beat the crap out of me. As Henlie walks away, I hear her boots crushing the hay and kicking what sounds like buckets.

This woman is beyond psychotic. She may have multiple disorders. I don't know, I'm not a psychiatrist. I've defended some mentally ill clients over the years, and several displayed symptoms similar to hers. The unpredictable behavior and the rambling, nonsensical words, referred to as word salad by the experts, indicate she might have schizophrenia, but I can't be sure. Whatever her mental health problems are, there's no doubt she's extremely dangerous and violent. Definitely unmedicated.

At this moment, I'm not sure Justin is the one I need to fear.

Removing the drenched robe, I dry off, wiping myself with the towel. My sweatshirt is still dry, so that's a good thing. Having the blanket will help me stay a little warmer. Feeling my way around, I spread the robe and towel on the ground, hoping the hay will help absorb the water and dry them quicker. Wrapping the blanket around me, I turn toward the other woman.

"Are you there?" I ask as my teeth chatter uncontrollably.

No answer. I try again, louder.

"Lady, are you there?"

Hearing a groan, I attempt to inch my way over to her, but the ropes on my wrists won't let me go far. I move closer to the wall the rope is attached to and stand. From here, I can reach what feels like a short wall but can't get close to the woman. Slowly, I inch my way in the opposite direction, using the wall for support. I move as far as possible but feel nothing, just open space. Recalling that the lady said we were in a barn, I think I might be in a stall. Justin must have the woman in the one next to me.

"Lady!" I yell, not caring if anyone hears me. "Lady, are you there?"

There's a loud moan followed by some whimpering.

"Are you okay?" I ask.

There are more crying sounds but no words.

"Lady, answer me! Are you okay? Tell me if you're okay."

"No!" she screams. "I'm not okay! This isn't supposed to be happening!"

She weeps loudly, a wail of despair mixed with agony. My heart breaks for her, but if I'm going to find out anything about what's happening, I need to get her to talk. Crying won't help. I know— I've done plenty of it.

I need to know what happened to her, where they took her, what they did, what she might have seen or heard. Anything that could help get us out of here or, at the very least, survive until help comes.

Placing my face against the spaces in the wall separating us, I try to console her. "I know you're scared. There's no way to imagine what you're going through. I want to help if I can." I pause, waiting for a response.

Her crying eases a little, and I can hear her inhaling quick breaths broken by tiny spasms as she struggles to regain control of her emotions.

"I'm Ivy, Ivy Preston," I state. "What's your name?"

"I know who you are, Ivy," she replies, her voice listless and strained. "I heard Justin and Henlie talking about you." Her broken breathing fractures her words.

"Who are you?" I ask once again. "What's your name? How'd you get here? How do you know exactly where we are?" A flood of questions flows from my mouth.

"Abby, Abigail. My name's Abigail. This wasn't supposed to happen. You were in the wrong place at the wrong time. You never should have tried to help me!" she yells angrily.

It sounds like she's angry at me for trying to help save her. "What do you mean, Abby? You are the woman I saw being kidnapped, right?"

"Yes, but it wasn't what you thought it was. It wasn't supposed to be this way. You aren't supposed to be here. None of this is right!" she screams. "None of it! I told them to stop, but they won't. I didn't know Henlie was mentally ill when I met her." Abby's voice is weak.

"I don't want to talk anymore right now. I'm too tired… I can't…"

Her voice trails off, and then there's only silence. Somehow, I know Abby has given in to her exhaustion and drifted into the same deep sleep I was in. I hope her dreams are as pleasant as mine.

That may be the only peace she'll find until we leave.

CHAPTER 27

4 Days 20 Hours 18 Minutes
18 Hours 58 Minutes

Sunday 6:40 a.m.

While sleeping, I dream of the kidnapping I witnessed. My mind replays the event as though I'm watching a movie. The man places a cloth over the woman's face. The woman struggles against the man holding her. The man shoves her limp body into the trunk of a car.

Flashing to the next scene, the man is in front of me, close to me. He says things that make no sense. "She made me," and "It's not what you think." He pushes me backward, and I fall to the ground in slow motion. I grab his jacket to keep from falling, but my hands catch only the wind as my feet fly out from under me. Just before I hit the ground, I jerk awake, my chest rising and falling rapidly in sync with my shallow breathing.

My thoughts float to Abby, and I wonder how much time has passed since I spoke to her. Thinking about what the kidnapper, Justin, said to me that day, I believe Abby said something similar, but I can't recall her exact words. I've got to remember to ask her more about it.

Awake, the blanket Henlie gave me is partially covering my face. It seems heavier than before. Although I'm still shaking, I'm warming up some. Rolling over, I open my eyes just beyond a slit. Even with all the swelling, I can see for the first time since I woke up here. A soft, warm glow of light spills into a section of the darkness, pushing the black into the recesses of the barn. The contrast between the dark and the light is so vivid. In its softest, most subtle form, even this light takes my breath away and renews my hope.

Slowly, I lift my head. The light comes from a corner a few feet from where I'm lying. I was right. I'm in a stall with hay covering the ground. It's just big enough for a horse to move around in. A rusted hay rack is attached to one wall with several feeding troughs near it. A few barrels sit close to the wall, likely holding food once. On another side, some ropes hang on hooks, and several large nails poke out of the wood. Some old, worn-out horse reins hang high near the wall where I'm tied. They're too far away for me to get to any of them.

The rope around my wrists is attached to a bullring anchor on the barn wall, several feet from the ground. The cord is long, giving me enough leeway to use my hands and move about ten feet in each direction.

Sitting up, I snuggle into the blanket and notice that it's not one but two separate blankets covering me. That's why it feels heavier than before. The blanket Henlie gave me is a thick flannel. The other seems much softer and warmer, like it's filled with down feathers or something similar.

Light emits from a kerosene lantern, the kind used for camping. It's small and doesn't give off much of a glow, just enough to see a few yards out. Everything outside the stall is still dark, pitch black.

I listen for any sounds; I can only hear the irregular breathing from the stall beside mine, where Abby is. A man's raspy voice unexpectedly comes forth from the darkness. Startled, I cringe, draw my legs up, and slide back against the wall, pulling the blankets tighter around me.

"I brought you some food," he says, his voice low as though he doesn't want anyone but me to hear. "It's there beside you. It's oatmeal. You might wanna eat it before it gets cold. I got you some water, too."

The shadow of a man emerges from the corner behind the light and leans toward me. His hand trembles as he hands me a bottle of water. His face becomes clear as he enters the illuminated area.

Moving slowly and leaning toward the left as he walks, he winces in pain with every step. His left arm rests in a homemade sling of torn sheets or pillowcases. I know who he is despite his swollen and bruised face. He guards his left side, protecting it from further injury.

"You're Justin," I state. My voice cracks.

I'm terrified. Our last encounter ended with him getting a couple of puncture wounds from a tire iron and me beaten to a bloody pulp and tied here.

"Here," he hands the bottle closer. "Take it. It's fine, I promise." He glances at the ground, avoiding eye contact. Then, he quickly swipes his eyes with his hand.

Justin clears his throat. "I brought you an extra blanket. It's goose down, so it should help keep you warm."

The light coming from behind him throws his face into the shadows. His chin drops to his chest, and he looks down at his feet. "I'm so sorry all this happened," he utters. "I'd take it all back if I could. This wasn't what we planned." Justin looks at me from beneath his raised brows, his head still down. Justin seems sincere, but I don't trust him.

My memory seems to be returning in small fragments. Here, with him now, I remember the look on Justin's face when I tried to stop him from kidnapping Abigail in the alley, the sadness in his eyes. I see that same sadness now. I feel that someone, probably Henlie, forced Justin to take Abby.

But why did he take me? I did nothing. I guess he saw me as a threat since I was a witness. But I couldn't remember much of anything after my second fall—not until now. He didn't know that part, though. I wish he had.

Thinking fast, I know I have to keep him calm. I want him to think I'm on his side and can help him. He gave me an extra blanket and brought me food. I saw how he petted the little dog, tender and loving. He has compassion, unlike Henlie. She must be the one controlling him.

I remember now. That's what he said to Henlie when I was still in the trunk. *You made me,* meaning Henlie made him kidnap the woman. Maybe that's what he was trying to tell me when he kidnapped Abby, that she, Henlie, made him do it. It's making some sense now. At least, parts of it are.

I've got to keep him talking and make him feel even more sympathy for me and Abby. "Thank you for the blanket and the food, Justin. It's very nice of you to bring them to me. I'm starving."

I am trying to show him I'm not a threat, so I keep my voice low. All the while, my insides feel tied in knots, like I'm going to vomit.

He picks up the bowl of oatmeal and hands it to me with a plastic spoon. "Here, it's delicious. Eat some."

Maybe I've watched too many murder mysteries, but I hope he hasn't put drugs or poison in the food or water. My gut says it's okay, so I'll risk it. I've got to get him to trust me, and eating the food is one way I can. Besides, I'm dying of thirst, and I'm starving.

My hands tremble as I take the bowl. "Will you sit and stay with me while I eat, Justin? Then you can take the bowl with you when you go, and you won't have to come back for it." Despite my best effort to sound typical, my nervousness is apparent.

I'm unsure I can eat with my face so swollen and painful. My lips feel about twice their size, and I can barely breathe, talk or see. All I want to do is cry, but I hold it in.

Justin looks around and then peers over his shoulder toward the center of the barn. "Just a sec," he says as he hurries out of the stall.

Not knowing where he went, I'm not sure he'll return. Because I'm so thirsty, I gulp almost all the water in seconds. The oatmeal is still warm, and I want to shovel it in as quickly as possible to quiet my grumbling stomach. But since I'm hoping Justin will return to sit with me, I try to eat it slowly. When about half of it is gone, I put the spoon in the bowl and save the rest. He left the lantern burning, so he must be planning to come back.

It's hard to judge time when you don't have a reference point. Minutes, hours, and even days could pass, and I wouldn't even know it. A minute can seem like an hour or a split second. It's peculiar. I've always been aware of the time, but somehow, time doesn't matter anymore. The only time I care about now is how much longer until I leave here. I want to go home.

After an eternity of sitting here holding a half-eaten bowl of cold oatmeal, the stall door opens. Unfortunately, Justin's not alone.

Henlie walks so close behind him that she could be his shadow. She seems calmer than the last time I saw her. She has on different clothes, and her long, beautiful hair, a mixture of brown and blonde streaks, hangs around her shoulders in soft waves, not wild and mangled like before when she was in such a rage. Her full lips and light brown eyes framed by perfectly arched brows emphasize the softness of her skin and face. She looks serene and very pretty. It's sort of spooky. Compared to how she looked when she attacked me, she could almost be two different people.

"Are you finished with your oatmeal?" Justin asks politely. "Do you need more water?"

My heart is stuck in my throat, beating a thousand times faster than usual. I swallow hard, trying to keep my fear hidden. Still trying to figure out how to respond to this situation, I hand him my bowl without speaking. We exchange looks, and I feel he understands my apprehension.

"Henlie's real sorry for all she did, Miss Ivy," he begins. "She's been off her medicine for a while now, but we got that straightened out, right, Henlie?" He looks at her for affirmation.

Henlie doesn't move, her expression flat. She stares at me, unflinching, unblinking, like she's in a trance.

"That's right," Justin continues, as though Henlie had agreed.

"She's better now, and we'll get this whole thing straightened out. Yes, sir. We're gonna take that money and run off like we planned from the beginning. That's how things were supposed to go, and we're gonna stick to the plan. Ain't that right, Henlie?"

Still, Henlie doesn't reply. She moves her gaze to Justin without acknowledging a word he said, then turns and continues glaring at me, her eyes now cold and empty, her face void of all emotion.

"We gotta ride this storm out first," he continues. He puts his arm around Henlie's shoulder and squeezes her affectionately. "Yep, it looks to be a bad one, too. It's supposed to start in a few hours. Weatherman moved it up. Gonna be some mighty wind, so if you ladies hear anything, that'll be what it is, just the wind."

Justin keeps talking rapidly, sentence after sentence, without a pause.

"Unfortunately…" Justin pauses. His mouth droops and his shoulders slump as he looks down, shaking his head, "You and Miss Abby have to stay here until this thing passes, and we can get on a plane outta here. But now, don't worry," he looks up, his face brighter. "You'll both be okay. We'll bring you some nice thick blankets and lots of good food. And when this thing's all over, and we get gone, we'll call the police and make sure they find you, the both of you." His face lights up with a wide smile. "We'll get those blankets out here real soon," he says as he picks up the lantern and leaves.

Turning to follow Justin out of the stall, Henlie casts a sideways look at me. A tiny sinister smirk peaks beneath the long strands of hair, partially concealing her face.

Justin leads Henlie out, then looks back at me.

"Oh, and one more thing, Miss Ivy." He brushes his finger across his nose. "I forgive ya for all ya did to me, you know, the stabbing in my stomach and slashing my arm, bustin' my nose." Justin moves his head up and chuckles low to himself. "You're a feisty little thing for sure, but I forgive you."

His head moves in a minuscule nod. His eyes squinch, and one side of his lip raises in a half smile.

"Yep, I forgive ya."

I don't think he does.

CHAPTER 28

5 Days 0 Hours 43 Minutes
23 hours 23 Minutes

Sunday 11:05 a.m.

Justin was right about the storm. The wind blows so hard that the barn creaks and groans with each gale-force gust whipping against it. A frigid breeze forces its way between the spaces in the wood, dropping the air temperature even more. Snuggling under the blankets, I pull my knees to my chest, hugging them, but there's no getting warm. Unfortunately, Justin hasn't made good on his promise to bring more blankets and food, and I doubt he will.

Tucking my face under the covers, I leave only my eyes exposed. I wish I could see something in the darkness other than the black bouncing dots and speckles of light darting across my eyes. My feet feel like popsicles, and my toes and fingers tingle. I'm concerned about frostbite with the temperature dropping since there's no heat source. There's a dull ache in my rib cage. My face hurts like hell, and my head pounds steadily. The oatmeal Justin brought me helped relieve some of my hunger, but I could use a good hot meal.

All I want to do is close my eyes and sleep, but I know I can't, not if I plan to survive. I have to make myself stay up and stay alert. I've never been this cold or in this much pain before. I never would have imagined this could be happening to me. It all seems like a bad dream, not reality.

Could this just be a nightmare? I hope so. And I hope I wake up soon.

Despite the pain it causes, I rub my arms and legs vigorously, trying to stimulate some warmth. Finally, I put my robe back on even though it's still damp around the top. The towel is almost dry, so I put it around my neck and chest to protect myself from the damp part of the robe. Placing the blankets over myself again, I pull them on my body and tent my face so I can breathe. I've got to get warm, or I'll die from exposure.

A tiny amount of light seeps through the cracks in the barn walls, and small bits of snow drop from the ceiling, floating onto my face. I don't know if the roof is about to cave in or if the snow has found a secret path to enter, like a top window or something. I hope it's the latter.

The dainty dancing snowflakes drifting through the air remind me of my walk with Detective Benson to the park. I had such fun that day, playing in the snow with the children and building that giant snowman. I giggle softly, remembering how silly Detective Benson was when he chased all of us during the snowball battle. He seemed happy and carefree. Just sitting with him, even in silence, was comforting. He's comforting.

Sometimes, I sense a sadness deep inside the detective. I can't quite figure it out. From what he's said, it must have something to do with a kidnapping. He didn't want to talk about it when we were in the park that day. And I didn't push him.

As hard as I try not to give up hope, I can't keep myself from wondering if I'll ever get out of here. I wonder if I'll ever see my family again, talk to my friends, or see Nick once more. I wonder, will I ever get to see Detective Benson again? I know he's looking for me. He has to find me soon, or it won't matter.

"Ivy!" Abby calls out. "Ivy, are you there?"

"Yes, I'm here. Are you okay?"

She breathes in deeply before she starts brutally coughing, gasping for air between the coughs.

"Try to relax, Abby. Imagine yourself breathing normally, in and out, slowly, controlled. Picture it: slow, relaxed breathing, in—then out. Like the waves in the ocean rolling onto the beach, in—then out." Speaking slowly, I control my breathing with her, coaching her, trying to help ease her coughing and fear.

Her coughing stops, and I can hear her breathing improve. Waiting for her to speak, I think about what we can do to get out of here. The weather is a big problem, so I don't know.

"Ivy?" she says again, her voice a little stronger.

"Yes, I'm still here."

"Do you think we'll get out of here?"

"Yes, I truly do," I say, wanting to convince myself as much as her.

"It wasn't long ago I didn't care if I lived or died." Her voice trembles as though she may cry at any second. "But now, I care. I think this has made me care."

Even though I've never felt that way, I understand what she means. Going through all this gives me new insight into the critical things in life and a renewed appreciation of simply living every day—free, warm, and loved. I've never had to endure anything like this before. I get what Abby means when she says this made her care about living.

"You must have been very depressed to feel that way, Abby. What made you not care?" I ask.

"I was depressed, severely depressed—for years. I could never move past the thought of my sister dying. I felt lost without her. We were twins, and I felt part of me died with her." Her voice cracks as she tries to hold her tears at bay.

After Henlie threw the water on me, she said something sarcastic about a precious sister freezing and partially eaten by wolves. Could Abby's sister be that person? But how would Henley know about that? How could that connect with this?

Abby has said nothing about her sister dying like that. Where am I getting thoughts like this? They're just popping up out of nowhere. My mind must be more scrambled than I thought. Regardless of how Abby's sister died, I need to keep her hopes up, keep her positive, and wanting to live, so she'll keep fighting and not give up.

"Tell me something about your sister, Abby, something special you remember about her."

"Oh, she was so beautiful, Ivy," she begins, her tone lighter, more joyous. "We may have been twins, but she was the prettiest one." Abby giggles. "We used to joke about it. And she had the gift of gab. She never met a stranger, always laughing. I can still see her beautiful face," her voice lowers. "We had great times together."

Although I can't see her, I believe Abby is smiling as she reminisces about her sister.

"She sounds like a nice person. I wish I could have met her. Maybe after all this is over, you and I can get together for lunch or something, and you can tell me even more about your sister. What was her name?"

"I'd like that, Ivy. Her name was Hannah. She was in college in Boston when she di—" Abby doesn't finish her sentence because the bright lights flash on, then off and back on again, just like the last time.

"No, no, not again," she cries, terror consuming her. "No more!" she screams hysterically. "It's over! No more, I've had enough!" She repeats the words multiple times, yelling loudly.

"This isn't how it was supposed to be! You're supposed to stop! Let—me—go! What's wrong with you?" Abby screams at the top of her lungs, emphasizing each word.

But the lights continue to come on and go off at random intervals until they finally stay off.

With no concept of time, it's hard to judge how long it's been since the lights flashed until we hear noises coming from the center of the barn, shuffling sounds followed by footsteps. No voice speaks, and no light shines. The footsteps stop as though the reaching their destination.

Abby doesn't scream like before.

I can't tell what the person is doing. There's only silence in the dismal darkness, complete and total silence—for now.

I know that whoever entered the barn is still here.

I just don't know where.

And I don't know why.

CHAPTER 29

5 Days 6 Hours 1 Minute
28 Hours 41 Minutes

Sunday 4:23 p.m.

It seems like hours have passed since the lights were on. After this long, it's impossible to know if someone is still in the barn or if they left. I know I heard footsteps, but I haven't heard them since. It's still pitch black in here except for the tiny glimmer of light from the cracks. Someone could stand right next to me, and I'd never know.

My imagination runs wild. I listen closely, but the only thing I can hear is the rapid thumping of my heart. I strain to see if someone is near me as I swipe my hands around to be sure it's clear. I'd have a heart attack if I felt someone. Fortunately, the area seems clear. The footsteps weren't coming my way, but it's impossible to be sure. I didn't hear Justin when he brought the oatmeal or Henlie when she threw the water on me.

Even the sliver of light that makes its way in through the cracks doesn't light the room well enough to see very much. Waiting, not knowing if someone's lurking in a corner or about to strike you or grab you, is terrorizing. I can barely breathe. My eyes dart around the darkness, but trying to see is useless. I'm wasting my energy.

The freezing temperatures have weakened my body, and the lack of food has stolen my energy. Those are types of physical torture. The flashing lights and pitch-black darkness are forms of mental torture. Everything these people are doing is torture. Why? What's their motive? Are they just sadistic killers who get pleasure from hurting others? Or is it something else?

Abby is the woman I saw Justin kidnapping. She said so. I understand why Abby thinks it's her fault I'm here and that I was in the wrong place at the wrong time. She even said that I shouldn't have tried to help her. Henlie told me the same thing—that I should've minded my business and, if I had, I wouldn't be here. I know they're right, but I had to help.

Abby's the one Justin kidnapped. But why? Was it for ransom?

Justin gave a couple of hints at the reason but has yet to say it directly. He said there was a plan and something about taking the money. He and Henlie must have made a plan to kidnap someone and hold them for ransom.

Abby must be wealthy or very important to someone with a lot of money. That's the only thing that makes sense. And they're planning to leave on a plane for a beach somewhere. It sounds like something two stupid kidnappers might try to do if they get away with it.

"They haven't even thought about extradition," I mutter.

But why did they remove her from the barn when the lights went out? She sounded like she was petrified. Why would they hurt her if they were using her for ransom? That wouldn't make sense, not if the kidnapping was about money.

Could she be in on it with them? I haven't seen Abby; I only talked to her. How can I be sure she's even in the stall next to mine? What if she's pretending to be hurt, pretending to be scared? Could she be coming in here, acting like she's a victim, and then leaving in the dark for the warm cabin while I'm left here to die from the cold and starvation?

No, none of that makes any sense at all. That's too far-fetched. Where am I coming up with this stuff? These are just unrealistic, baseless thoughts. Abby's kidnapping has got to be for ransom. These two lunatics could be sadistic killers who enjoy torturing and violence. They don't care if she dies, not as long as they get the money they want. The way Justin talked, they've already got the money. They're just waiting for the weather to clear so they can leave. If we both die, there are no witnesses to testify against them.

"Wait a minute," I utter softly.

Everything becomes clear to me. Now I understand. I was the only witness that could testify against Justin. That's why he took me—*to kill me*—to eliminate the only witness. That was his intent all along. Why didn't I realize that before now? My mind has been so mixed up, so confused. I haven't been thinking clearly.

Justin doesn't know that I can't remember much about the kidnapping, only a few memories that make little sense and what Detective Benson has told me.

If I can't get out of here, I will die. They will kill me. I know it.

There's no more wondering what Justin and Henlie will do next. Whether I escape or fight my way out of here, I have to make a move soon, or there won't be a move to make. I'm getting weaker with every precious minute that passes. I have to act while I still have some strength, some life left in my body. I have to come up with a plan.

The sound of the wind outside draws my attention. I can hear trees popping, limbs cracking, and a thundering crash as one falls to the ground. As more snow falls in my stall, the wind whips eerily through the rafters above me. I can't see it, but I hear its horrifying howl. I feel its wetness gently kiss my broken nose, swollen cheek, bruised eyes, and battered body.

As hard as I try to stay awake, my eyes close, and I hide in the solitude of darkness. The snow caresses my face. I'm not as scared of the dark when my eyes are closed. I guess that's because I can't see it.

A high-pitched scream yanks me from my slumber, snatching me back to reality and the nightmare I'm living. The sound of a whip whistles through the air, striking its target with a hard snap. Screams and moans follow, then another round of whistling and snapping; again and again, another scream and another pop.

"Stop it!" I scream.

My hands tighten into a fist. Desperate, I pull myself up the stall wall near Abby, the rope cutting into my wrists.

"Hey! Justin! Henlie!"

I scream from the pit of my stomach. I pound and kick the wall with all the strength I can summon.

"You cowards! You sorry pieces of shit! Leave her alone! You wanna fight? Fight me! Leave her alone! You hear me?"

Once again, my instinct to save and help someone in trouble kicks in without me considering my self-preservation. I don't know why I react this way. It may be a foolish thing to do, but something inside drives me to do it. It's almost impossible for me to stop myself from getting involved. I can't stand by and watch something terrible happen to someone. I couldn't live with myself if I didn't at least try to help.

Exhausted from screaming and yelling, I finally give up. I cry using the little energy I have left—a heavy, heaving cry. My legs are too weak to hold me up, so I sink to the floor, my hands sliding down the stall wall onto the dirt and hay. Lying there, my face on the ground, I wail uncontrollably. Spit drools out of my mouth. Tears flood down my cheeks. The dirt under the hay becomes muddy and sticks to my face, coating the bruises like makeup and sealing the gashes where blood once flowed.

They're going to kill her. They're going to kill her, and then they'll kill me.

At some point, I realize I don't hear the whip or screams any more. Everything is silent. There are no sounds from Abby's stall. She must be dead or unconscious. I can't tell if Justin or Henlie are still in the barn. I didn't hear them leave, but I wouldn't have over my screaming and crying.

"Wait a minute," I whisper. Remembering I took some things from the car's glove compartment, I search the pockets of my robe for the flashlight. I only find some paper and small rags of cloth. Where could I have put it? Maybe Justin found it on me.

Remembering the large inside pocket of my robe, I pat low on my waist and hips. I open my robe, reach into the deep pocket, and find the two lighters, the wrench, the small flashlight, and the cigarettes.

My hand shakes as I place a cigarette between my lips. After a few strikes, the lighter flares, and the flame almost instantly brings the tip to a fiery red. The rich smell of the tobacco burning reminds me of my college days. I would stay up till all hours of the night, drinking coffee and smoking cigarettes, studying for exams.

I reminisce about all the good times I had, all the late nights and early mornings. I wasn't much of one for partying. And I didn't jump from guy to guy. I was always selective about my friends and who I dated. After I graduated, I quit smoking cold turkey. It was just a crutch to get me through the exhaustive college years. It may be the crutch I need to get me through this.

At first, I draw the smoke into my lungs lightly, hoping not to get choked. Unfortunately, it doesn't work, and I cough spasmodically for a few seconds. After a couple of tries and coughing episodes, I inhale a little deeper and become lightheaded but feel calmer and relaxed.

The smoke encircles my head, leaving behind a musty odor as it drifts into the rafters. I take another draw, tip my head back, and close my eyes. Somehow, my battered, swollen face stretches into a small smile.

These few cigarettes could be my salvation.

CHAPTER 30

Sunday 6:36 p.m.

Light no longer peeps through the cracks, so I know it's dark outside. The barn walls moan and creak as the powerful gusts from the storm pound against them. The wind whistles, shoving its way through the gaps in the wood. The loud bangs and thumps of objects thrown violently against the side of the barn keep me continually on edge. Instinctively, I jump at every pop and crack I hear.

The swirling wind in the trees sounds like what I imagine a tornado would. I've listened to more than one tree fall to the ground since this storm started, and I halfway expect one to crash through the barn at any minute. It won't surprise me when it does.

There's no way to know how deep the snow is outside, and I can only imagine the size of the drifts the storm is creating. It's unlikely Justin and Henlie will be flying anywhere soon or driving in a blizzard like this. They're stuck here just like we are.

Serves them right. I can't help but smirk.

In my heart, I wish they would go away and leave Abby and me here alone. We'd get loose somehow. We could get out of here if we weren't expecting their physical attacks anymore.

Abby hasn't responded to any of my calls to her. I wonder if she's dead. Who knows what they've done to her. I don't see how anyone could survive all she's gone through. It's as though they have some kind of personal vendetta against her. She's been the target of all their abuse, at least so far, except for the beating I got from Henlie when I first got here. Knowing Abby has received them all, it's hard to be thankful for the attacks I've not gotten. What they've done to her is barbaric.

Unable to see in the darkness, I look down at my hands and visualize them bound by the rope. I don't understand the minds of people like Justin and Henlie. I know why Justin sees me as a threat, but what's up with Abby? Why are they torturing her like this?

Burying myself deep into my covers, I consider giving in to the despair tugging at my heart. If I keep thinking this way, I'll only get more depressed. I have to figure out how to get out of here. I've got to make a solid plan and take action, not dwell on things out of my control.

Leaning back against the wall, I straighten my shoulders and set my jaw in defiance of my dismal circumstances. I'd rather die in the woods than suffer any longer at the hands of these psychopaths.

There's some comfort in knowing I have the flashlight and the lighters. I know I have to be careful when using them. If they find out I've got them, Justin and Henlie will take them away. I have to hide them somewhere. That way, they won't know I have the other items if they catch me with one.

Since I need to know if anyone is in the stall with me before I search for a place to put them, I take a chance and use the flashlight to look around. A lighter wouldn't give off enough light for me to see far enough to know if anyone was near, so I don't have a choice.

I call out to Abby one more time. Still no response. I don't know if she's even in the stall anymore.

Taking a deep breath, I hold the flashlight in both hands, point it straight ahead, and press the spongy button once. The area around me illuminates, and I can see everything. It's a powerful little flashlight. Fortunately, no one's in my section of the barn. The stall gate is open, giving me a limited view of the center of the barn. I don't see anyone there, so I push the light off.

Holding my breath, I listen intently for any sounds, hay crunching, footsteps, breathing, anything. Everything's still and quiet, except the storm raging outside.

After a few minutes, I take another chance using the flashlight. Turning it on, I point it to the gate, then around the walls and ceiling. Some rafters are sagging in the barn's top, rotting from water leaking through the roof. I can see snowflakes swirling in the wind, seeping in from the side of the roof where it meets the side wall. Judging by the amount of snow dancing above me, there must be an enormous gap.

The wall separating Abby and me has several large cracks and holes in the wooden planks. Shining the light through the closest opening, I peer into her stall. She's lying on the ground with her back toward me, her body still—like a doll.

"Abby," I call. "Abby, wake up."

There's no movement at all. Abby's long chestnut hair lies tousled on the hay, dirty and matted with what appears to be blood. Several blankets cover her. Abby's right arm is on top of the covers across her waist. It's ashen, bruised, and bloody. It's impossible to tell if she's breathing or not. As much as my heart breaks to think about it, she looks dead. I turn the flashlight off, my chin drops to my chest, and tears drip silently off my face as I grieve for a friend I'll never have.

Knowing I must get out of here as quickly as possible, I allow myself only a moment to mourn, then shine the light at the wall where my rope is attached. Spotting a couple of holes at the bottom of the wall where it meets the ground, I pull out the lighters and tuck them away, concealing them with hay. Maybe I can use the wrench to remove the bullring. I could try to untie the rope from my wrists, but the knots look pretty solid, and I'm not sure I have the strength.

Can I burn the rope with a lighter? It would be quicker, but there's always a chance I could burn the barn down. There's hay everywhere, but there would be less chance of starting a fire if I clear away some of it. And, if I got free, I could always put a small fire out by beating it or smothering it with the blankets. I would just have to keep the rope away from the wall and over the clean area on the ground so no sparks got on anything.

There's also a risk of Justin walking in and spotting a fire. I'm not sure how long it would take for the rope to burn in half, but I imagine it would be pretty quick.

I don't know what to do. I need to think before I do anything I might regret.

Turning the flashlight off, I return it to my hidden pocket and put the wrench in my left boot, inside my sock. The blankets don't warm me thoroughly, but they help keep some of the wind and coldness out, so I snuggle under them, staring into the dark.

I've never been afraid of the dark before, not until now.

CHAPTER 31

5 Days 10 Hours 56 Minutes
33 Hours 36 Minutes

Sunday 9:18 p.m.

Knowing I must have fallen asleep, I try hard to fight the urge to close my eyes again. I push the covers off so I won't be as warm and comfortable, hoping the cold will help me stay awake. No matter how hard I fight to stay alert, my body yearns to lie down, shut down, and drift into a warm, happy world filled with raspberry cream-filled cake.

Man, I'm so hungry. The half bowl of oatmeal is long gone, and my stomach aches and growls, begging for food it's not likely to get. Is there anything I can give my stomach to make it quiet down? Maybe the hay? Horses and cows eat it. I know it's used in cooking in some European countries. There's no telling how long this hay has been lying here, but some of it looks fresh. It might be clean. There could be bugs and stuff in it, but that would just be some protein, right? People eat wheat, corn, ants, grasshoppers, and other things. Maybe hay is not so bad.

I need something to replenish my energy. With no other options, I scoop up a small amount of hay. Hiding under the blankets, I use the flashlight to inspect it for unwanted critters. I can't see any moving ones, and I carefully pick out anything that doesn't look like hay, trying not to think about what it could be. Putting the flashlight back in my pocket, I place a small chunk of the dried grass in my mouth and chew slowly. My lips snarl at the grainy, herbal taste. My already dry mouth becomes a dust bowl as the hay steals every drop of moisture. The more I chew, the bigger the small chunk gets, becoming a thick, hard wad, like bubble gum with sticks.

My face twists and my lips pull apart with disgust as I push the mass out with my tongue. Peeling it from my mouth, I hold it with my fingers. Trying again, I pinch off a tiny piece of the wad and place it back in my mouth. My lips refuse to meet when I chew, so I bite down twice and swallow hard. The thought of chewing cud like a cow makes my belly lurch into dry heaves. Retching my guts out, I don't hear the footsteps approach.

I roll onto my back and pant like a dog between stomach spasms. Without warning, there's a sudden blow to my right side. A sharp pain shoots through my ribs. I let out a moanful yelp like an injured animal and roll to my side, gasping for air. It takes a second to realize the pain came from someone kicking me.

Someone is here. Someone I can't see or hear is in the darkness with me.

About a minute or two later, the person kicks the right side of my back with their foot and follows with a brutal stomp on my hip and buttocks. Somehow, I get on my hands and knees, tuck my head toward my chest, and cover it with my hands, trying to protect it from further injury.

Unrelenting in their attack, a boot lands hard on my left upper back. I let out a high-pitched cry as my left shoulder plunges to the ground. Without pausing, I roll to my back, continuing to my right side, and end up under the person's feet, entangling their legs in mine. Thrown off balance, they fall to the ground with a loud crash. Hearing a gruff moan and gasps for air, I'm pretty sure it's Justin and he landed on his back, unable to breathe for a minute.

Without hesitation, I go on the attack. I feel my way on top of his body and punch what I think is his face as hard as I can, pounding over and over with my fists. My hand hits something hard, and I hear the crack of glass or plastic. Something sharp cuts through my glove and rips the flesh on my knuckle.

Moving my hands over his face, I find what feels like glasses or goggles covering his eyes. Sliding a finger under one edge of whatever it is, I pull, but it's attached tight and doesn't slide off. Placing one hand on his throat, I squeeze and push down with all my weight. Quickly, I grab the goggles with my free hand and push them up and off his face. Before I can get them over his head, he grabs my arm and pushes my hand away.

With an almost supernatural strength, he uses his legs to lift me above him and launch me backward through the air. The sudden impact of my back crashing into a wall brings me to an instant stop. My ear-piercing scream echoes through the rafters when a large nail punctures my back just above my shoulder blade, ripping the tissue and skin as I slide down the wall and fall to the ground.

Helpless, I reach into my boot and pull the wrench out as I wait for Justin to come for me again. It's a pitiful weapon, but it's all I have. Suddenly, I hear him running from the barn and breathe a sigh of relief, knowing the battle is over—for the moment.

Now I know how Justin and Henlie see in the barn's darkness. They're wearing night vision goggles. If I can get close to one of them again, I will rip those goggles off, so at least we'll be fighting on equal ground. Well, as even as possible. It'll be even more fair if I can free my hands without them knowing it.

And I'll need a weapon. The wrench is just not big enough to do any damage. I have to find something better, but what? My mind's jumping; every synapse in my brain sparking at once. I'm barely even aware of the pain ravaging my body. Freezing, I struggle to return to my spot and crawl under the covers, holding the flashlight in my hand. The wound on my back is throbbing. I can tell it's bleeding, but I can't see it because of its location, so I don't know how bad it is.

A small piece of glass about two inches long cut through my glove and slashed my knuckle. Using the flashlight, I pluck it out and lay the shard to the side, out of reach, so I don't cut myself on it again. I apply pressure to the minor wound with my glove to stop the bleeding. Fortunately, the glove got most of the damage, not my hand.

A thousand horses are racing in my chest as adrenalin continues flowing through my veins. My throat tightens, and my muscles feel like Jello. Every heartbeat throbs within my head. To calm myself, I try to slow my breathing by taking one deep, controlled breath and then another, as I always do when in a stressful situation. However, I breathe in once this time, then dry heave uncontrollably. The sharp pain in my ribs intensifies with each breath, the pain branching into my chest and back. I think my ribs are fractured, but there's nothing I can use to wrap them.

Although I hurt more when lying down, I don't have the strength to sit up. As I roll to my side, arms wrapped around my ribs, I bend my knees, trying to get comfortable. I allow the pain to settle as much as possible before snuggling under the blankets.

Once more, snowflakes fall onto my face. The sounds of the storm growing louder and stronger surround me. Silently creeping from the barn's darkness, the blackness washes over me. Taking a couple of shallow breaths, I black out again.

The dark holds a power of its own.

CHAPTER 32

5 Days 13 Hours 45 Minutes
36 Hours 25 Minutes

Monday December 5
12:07 a.m.

Awakened by the thundering sound of a tree crashing on the barn, I bolt upright and stare into the sea of darkness, trying to spot where the tree hit. I can feel the harsh wind moving in gusts, but without light, I can't fully know what happened, whether a tree just fell on the roof or crashed through it.

Despite being covered by the blankets, my teeth chatter, and every hair on my body stands on end from the chill of the icy air rushing through the stall. I've been unimaginably cold since they put me in here, but now the temperature is falling lower and lower by the second. If it continues to drop, I'll become hypothermic soon. I've already been worried about frostbite. Colder temperatures with no heat are all I need.

Fumbling in my pocket, I find the flashlight and click it on, not giving a damn who might be around to see it. Pointing the beam toward the ceiling, I search for where the wind is coming from.

About ten feet to my right, large ice-covered branches protrude through the roof with only a couple of old cracked rafters supporting them. Chunks of wood and tin fall to the ground, the sound of their crashing silenced by the howling of the wind. Heavy sleet pelts the tin roof, sending ice pellets ricocheting around the tree limbs and into the barn, collecting, unmelted, in piles on the ground.

If the barn cannot bear the tree's weight, there's a good chance I'll get crushed when it falls. I've got to get this rope off my wrists anyway I can and get out of here.

Thinking about Abby and how cold she must be, I shine the light through the hole in the wall and call out to her. Her back is still toward me, her legs drawn up toward her chest, and the blankets now cover her arm. Her position change is a sign that she's still alive.

"Abby," I yell as loud as I can, knowing Justin wouldn't be able to hear me over the storm unless he was right next to me.

"Abby, can you hear me? Wake up!" My voice is low and croaky, even though I'm screaming as loud as possible.

She moves ever so slightly. She might be unconscious or drugged, but at least she's not dead. Who knows what these lunatics have done to her? I know I have to get loose so we can get out of here.

Looking closely at the bullring, I can tell it's attached to the wall with four large nails. Damn. I don't have a screwdriver or anything to drive behind the plate to get it loose. And with the way the rope loops through the ring, it's too snug for me to pry it up with the wrench. The nails are sturdy, so I doubt I'd be able to get it off anyway. Besides, I don't have the energy to try such a strenuous task. The pain in my body holds me hostage, renewed by the recent attack.

I move on to my second option: push my fingers through the hay at the edge of the wall and retrieve a lighter from its hiding place. I'm not keen on burning through the rope, but that may be my only choice. If only I had something to cut them.

Shining the flashlight around the stall floor, I look for anything to make a cutting instrument. Pointing the light up at the roof where the tree is ready to plummet to the ground with the next powerful gust of wind, I wonder about the tin roof. Would a piece of it be sharp enough to cut through the rope?

Shining the light at the floor where the ice pellets are gathering, pieces of the roof and split pieces of barn wood lie scattered about. If I get some of the tin, I can try to cut the rope. Or if I can get a piece of the wood, I can use it as a weapon. I stretch my body as far as possible, but I'm about a foot too short to reach anything. I'd love to get a hold of that ice. It would feel so good in my mouth.

Exhausted just from what little I've done, I sigh and move back to my spot. The pressure and sharp pain behind my eyes have been gradually building for days. I think it's from my concussion. I seem to recall Detective Benson telling me I had one. It's getting harder to remember things. My eyes are heavy, and I want to close them, but I'm afraid to. I'm worried if I do, I'll never open them again. So I push myself to keep going, my mind on freeing my hands and getting out of here.

As I skim the floor with the light, I spot something glistening not far from me. It's a piece of glass. A good chunk of glass, buried in the dirt, but it's not from Justin's broken goggles. It's something else, something buried in the ground.

Squirming to it on my belly, I dig around the edge of the glass with the wrench. When I wiggle it from the ground, excitement ripples through my body. The glass is a piece of an old brownish bottle. It's thick glass, an old beer or soda bottle. The round top of it is intact, but about four or five inches down, it's broken and jagged.

Maybe I can use this as a weapon. It could do some damage if used right. Taking the bottle with me, I crawl back to what I consider my bed area and pull the blankets tightly around me, trying to warm my trembling body.

I use the flashlight to see under the covers and try rubbing one of the sharp edges on the rope attached to my left wrist. Cutting the rope this way is a tedious task that takes a lot of time and a lot of concentration. It's getting hard to breathe, covered with blankets like this, so I push them off my face to get some air and change my position to continue freeing myself.

The longer I stare at the rope, the more my eyes blur and long to close. I blink several times to clear the haze. My mind stays fuzzy, so I look up toward the roof, hoping snow or ice will fall on me, refresh me, and remove my fatigue. The colder I get, the more tired I am and the more I want to sleep.

The tears I desperately try to keep inside cling to my eyelashes and freeze into tiny crystals. My breath forms white frosty clouds that hang in the air. I've got to have some heat. Giving up on cutting the rope, I make a small fire in the hay and try to burn the rope in half. I tuck the bottle near me, within easy reach, and gather some of the straw into a small pile, clearing a large area around it so the fire doesn't spread.

Taking out the lighter, I roll the striker but only sparks dance from the top of it. I strike it again, but it still doesn't light. Blowing it to clean out dust or dirt, I flick it twice more, and a beautiful blue flame burns bright.

My hands shaking from the cold, I hold them above the small pile of hay and place the lighter close to the rope. Smoke rises, and tiny threads of red appear in the cord. The burning strands enlarge, and the rope flames like it's been soaking in gasoline. Black smoke billows into the air, disappearing in the wind and darkness above me. Pulling my wrist away from the fire, the rope snaps, and my left hand is finally free from bondage. A small part of the rope still dangles from my wrist, the end of it glowing bright red. I rub it in the dirt next to the pile of hay, and the fire goes out.

The other section of the rope bounces against the side of the barn and burns up the wall, traveling back to the bullring. As dry as the barn wood is, I'm afraid it will catch on fire, so I grab the flannel blanket and beat it against the wall, smothering the flames. Shining the flashlight, I see black charred wood on the wall still warm to the touch, but I think the fire is out.

That was close. At least I got one hand loose. Even though the rope burned in half, I'm still not wholly free since a knot in the cord is stuck in the bullring. It slipped enough through the ring that I can move farther out than before, so that's a good thing. I'll work on cutting the other rope with the bottle. It may take a little time, but cutting through one will be easier than two. Besides, after this little round of excitement, I'm not sure I can handle another one, at least not yet. I don't want to burn the barn down around me.

With more freedom to move further from my spot, I crawl toward the debris left by the fallen tree and gather some of the wood pieces and broken tin from the roof. Scooping up as much of the sleet mounds as possible onto the roof part, I toss a few pieces of the ice into my mouth. Wasting no time, I crunch down on the ice and swallow, relieving the scorching rawness in my throat. Adding a few more pieces, I allow them to melt naturally, lubricating my dry mouth and rehydrating my body with every melting morsel. Then, slowly, wincing with each movement, I get everything to my spot.

The wind blasts into the barn as the storm gains intensity. I want to free my other hand, but my most pressing need is warmth, and I need it now.

Given my current situation, I'm not concerned about Justin seeing the fire. I have to have heat, or I will die. Besides, if I have a fire, I'm more likely to see him when he shows up to take another run at me. I'm much better off with a fire than without one.

I rake up more hay and clear out a larger area around it. Holding the lighter to the dry straw, I shiver intensely, making it almost impossible to strike it. Finally, I clamp my hands between my knees to stop the shaking, snap the striker once, and watch it burst into a beautiful, flickering flame.

The small pile burns fast, so I gather more hay and place it on the dying fire. Removing my gloves, I warm my hands and face over its heat. I use some of the wood brought down by the tree to make a teepee of wood over the fire, adding more wood to keep it burning. I put my gloves back on, pry pieces of the splintered and cracked wood from the boards separating the stalls, and place them on the fire. A nice-sized campfire takes shape, providing the warmth I need to keep from freezing.

Since being kidnapped, this is the first time I have come close to being warm. Staring into the fire, I become more despondent. I think of Nick and wonder if I'll ever see him again. I have a feeling we won't be together much longer.

CHAPTER 33

5 Days 17 Hours 6 Minutes
39 Hours 46 Minutes

Monday 3:28 a.m.

Cocooned in both blankets, I begin slowly waking from the best sleep I've had in what has to be days. My eyes are heavy, swollen, and crusted. They don't want to open, and I don't want to move from my halfway warm, comfortable spot.

"Move!" I command myself out loud. "Move your sorry ass and get out of here!"

Slowly, with every muscle screaming in agony, my body moves. With each jolt of pain, I groan, squinching my eyes and twisting my face. My legs quiver and feel limp when I try to stand, so I use my hands to help lift them.

Finally, I get myself to a sitting position and fall back against the wall. The longer I sit here, the stiffer my body gets. Growing colder by the minute, I force my eyes open and blink several times to clear the film covering them. Only a few fading embers remain of the fire that warmed me while I slept. I'll be in total darkness and frigid cold when they die again. I'm getting weary of the struggle.

"You're not a quitter!"

The voice is nearby, so clear and distinct. I look around to see who's there, but all I see are shadows created by the faint light of the fading fire.

"Get your butt up and get going. You've got work to do, young lady!"

The voice is so familiar. Is it possible someone is here with me? No, I'm just imagining it. No one's here, at least no one to encourage me. Only Abby, who's probably unconscious or dead by now, and Justin and Henlie, who are frigging lunatics that want to kill me. I laugh out loud at how ridiculous this scenario is as my mind continues playing tricks on me.

"I said to get up, young lady! You've been asleep long enough. It's time to put your plan into action."

I squeeze my eyes tightly and pinch the bridge of my nose. Blinking repeatedly, I move my head slowly back and forth, trying to unscramble the confusion in my brain. What I'm seeing doesn't make any sense.

"Dad? Daddy, is that you?"

"You don't have time for all of this. You've got to get started!"

Taking the flashlight from my pocket, I shine the light around the stall. My dad stands in the corner where Justin once stood. He holds his back straight with his arms by his side. He looks dignified and brave in his Air Force uniform. But how can my dad be here?

"Daddy?" I whisper, barely able to speak. "I've been wanting to see you. Where have you been?"

"I miss you, Ivy," Dad smiles sadly. His inside brows rise, and the corners of his mouth sag. "We've got to get you back home, and we don't have much time left. Will you do this for me, little one? Will you get up and get to work on your plan?"

"What plan, Daddy? I don't have a plan." I raise my shoulders as I shake my head slowly.

Daddy playfully purses his lips, suppressing a mischievous grin, as though he has a secret he wants to share.

"Oh yes, you do, Ivy. You have a good plan."

His demeanor changes from sadness to encouragement. He squinches his eyes and assumes the role of commander as if he were giving a pep talk to his troops.

"You've got a good weapon in that bottle. It'll cut through skin in a heartbeat," Daddy tips his head sideways. "And speaking of heartbeat, that's always a good target." He winks. "I taught you about self-defense and survival, and you've used your training well.

But the big test is coming soon." His eyes widen, and his eyebrows lift.

"What big test, Daddy? I'm so tired. I don't think I can take a test right now." Tears drip from my eyes, and my chin quivers.

Moving closer, Daddy wraps his arms around me. "It's okay, little one," he whispers, hugging me tight. "I'm with you every step of the way." He tilts my chin, looks into my eyes, and then pushes my hair back, tucking it behind my ears. "We're not quitters, Ivy. We've never folded under pressure, and we're not going to now. No matter how hard you have to push yourself, you push," he insists. "I'm going to send you some help, but you must do your part first!"

I nod, sucking up my tears like always when the odds are against me. "We're not quitters," I repeat to him, straightening my shoulders, my jaw tucked and firm. "I'm going to push myself as hard as I have to, and I *will* win."

"That's my girl," Daddy grins. "Now, you get started. I'll see you when you get home," he smiles sweetly, kissing me on my forehead.

BANG!... BANG! BANG!... BANG!

The loud noise of gunfire in the distance rumbles through the barn. At least it sounded like gunshots. It's hard to tell what the noise was with the wind howling and trees popping and snapping.

Surprised by the noise, I jump. My eyes open as wide as possible, and I jerk my head toward the sound. Whatever it was, it was loud, and it was close. After a few seconds, I look back at my dad.

He's gone. Disappearing in an instant, Daddy's no longer sitting beside me, holding me. I still smell the musky odor of his cologne lingering in the air. Or do I?

My mind is all messed up. I know I've got to be hallucinating— but it seems so real.

Real or not, I made him a promise not to quit, a promise to push myself and keep fighting, a promise to get started on my plan. A promise to win.

Now, I'll start… if I can just figure out my plan.

CHAPTER 34

5 Days 17 Hours 41 Minutes
40 Hours 21 Minutes

Monday 4:03 a.m.

Knowing that my dad was a hallucination doesn't make me feel good about my mental or physical state. I thought I was doing okay, but hallucinations are not typically a good sign. Am I having a mental breakdown, or is it the effect of the icy temperature, hunger, or dehydration? I'm experiencing all these things, not to mention the injuries inflicted by Justin and Henlie.

And now, hallucinations? What could possibly happen next?

I could have sworn I heard gunshots a few minutes ago, but I'm doubting myself and my judgment. It was probably limbs popping. They can be very loud and easily mistaken for gunshots when they snap.

I know Abby has endured more physical and mental trauma than I have. I don't think I'm as strong as Abby. I don't know how much more I can take.

"Damn, Ivy, just how self-defeating are you gonna get?"

Wow, I'm talking to myself regularly now. I bet that's another sign of mental collapse. I've got to pull myself together, or I'll be acting like Henlie before long.

The fire has been out for a long time, and I'm losing body heat again. My shivering is getting worse, and I can't feel my toes wiggle in my boots. Concealing my actions from Justin and Henlie isn't even a concern anymore. What difference does it make if they catch me with a fire? If they kill me because of it, at least I'll die warm.

Gathering more hay and wood, I prepare my little campfire and remove the lighter from my pocket. All of a sudden, there's a soft whimper outside my stall. Glancing that way, I don't see anything, so I return to the fire and hold my hands out to warm them. A small creature darts through the door. I cringe as I pull the blankets around me and prop against the wall.

My swollen eyes strain to see the animal in the glow of the firelight. My fear of what it could be grows, and my imagination takes flight.

It could be a giant rat come to feast on my dying flesh, or perhaps a sly fox or rabid raccoon? A bat? A squirrel? No telling what kind of varmint has found its way in to nibble on my rotting flesh. I shudder at the thought.

Stop it. That's so morbid. I can't let my mind go there. It reminds me of what Henlie said about the sister eaten by wolves. That's such an awful thought, and here I am thinking the same thing might happen to me, just like Henlie said.

The flames of the fire grow, casting light on the creature. I smile. It's not a rat or a raccoon. A small brown and black, long-haired dog crawls on its belly toward me, its head down as though it's afraid. The dog is so tiny, weighing maybe five or six pounds. The little thing is soaking wet, visibly shivering from nose to tail. Its big brown eyes look so sad. My heart crumbles with each whimper. It seems as terrified as I am.

The dog is the same one Justin was petting. Only it's not bubbly and bouncing happily anymore. It's scared and lonely, just like me. It must have gotten out of the cabin somehow. I cringe, knowing Justin will be looking for it.

The storm grows louder, expressing its wrath as it becomes stronger. The wind tears at the barn as though it wants to rip it apart. The walls moan, trying to withstand the violent attack. Looking around at the gray, weathered barn and its years of decay, I admire its grit and resilience, holding its own against the destructive forces of the storm.

I look down at the frightened, sopping-wet dog. It could never survive outside in this kind of storm. As long as Justin and Henlie stay away, I'm glad we're together, sheltered by the sturdy barn.

"You poor thing," I murmur, barely able to squeeze out my words. My voice is gritty, my throat burning with each utterance. "Come on, come here." I pat the blanket and make a kissing noise with my dry, shriveled lips. "Come here, baby," I coax.

Slowly, the little dog creeps closer and then pounces onto the covers. The pup smothers me with licks, its tail flipping back and forth with excitement. I pet and snuggle with the furry creature before tucking it inside my robe and covering it with a blanket. Holding the tiny thing against me, I feel its heart beating rapidly against my chest. I move closer to the fire and dry its fur with the flannel blanket. Talking to the dog constantly while I stroke its fuzzy body, it eventually curls up in my lap and closes its eyes, content with the warmth and affection it's getting.

My eyes become cloudy as I hold the small dog in my lap. Realizing I treasure its presence, I look up into the blackness above me. Closing my eyes, I pray it doesn't run off and leave me alone in the foreboding darkness when the fire goes out.

If this sweet creature is the help Daddy said he would send, he probably just saved my life. I cuddle the dog in my arms and nuzzle it with my face, its life rejuvenating mine.

CHAPTER 35

5 Days 19 Hours 11 Minutes
41 Hours 51 Minutes

Monday 5:33 a.m.

Startled by a loud crash and the popping sound of wood breaking high above me, I grab the dog and the blankets and retreat to the corner of the stall. The tiny dog growls softly and hides under the covers.

"That scared the hell out of me," I pant. "Looks like it scared you too, huh?" I move my trembling hand over its soft, furry head and stare into the lonely darkness above me. I swallow hard, trying to push my bounding heart back into my chest.

Even in the dark, I know another tree has fallen on the barn. The soft glow from the fire is not bright enough to lighten the emptiness in the rafters. The crunching and cracking sounds continue, coming from the same area where the tree crashed through the roof before.

I take out the flashlight and aim it in that direction. I was right—another tree has broken through the barn roof next to the first one. It looks like a single rafter is holding it up, preventing it from removing the entire top above my head. Part of the roof and wood from the barn wall continue to spill to the ground as the tree shifts, allowing more branches to plunge deeper into the barn. The structure groans and creaks, giving its all to support the weight of the enormous giants leaning on it.

Heavy snow flows between the branches, and the wind swirls the flakes, creating small white tornados. Many limbs are thick and close together, forming a thatch roof for the snow to pile on. If the snow continues to fall as heavily as it is now, the extra weight will cause the tree to drop farther into the barn. Eventually, part of the roof and the entire wall will collapse. That won't be good for me.

I can't get distracted by something I have no control over. I have to stay on task and stick to my plan. Now, what is my plan again? Daddy said I have one, and that it's a good one… but I can't recall what it is.

I'm so cold and hungry. And I'm so *very* sleepy.

As I put the dog under the edge of the blanket, I think about how to fight my intense desire to sleep. I glance around and notice the ice pellets I collected earlier have melted. Removing my gloves, I place my hands flat in the small puddles of water on the tin roof pieces and rub the icy liquid on my face. The shock of the cold stimulates my body to wake up, and I'm more alert and able to think clearly.

Sure the dog must be thirsty, I pick the tiny furball up and place it in front of the puddles of water. It quickly laps every drop, leaving the tin completely dry. Scooping the doggy up, I hug it to my neck and gently place it back under the covers.

My breathing is rapid and shallow. My shivering becomes more intense. I need the hydration of the frozen water, and I need heat. I can do without food for a while longer, but I can't do without these two essential things if I'm going to survive.

There are still piles of sleet underneath the tree, and I've got to get it. Pushing through the pain surging through my body, I crawl across the dirty, hay-covered floor toward the sleet. I stretch as far as possible and rake some toward me. Piling it onto a piece of the tin, I push it, inch by inch, back to my spot.

Even though my teeth are chattering, I place a large chunk of the ice in my mouth and close my eyes, relishing every melting drop as if it were a fine wine at dinner. I circle my shoulders several times to release the strain and tension in the muscles and relax for a moment, stroking the soft fur of my new friend. The ice in my mouth melts, so I shove another piece in. I replace the melted ice as often as needed until my body no longer screams for water.

Needing to keep my fire burning, I break apart the wood I

collected into small sticks and stack them on the dying embers with a small amount of hay. The dry grass ignites quickly, and the wood glows red as the flames climb. With each piece of wood, the embers glow hotter and brighter until, finally, I can warm myself with the heat produced by the fire. My little friend pokes its nose from under the covers, moves closer to the fire, and closes its eyes.

"Are you a boy or girl?" I ask, petting it above its eyes and touching its nose gently. "You need a name." I move my hand down the little doggy's neck, feeling for a collar, but there isn't one. "Well, no luck there," I whisper. "Let's see if you're a boy or a girl before I give you a new name."

Cradling the pup in my arms, I flip it onto its back. I scratch under its chin as I quickly peek at its gender.

"Oh, I see." I giggle as I snuggle close to my little fur ball. "So, you're my little man, huh? How about I call you Apela? That's a great name," I whisper, lifting him in front of my face. "It's Hawaiian, and it means Breath of Life. That's just what you are, too."

My voice cracks while I choke back tears. "You're my breath of life, Apela." Sniffing hard, I hug him tight and lay him by my side. "We've got work to do..

Removing my boots, I move closer to the flames, careful not to burn my feet. The ends of my toes are bright red, but the rest of my feet are an ashy tone. They sting from the cold. Warming them helps, and I can finally wiggle my toes and move my feet without a problem. They still feel numb and tingly, so I'm afraid to rub them since it could cause tissue damage. I keep them near the fire, warming them slowly while Apela lies comfortably beside me, watching my every move. I know the little dog is hungry, but there's nothing to feed him.

"We'll get some food soon," I say, stroking his back. He closes his eyes, content with the warmth of the fire for now.

As I think back, I remember the rags and papers I found in the car and take them from the pockets of my robe. The rags are just old pieces of cloth ripped up. I sniff them and detect a sweet scent I can't identify. Justin may have poured whatever substance he used to knock Abby and me unconscious on them. They're not wet anymore, and the odor is weak, so I doubt they will help me in any way. They're too short to use as a bandage, and I can't reach over my shoulder to cover the gaping gash left by the nail when I fell on it.

Laying the rags to the side, I move on to the papers. They are much more revealing. One is a printout of a picture of Justin. It looks like a copy of the sketch drawn by the police artist based on my description. I don't remember meeting with the sketch artist, but her initials and date are on the bottom. I lay it down and continue sorting through the papers.

A small yellow sticky note is stuck on the next piece I pick up. This one looks like a torn part of a contract or agreement. The words *'gree to pay one hundred thousand dollars to Ju'* are the only words I can make out. Some kind of water or liquid has caused all the other words to fade and run, making it impossible to read.

It doesn't make any sense. The Ju could be Justin. If it is, it looks like he would receive a lot of money from someone. I wonder if this is the ransom he wanted for Abby. I've never heard of any kidnapper having a written agreement for ransom money.

I shrug my shoulders. "That's weird."

The yellow sticky note has the name and address of a hotel written on it: the Shadyside Inn, 1252 Mocking Wood Lane, Room 216. I wonder if that's where Justin was supposed to pick up the ransom? That doesn't seem likely since he could get caught so easily that way. Most ransoms are done in public places, inconspicuously. But, then again, Justin and Henlie aren't the brightest bulbs on the tree.

It could be where Justin and Henlie were staying before the kidnappings. But wouldn't they have been staying here, at this cabin and barn? Does it belong to them, or was it abandoned and they just happened to come upon it?

There are simply too many unanswered questions to worry about right now.

The last paper looks like a piece of a newspaper article. Since my vision is still blurred, reading the small print is tricky. I adjust the distance from my eyes and blink several times, and the letters become more defined. Reading softly to myself by the firelight, the article tells about a murder.

College student Hannah Bellston was kidnapped, tortured, then brutally murdered. Her body was found late Saturday night in an old barn off I-90. The police chief stated that the FBI is involved since this crime might be part of a series of murders. The victim's sister, Abigail Stephens, remains under a suicide watch at a local hospital. We'll have more updates as information is released.

"Oh, shit!"

I quickly clamp my hand over my mouth. Apela lifts his head, his ears alert, looks at me, then lays back down, reassuring me no one is there.

These people might be serial killers. What the hell have I gotten involved in? Panic surges through me, and I freeze, unable to move, staring into the center of the barn. Tears pool in my eyes, releasing with every blink. Finally, I build up enough courage to glance at the stall Abby is in. My breathing is rapid and erratic. My thoughts are all over the place, jumping with nowhere to land.

No, no, no! Get a grip. Don't let panic take over. I can't let this happen. I have to keep focused on my plan, on developing a plan. I have to stay away from anything that might distract me.

Quickly, I wad the papers up and shove them in my pocket. It doesn't matter that Abby's sister was kidnapped too, or that it may have been by a serial killer. It doesn't matter if Justin and Henlie are serial killers. The *only* thing that matters is that I get out of here.

I think about what Daddy said. He said to *push* no matter how hard it is. So, I'm going to keep trying. I'm in control, and I don't quit. I will get out of here—alive.

CHAPTER 36

5 Days 21 Hours 39 Minutes
44 Hours 19 Minutes

Monday 8:01 a.m.

My focus is only on staying alive and going home. I have water in the form of sleet and snow. I have warmth in the form of fire. I have other protection from the cold, like my robe, clothing, and the blankets. Plus, I have weapons I can use to fight back.

Sorting through my simplistic weapons, I use a blanket to shield them from the view of anyone coming in and lay them out side by side. First, I check out the broken bottle I dug from the ground. Daddy said it would be great for cutting skin. It's very sharp and jagged, and I can tightly grip the bottle's neck. It could do some damage if used right. The bottle may be my best weapon.

Putting another piece of ice in my mouth and giving one to Apela, I pick up the wrench, examining it closely. Shifting it from hand to hand, I decide it's not much of a weapon. It's just a miniature wrench, one of those small ones just to get you by in an emergency. It's not very sturdy or heavy. I don't think it can be used effectively as a weapon, so I lay it to the side with the lighters.

Pushing a loose strand of hair behind one ear, I spot a couple of pointed wooden stakes about ten inches long stacked with the wood I plan to burn. I pull them from the pile and look closer at their shape. They might make good stabbing weapons. They're pointed and sharp enough to penetrate skin and tissue and long enough to hold in my hand, but I'll have to use my gloves to protect myself from the splinters. The only problem I see is that they're pretty thick and wide.

Gripping one stake in my right hand, I mimic several stabbing motions. Unless I trim the width, I would have to use both hands to jab them far enough to cause damage. I don't know if I would get an opportunity to use both hands or if I have enough strength to push that hard. Still, I place them in the weapon pile next to the bottle since they have potential.

"What's your preference, Apela? Any thoughts on which weapon is the best?" I ask the furry creature curled up next to me.

The sweet dog raises his head, cocking it sideways like he's thinking about what I said. Moving closer, he pushes his nose under my hand, and I pet him gently while sorting through my items.

"No opinion, huh? It is a hard choice," I say, raising my eyebrows. "But I think I'll use the bottle as my first defense. I'll work on trimming down the stakes if I have time." Half smiling, I continue to rub his soft, furry head. It's comforting just to have him here.

Besides the weapons, I have two lighters and a flashlight. The small pocket-type flashlight's only purpose is to help me see in the dark. I'll need it at night when I make it to the woods, so I've got to preserve the battery as much as possible.

There are several ways to use the lighters. I flick the striker to be sure both work. They're the cheap lighters you can see the fluid level in. That's handy. I can tell how much fluid is left when I use them. I can use the paper and rags in my pockets to help start a fire.

The loud crunching sound of the massive tree plunging lower into the barn echoes through the rafters, frightening Apela and me. Apela growls at the sudden noise before climbing into my arms for protection. My heart thumps wildly, banging on my chest like a drum. The tree may fall soon, crushing me, before I can escape. I'll never get to go home.

Sucking up my tears, I know I must make a choice. I can give in and give up, letting fear, doubt, and all the obstacles I face defeat me, or I can do what Daddy said for as long as possible.

I choose to fight. I prefer to live.

Securely tucking all my items away, I deliberately ignore all the creaking noises, all the snow swirling in the air, all the ice crashing to the ground, and the eerie noise the wind creates as it circles through the rafters. I sit for a few minutes, gazing into the already dying fire.

As much as I want to, I can't keep the fire burning constantly. I'd run out of wood. I still have to get my other hand free to get out of here before Justin returns. I don't know if I can take another beating and survive as weak as I am.

I don't know how Abby has held on as long as she has with all she's been through. If I'm honest with myself, I'm not sure Abby will make it much longer. I should look into her stall to check on her, but I dread what I might see. I don't think I want to know if she's already dead.

Inching closer to the fire, I shake my head to clear the fogginess from my mind and think about how to get free of the rope. I don't want to try burning it over the fire like I did before. It did get the rope off, but I almost caught the barn on fire, so I'm not sure it's a good idea to take that chance again.

Okay, so it's not good to burn the barn down. When I tried cutting it with the bottle, my concentration wasn't good, and it felt like it would take forever to cut it off. Unfortunately, I didn't have much time then and even less now, so if I'm going to get this rope off, it's got to be quick.

Unable to think of another option, I brace the bottle between my knees and place the rope against one of the sharp edges. Holding the rope with both hands, I move it over the raw edge of the bottle in a sawing motion. Getting a sudden burst of energy, I saw more fervently, and the rope threads begin to separate.

"Yes. Yes!" I clench the rope tighter.

My breathing becomes more rapid. Sweat beads pop out on my forehead. The salty drops wiggle into my eyes, stinging and burning them, blurring my vision. I stop momentarily, take one of the rags from my pocket, and dab it over my face and eyes to dry the sweat.

"Shit!" I scream, dropping the rag and slapping my hands over my eyes.

My eyes burn like a hot poker is stabbing into them. I forgot that the rags had some kind of smell on them, possibly from a chemical.

"Please don't let it be acid!"

The longer the chemical stays in my eyes, the more intense the pain. My whole face feels like it's on fire. Letting out a loud shriek like a cat with its tail caught in a vice, I fall to the ground, squeezing my eyes closed and clutching my face.

My behavior is scaring Apela. He scurries around me, whimpering like he wants to help. I'm sure he's seen Henlie act much like this when she has psychotic spells. I don't want him to be afraid of me. Keeping my eyes pressed tight, I feel for him with my hands and pick him up to soothe him.

"Shush," I whisper repeatedly. "It's okay, boy. It's okay. I'll be okay," I whimper.

Holding Apela in one arm, I sweep my other hand around the floor, trying to find the pile of sleet I gathered. I grab a handful and press it on my eyes, hoping it melts the pain away. Rubbing ice over my swollen face, I curl up on the ground and pray the burning eases. I place more ice on my eyes and just lie here. Freezing and scared, I tug the blankets over me.

My greatest fear is that the chemical may have permanently stolen my sight. The pain gradually eases, and I fall asleep crying, cuddling my little friend.

CHAPTER 37

Monday 9:32 a.m.

Apela wakes me from my sleep by nudging my face. He jumps up beside me, stands alert at the edge of the blanket, and growls as he stares at the stall door. Instinctively, I pull him to me to protect him from whatever he sees or hears.

"It's okay, boy," I murmur. Resisting the urge to rub the crust from my eyes, I blink rapidly to remove the hazy film clouding my vision.

"It's okay," I repeat. Holding Apela close, I tuck the blanket around him, clutching him securely in my arms.

The storm rages, and I hear the angry wind howling through the trees. I can only imagine how intense the blizzard has become and the damage it's doing. I'm surprised this old barn is still standing with the battering it's taking.

Squinting my eyes to see, I'm not staring into blackness anymore. Daylight trickles through the fallen tree branches near the top of the barn. This is the first natural light I've seen since I got here. My gaping jaw becomes a broad, open-mouth smile. Bouncing Apela, I squeal, barely able to contain my excitement.

All of a sudden, the lights in the barn flash brightly, blinding me and forcing me to close my eyes. Placing my hand over my eyes, I separate my fingers slightly to filter the light, hoping to see what's happening. The last time the lights came on like this, they went off again, then back on several times before Justin came and attacked Abby with the whip.

My chin sinks to my chest, and I close my eyes, holding Apela tightly in my arms. Abby's not made a sound for hours and hours.

I'm ashamed of myself for not having checked on her. My heart hopes she's okay, but I know she's dead. Without warning, my face scrunches as though I'm going to cry, but no tears come.

My jaw set, my shoulders straight, I gaze unblinking at the light above me weaving its way through the darkness. The bright spotlights go off in the barn, but the menacing fear the dark brings no longer dominates me. Again and again, they go on and then off. Still, I'm unaffected—no longer flinching, cringing, or cowering in fear. My eyes focus only on the light peeking between the tree branches resting on the rafters.

Stroking Apela's soft fur, a tiny smirk creeps over my face.

I'm out of tears and fear, but *not* out of fight or hope. I'm ready to go home.

CHAPTER 38

5 Days 23 Hours 55 Minutes
46 Hours 35 Minutes

Monday 10:17 a.m.

The lights no longer flash on and off, and I know what comes next. Returning to my corner, I pull the blankets around Apela and me, then gather my weapons. If Abby is dead, Justin will go for me, and I won't just sit here defenseless and do nothing.

There's some light from the roof, but it's not bright enough for me to see Justin enter the barn. Taking the small flashlight from my pocket, I turn it on and prop it on a piece of wood, aiming the beam directly at the stall door. I wanted to save the battery for later but sometimes plans change. I'll take my chance in the woods when I get there.

The broken bottle is my best weapon, but it's also the best chance to free myself of the rope before Justin arrives. Once again, I prop it between my knees under the covers, hold the rope between my hands, and move it back and forth over one of the sharp edges of the bottle. A few more strands of the rope break, motivating me to keep sawing.

My muscles scream to stop, and sweat drips into my eyes, but I'm not foolish enough to wipe my face with the rags again. Using my forearm, I sweep the beads of sweat across my forehead and from my eyes. Slinging my hair out of my face, I pause to catch my breath. Everything I do, every move I make, every task I perform, and even the slightest activity quickly drains what energy I have left. Tiny drops of blood appear on my hands and fingers from cuts made by the sharp edges of the bottle as I saw the rope.

"Funny," I say to Apela. "I didn't even feel it."

Without hesitation, I return to cutting the twisted strands of cord, not considering the bleeding or pain pulsing through my body. I have only one thought—get free from this rope and fight as hard as possible to live.

Apela may be tiny, but he seems to be a good watchdog. He jumps to attention, his ears twitching, as he radars in on the noise he hears. Noticing his behavior, I stop sawing the rope and grip the bottle in my left hand. Apela snarls his lips, teeth showing, and growls softly under his breath. I place the little fella behind me, then grab the thinnest wooden stake with my right hand. Keeping the covers over me to conceal my weapons, I steadily watch the stall door, waiting for the battle to begin.

Undoubtedly, this fight will end in death—either his or mine.

CHAPTER 39

6 Days 30 Minutes
47 Hours 10 Minutes

Monday 10:52 a.m.

A sinister silence cloaks the barn. The storm outside is eerily quiet. There are no outside sounds. No howling of the wind through the trees, no branches squeaking as they rub against each other, no popping of limbs snapping from the weight of the ice and snow sleeping on their branches. The snow no longer swirls through the barn. It's as though time is frozen, temporarily pausing the storm's fury. Having experienced the wrath of a nor'easter once before, I know this is its eye, warning that the worst is about to come.

Unfortunately, a storm is about to rage inside the barn as well. I prepare myself mentally for the battle, reviewing all the self-defense and attack moves Daddy taught me over the years. At times, being the daughter of a military man had its advantages.

A few moments pass before I see an ominous figure slink past my stall, hidden by the shadows in the center of the barn. The thunderous roar of my heart pounds in my ears. My throat tightens, and my breathing becomes shallow and rapid. I can't find a drop of spit to wet my arid mouth. Gripping the neck of the broken bottle tightly, my hands tremble, knowing I may be using it at any moment.

Apela peeks his head from under the blankets, his gaze steady on the stall door, his growl fiercer than before.

"Shush," I whisper. "Stay back, boy."

He looks up at me, his eyes big and round and scared. Tenderly, I hug him and stroke his soft face, then gently push him behind my back into the corner of the stall.

"Stay," I command firmly.

He lies down, and I feel Apela's frightened brown eyes still gazing at me.

"It'll be okay, boy," I promise. "It will all be over soon."

Apela's soft growls become shrill barks when an obscure, sinister figure emerges from the darkness. Dressed in a heavy coat with a thick wool beanie pulled over his ears, Justin stands motionless, not uttering a sound, wearing night vision goggles. He moves silently to my right toward the flashlight, then rushes forward, kicking it into the wall. The small light breaks apart on impact, pieces flying in every direction.

Alarmed at his unexpected movement, I retreat farther into the corner, blocking Apela so he doesn't get hurt. I'm not sure Justin is aware that, even though it's still very dark and I can't see his face clearly, the light from the roof dilutes the darkness enough for me to know where he is. Knowing where he's at gives me an advantage I haven't had until now. This time, the playing field is more level.

Taking a deep breath, I grip the bottle securely and stand slowly, keeping my weapon hidden beneath my robe. Justin scurries, jumps at me, and yanks my robe, slinging me to the ground with barely any effort. He follows with a ruthless kick aimed at my left rib cage. Avoiding solid contact, I roll onto my knees away from the hit, preventing more fractured ribs. I felt prepared to defend myself, but Justin's aggressive actions and strength are overwhelming.

Having dropped the glass bottle when I fell, I rake my hand over the ground, searching for it. Finding it near the blankets, I grab it tightly by the neck and stand, ready to face my attacker. The rope, still binding me to the wall, hinders my defense by limiting the distance I can move.

Apela growls ferociously. From the corner of my eye, I spot him attacking Justin's leg, snarling and biting as viciously as the little dog can. The tiny creature is no match for Justin's strength. He picks Apela up by his neck and brutally hurls him into the wall. I can't believe Justin would do such a horrible thing to the tiny dog, the same little dog he was so affectionate toward when I first got here.

"No!" I scream. Dropping my weapons, I dive for Apela, trying to catch him before he lands, but the rope jerks my arm back, and I tumble to the ground.

Thud.

Apela slams against the wood so hard that the old horse harness hanging on the wall falls to the ground. My heart breaks when his little body strikes the wall. A sharp, shrieking yelp escapes his tiny body. Falling to the ground in the dark shadows, I can barely see him crawling away, his movement slow, his whimpers weak. I know Apela is injured, but alive. I just don't know how badly he's hurt.

Why? Why did Justin do this to the poor little animal? How could he do what he's done to Abby and what he's done to me? How sadistic is he? All of this for what? Fun? Money? What?

The more I think about it, the angrier I become—the more inflamed my wrath.

My heartache turns into rage, and my anger into revenge. The violent storm is no longer just outside; its fury is within me.

Standing, I face Justin, and all I see is *red*. My swollen eyes blaze with the fiery fury burning deep within me. The muscles in my jaw twitch from my tightly clenched teeth. I feel like my insides are going to explode.

I charge Justin, but he catches me by the arm and flings me to the ground again like I'm no more than a wet paper towel. He thrusts his leg back, preparing for another kick, but before he makes contact, I roll to the side and trap his leg between mine. He falls with an echoing thud to the ground beside me. His head bounces on the frozen ground, and he struggles to breathe. Sprawled on the hay, Justin moans, rolling his head from side to side.

Seizing my opportunity to remove his goggles, I squirm towards him and reach for his face. Justin's hand grabs mine and forces me to my back, then throws one leg over my stomach, pressing down on my left hand. The pressure of his weight on me pushes the air from my lungs, and I can't breathe. I hear a pop as another rib breaks, but the pain does not deter my determination to fight, win, and escape.

He mumbles words I can't understand in a gritty, garbled voice. Then he moves his hands to my throat, squeezes, and presses down, his intent—killing me.

I drop my chin and tighten my jaw and throat against the pressure on my neck. Unable to breathe, I grab his hands and pull his thumbs out to break his grip, but he's too strong. I force my arms between his and push out, and his grip loosens for a second, allowing me to grab a quick breath.

Unable to get his hands off my neck, I claw at his face and push the goggles to his forehead. I press both of my thumbs in his eyes until I feel them sink into their sockets.

His horrifying screams explode through the barn, reverberating into the rafters. Justin releases the grip on my neck and arches backward. Covering his eyes with both hands, he howls in horrific pain as drops of blood seep from under his hands.

Struggling for air, I cough violently. The pressure of Justin's body, still crushing me, cuts off my breath. His attention is only on his eyes and the damage I've done to them. I bend my knees, arch my back, and rapidly roll to the side, using one leg to push him. Justin tumbles off, still holding his eyes. Crying out in pain, he curses me with every scream.

Crawling around on the floor, I sweep my hands over the hay, searching for one of my weapons before he launches another attack. Before I get two feet away, Justin stomps me on my back. Filled with adrenaline, I ignore the pain, flip over, and deflect his next kick by swinging my legs up and out as his foot comes down. He crumbles to his knees, mouth open, howling in agony.

I try to crawl away from him, but the rope on my wrist refuses to release its grip. Justin grabs my robe and pulls. Letting the robe slip off my arms, we both become entangled. We struggle on the ground, each trying to get the upper hand. I slap and kick at him, punch and claw at his face as he drags me closer.

Justin manages to get himself to a standing position, then grabs me by my shirt and jerks me up, holding me in front of him. He lifts me off the ground with unimaginable strength and sends me flying across the room.

The stress on the rope is too much for the last strands to take, and it snaps with a loud pop, freeing me from my bondage. My shoulder takes the brunt of the hit as I strike the wall with a loud *bam!* Stunned, I lie on the ground, still refusing to give in or give up despite the pain.

I'm in a live-or-die situation and have no plans to die.

The snow coating the branches of the trees above me tumbles down in a flurry. The barn becomes darker as gray clouds conceal the light once visible between the branches. The wind blows violently, rumbling like a train out of control. The last tree that crashed onto the barn groans and then shifts with a loud crunching sound, its branches descending lower into the barn. The rafter supporting it breaks, crashing to the ground a few yards from me. The wall it's leaning on begins to crumble. Caught in the savagery of the wind, pieces of old gray wood shoot through the air like arrows from a bow.

Quickly, I dive to the side, moving away from the tree and falling wood, and lie face down on the ground, protecting my head with my hands. With everything going on, I've lost track of Justin.

The tree plunges deeper into the barn, its trunk bursting through the wall, thunderously vibrating the ground when it lands. The ferocious wind sweeps in the large opening left by the fallen tree, howling more fiercely than before. Wood and other debris hurl through the air. Pieces of the tin roof become missiles as they soar across the barn, striking anything in their path, some with such force that they penetrate the wall, lodging in the wood. Blinding snow beats through the open roof, forming a thick layer of ice and snow on the ground in seconds, and the temperature plummets. My skin burns from the half-frozen snow, and the freezing wind slaps across my face.

Even though some light flows through the open roof and wall, I have trouble seeing clearly because of the injuries I've sustained to my face. I notice movement behind me and spot Justin struggling to pull himself from under the edge of the fallen tree. Snow and debris cover his back, and a piece of the tin roof is sticking out of his right calf. He stands, looks down at his leg, and jerks the tin out, seemingly impervious to the pain and ignoring the blood soaking his pant leg. Although I can barely make out his face in the dim light and blowing snow, I can tell that his eyes are swollen, almost completely closed, and blood is dripping down his cheeks.

I don't know how Justin can even see, but somehow, he spots me close to the blankets. With all that's happened, I'm still his primary objective. Parting his coat, he removes a hunting knife from a sheath attached to his belt. He moves swiftly toward me, the sharp, thin blade poised to strike. Quickly crawling across the floor, I grab a piece of wood from the broken barn wall to use as a shield. Unable to stand before he gets to me, I grip the wood firmly with both hands and swing it like a bat at Justin's arm just as he plunges the knife down. The board hits Justin's hand, and the blade flies across the stall into the dark shadows, no longer visible.

Continuing his attack, Justin flings himself on me, straddling my waist as before, then grabs me by my shirt, pounding the back of my head into the ground.

"It's all your fault!" he growls.

Hearing his voice clearly, I don't recognize it.

"You made me do it!" he screams shrilly, then laughs

hysterically.

"Shamba force kiltsha!" He rears back and spreads his arms wide as though he is worshiping an unknown demon god or something, yelling words that make no sense into the air.

His crazed behavior removes his attention from me, so I use it to my advantage. I rake my arms and hands over the ground, searching for anything I might hit him with. My hand runs across a jagged object I recognize as the broken bottle. Justin leans down over me, his face shadowed. He grips my neck, squeezing tightly, a broad, sinister smile plastered across his face.

Closing my eyes as my breath leaves me, I hear the swish of the bottle splitting the air and feel a warm liquid flow down my hand, falling like rain onto my chest. There's no weight pressing down on me anymore, no squeezing on my neck, and I feel the air enter my lungs again. Rolling onto my side, numb from the frigidly cold storm engulfing the barn, I see the blankets lying near me about an arm's length away. I slowly pull my exhausted, bruised body toward them, hoping I don't die before I get there. Justin must have left the barn. I don't hear him anymore.

The wind whips and the snow continues falling. I wrap up in the flannel blanket and down comforter Justin had graciously given me. At one time, he seemed like a victim, too, and I even felt sorry for him. Funny how people aren't always who you think they are.

Whimpering, Apela slowly crawls from the shadowed corner of the stall where I had told him to stay. Holding him in my arms, we cuddle under the blankets, no longer aware of the storm, cold, or violence surrounding us. We close our eyes, waiting together for whatever comes next.

CHAPTER 40

6 Days 1 Hour 13 Minutes
47 Hours 53 Minutes

Monday 11:35 a.m.

My eyes open briefly. Everything around me is white: people wearing white, a white sky, white blankets that sparkle like silver. There's so much commotion, everyone talking and moving about so quickly. The room starts to spin, so I close my eyes again.

Arousing me from my deep sleep, someone's caressing my face tenderly, stroking my hair, and I hear murmuring but can't make out the words. Opening my eyes to a slit, I see a man's face, soft and tender, mouthing words I can't understand. I reach up, touch his face, then his eyes, and wipe the tears away. He smiles, caresses my hand, and kisses it lightly.

I close my eyes, knowing *he* found me.

* * *

Apela is being lifted from my arms, pulled from me. I can hear him whimpering. I open my eyes as much as possible and see the man holding him. I feel a tiny prick in one of my hands. Even though everyone's trying to help me, I'm still afraid.

"No, don't take him," I murmur. "He's mine." Tears collect in my eyes. "Apela," I cry.

"It's okay, Ivy. He needs help, too. He'll be safe, I promise. We're gonna get you both out of here," the man assures me, rubbing my cheek gently with the back of his fingers. "Everything's okay. I'm not going to leave you again."

I know this man. It's the detective, Detective Benson. He's come for me. I knew he would. I drift back to sleep, trusting he will keep my Apela safe and be true to his word—he won't leave me, not again.

CHAPTER 41

Saturday December 10
9:05 a.m.

Sweet violin music drifts into my sleep. I recognize the song. Galvin has played it for me many times. It's a beautiful meditative violin solo, one of my favorites, *Spiegel im Spiegel, Mirror in the Mirror.* Imagining myself sipping sherry by candlelight in a hot, relaxing bubble bath, all the tension in my body dissolves with every stroke of the bow, and I sink back into my dreams.

* * *

Slowly, I wander back to reality from my unconscious state. A violin plays softly. The sound of a heartbeat in perfect rhythm suddenly stops. Opening my eyes, I see a woman in light blue scrubs moving away from a heart monitor mounted on the wall behind me. Her long, braided hair sways from side to side as she walks around the bed and checks the IV infusion pump.

Noticing my eyes following her from one side to the other, the woman looks at me and takes my hand. Her wide smile makes her eyes squinch together.

"Hello, there!" she says, her voice slightly high-pitched, baring a note of excitement. "We've been waiting for you to come back to us."

I try to speak, but my voice won't come.

"Here, let me get you some water. I'm sure your mouth is dry."

The lady in scrubs brings me some ice chips and a spoon, scoops some out, and places them gently in my mouth.

"It's usually better to start with a few ice chips," she explains. "Sometimes it's hard to swallow when you first wake up. Can you tell me your name?"

It's difficult to sort my thoughts, but I answer the lady's question correctly. "Ivy," I say, my voice gruff and dry. "It's Ivy Pr…

Preston."

Her smile widens, and she pats my hand approvingly. "Yes. How nice it is to meet you finally, Ivy Preston!" she exclaims. "Now, do you know where you are?"

Looking around at my surroundings, I notice the dim lights above me soothe my swollen eyes. I follow the violin music to a small CD player sitting on the table with the pitcher of ice. Large windows with curtains replace walls on two sides of me. Other people wearing light blue scrubs, some with white jackets on, some carrying clipboards or brown folders, are walking outside one of the windows.

Shaking my head, I squeak out the word, "Apela."

Her mouth drops into a frown, and with a quizzical look, she shakes her head slightly. "I don't understand," she says. "Apela? Is that the name of someone?" she asks as she places the cup of ice on the table. "I'll see if any of your visitors know who Apela is or what it means, but first, I must let the doctor know you're awake."

The woman pats my hand and steps just outside the room to a table, makes a call, and then returns to my side. Her face becomes soft and relaxed, and she pulls a chair beside me.

"You're in the Intensive Care Unit at Bainsview Medical Center just outside Boston. You were brought into the hospital six days ago with multiple traumatic injuries and a couple of fractures. You've been in and out of consciousness since you came in."

She pauses a second, giving me time to process the information, and continues. "My name is Polly. I'm your day nurse. The clock on the wall will help you stay oriented." She points to a large digital clock displaying Saturday, December 10, 2022, and the time 11:03 a.m. in blue, glowing digits mounted above the door. "Do you have any questions?"

Indicating 'no,' I clear my throat and whisper, "Apela, where's Apela?"

Confused, Polly says again, "I'm sorry, Ivy. I just don't know who you're talking about, but you have lots of family and friends waiting to see you. Your mom and dad are here, and your siblings. Oh, and Detective Benson has been here to see you every day. He's constantly calling to check on you."

A tall, lean man in cowboy boots walks up to the desk outside the room and begins scrolling through the computer. He looks like he fell out of an old western movie, scruffy beard, unkempt hair, and jeans. The nurse notices him immediately and excuses herself to speak with him. I can tell they're talking about me, but I can't hear what they're saying. The man spots me looking at him. The corners of his mouth turn up, his cheeks lift, and small wrinkles appear at the edge of his eyes as a smile sweeps across his face. I respond with as much of a smile as my still-swollen face can form.

Entering my room, the gentleman introduces himself. "Miss Preston, I'm Dr. Colin Ellis. I'm so glad you finally decided to join us! We'll talk about your injuries and all that a little later. For now, you have lots of people who are very anxious to see you," he states. His Australian accent fascinates me as much as his gorgeous, genuine smile.

"I'll schedule more tests for you now that you're awake. Several other specialists on our team will be by sometime today or tomorrow to see you, too. I'll be back later today. I want to talk with you and your family about your treatment and care, if that's okay," Dr. Ellis continues, arching his eyebrows as though he wants me to indicate my approval.

Nodding, I whisper, "That's fine," then I ask who's here to see me. It's easier for me to whisper than to use my normal speaking voice. My throat is extremely raw and sore.

Dr. Ellis looks at Polly, then back at me. "Your parents are very anxious to see you, as is everyone waiting in the lobby. And Detective Benson certainly wants to talk with you."

"Where's Apela?

His brows raise, and his eyes widen, signaling he knows who Apela is. "Ah, yes," he nods as his smile widens. "Your little dog. He's fine from what I've heard." He scratches his scraggly beard. "I believe your friends have cared for him while you've been here. Let's see, the violinist and the two ladies. They're all here, anxious to see you, too."

My heart longs to see Apela, to be sure he's okay. I believe he was sent to me to save me, to give me hope, and to renew my desire to live, to have someone—something—to care for and protect besides myself.

"Animals are not allowed in the hospital, but," Dr. Ellis grins, his blue eyes gleaming mischievously. "I might be able to arrange for Apela to make a special visit." He places his finger on his lips. "It has to be hush-hush." He winks.

"I won't say a word," I whisper, crossing my heart with my hand. "Promise."

He nods, suppressing his smile. "I'll see what I can do. Now, let's get that line of visitors started. Remember, Ivy, no one can stay very long. I don't want you over-tiring yourself. You'll have plenty of time to visit in a few more days. I'll see you later," he states as he stands and leaves, Polly at his heels.

I close my eyes briefly, and, as hard as I try not to, I still fall asleep.

CHAPTER 42

Saturday 12:07 p.m.

Someone speaks softly.

"She'll wake up soon. I know she will. She's just sleeping now. She's not in a coma anymore. She's just sleeping."

Opening my eyes, or eye as the case may be, Mom and Dad are sitting on each side of me, holding my hands tenderly. Mom is usually fashionable with every hair in place, but today, her dark curly hair is flat on one side and pinned off her face with two mismatched hair combs. Her eyes are swollen and red, her face damp from her tears.

The strained look lifts and Mom's face glows when she notices I'm awake. She dabs a tissue at her eyes and shakes Daddy's arm.

"Look, look! She's awake, Noah! Oh, Ivy, my baby, Ivy," she says as she leans closer and cups my face in her hands. Mom touches my nose with her finger and kisses me on my forehead—our ritual of affection since I was a baby.

"It's all okay, Mom. I'm okay," I whisper. "You look tired; you need some rest."

She holds my hand against her cheek and kisses it multiple times. "I'm fine." She brushes my comment away. "You're the one we've been worried about." She sighs, swallowing her tears.

Dad moves to comfort her, but not before he bends over and kisses me on the cheek. "We've been waiting for you to come back, baby. I knew you'd be okay." He presses his mustached lips tight and blinks hard, sniffing back the tears in the corner of his eyes. "You're a fighter, little one. You always have been!"

"I pushed, Daddy, just like you told me. I pushed myself hard. I didn't quit," I say proudly, pinching my lips together. All that happened in the barn flashes through my mind like flipping pages in a magazine.

Daddy wraps his burly arms around me. My body heaves as the floodgates open, and I bawl like a baby, held in my daddy's comforting embrace.

Looking up at his tan face, I place my hands on his cheeks, look directly into his sky-blue eyes, and whisper, "If you hadn't come, Daddy, if you hadn't sent Apela, I wouldn't have made it." Dropping my face down onto his chest, he cuddles me like when I was little, and I feel safe. Just his presence alone makes me feel safe.

"It's okay, little one," Daddy says. "You're going home with us for a while. We're going to take care of you. You and Apela." He smiles. Pulling back slightly, he places his hands on my shoulders. "We have strict orders from the doctor not to stay too long. Others want to see you too, so we can't be too selfish, isn't that right, Mama?" he looks at Mom and nods.

Reluctantly, Mom nods back and agrees. "Yes, Noah, you're right. We can't be selfish, but we'll be here all day and night. I'm not leaving you alone. We're going to be close by. We'll be back every time the nurses let us come in. In fact," she scrunches her nose and pulls her shoulders back. "I'm going to see if the nurses will let me sit with you for a little bit later," she states confidently.

I nod. "That would be nice, really nice, and I have no doubt you'll convince the nurses to let you. You can be very persuasive." I smile.

After some more kisses and a lengthy goodbye, hurried on by the nurse, Polly, Mom, and Dad leave, and my brother and sisters come in together.

"What the hell, sis!" Ben exclaims, pushing himself past Anita and Emily to be first in line.

That's my big brother—always taking the lead. Watching him reminds me of when we were little and how he'd always push us aside to be in charge. He never stopped reminding us he should go first because he was the oldest. I can't help but grin. Those are good memories.

"We've all been so worried!" He bends down and kisses me gently on the cheek. "You've always had the big head, but wow," he jokes.

Reaching up, I feel and find what seems to be a turban, but I know it's a bandage. Until now, I haven't thought about how I must look. I can feel a patch covering one eye, and someone taped my ribs, but I haven't looked in a mirror and don't want to.

Anita and Emily shove Ben out of the way, and each takes a turn hugging and kissing me.

"We're just thankful you're alive," Emily says. "You've been through a lot. I never knew how tough you were, Ivy," she raves. "You're amazing!"

Despite Ben being the oldest, Anita, who always takes care of everyone, my middle sister, takes charge. "We're not going to stay long. You still have your friends who want to see you. We just want to make sure you are okay," Anita says, a forced smile frozen on her face.

Finally losing it, Anita bursts out crying. "We thought you were dead!" she wails, flinging herself across the bed, clinging to me as though I was about to dash out of here.

"Alright, Anita, that's enough hysterics," Ben says, pulling her gently away. "You're gonna scare poor Ivy to death with talk like that."

Realizing how dramatic she's being, Anita pulls herself together and dries up her sobs. "I'm sorry, Ivy. I've just been so scared for you, not knowing where you were or if they'd find you alive." She bursts into tears again.

Emily, the more level-headed of my two sisters, jumps in. "Anita! Get yourself together and stop all this! We only have a few minutes with Ivy, and it's not all about you," she states firmly, staring poor Anita down. "We're going to go, Ivy. Your friends are still waiting to come in. They're as anxious to see you as we were."

Smiling sweetly, Emily brushes her long dark hair behind one ear, bends down, and kisses me. She leans close to my ear and whispers, "I knew you'd be okay. You're too much like Dad not to be. I wasn't worried a bit!" She stands just as Polly comes in to shoo them out.

"Wait!" I say as loudly as I can, my voice still squeaky and weak. "Is Nick here?"

All three look at each other with a *what do we say* look on their faces. Ben walks back to the bed and sits on the edge. Taking my hand, he looks down, his face drawn.

"He's been calling to check on you, but he got tied up and hasn't got here yet. He's supposed to be here by the end of the week."

My heart is breaking, but I don't cry. I knew Nick and I were drifting apart, but I thought he cared about me, that he loved me even if it wasn't the 'I want to be with you forever' kind of love.

My lips tighten. "It's okay," I say, trying to smile. "I know Nick has a lot of responsibility on trips like this. Thanks for telling me." I squeeze Ben's hand, nodding my head.

"You're too good for him, Ivy," he says, his face red. Looking at the others, he continues. "We all feel that way and have for a long time, but we didn't want to say anything. Nick's not worth crying over. He would have had his sorry ass here if he was a decent man, but he's not. He's all about Nick!" Ben pounds the palm of his hand with his fist. I can almost see the steam coming from his ears.

"It's okay, Ben, really," I assure him. "It's been coming for a while now; we've both known it. I've cried so much this past week; I just don't have any tears left, not for this. It just hurts a little, but I'll be okay."

After Ben, Anita, and Emily leave, Polly asks if I want to see Mickie, Alana, and Galvin. "Yes. Yes, very much," I tell her. Adjusting myself in bed and smoothing the covers, I anxiously wait to see my long-time friends again.

Alana bounds in the door first, practically diving for the bed to hug me. Mickie's hot on Alana's heels, her broad smile trying to conceal the tears she's cried. Expecting Galvin to be right behind the girls, my moment of joy turns sour when I don't see him.

My smile drops, and my shoulders slump. "Where's Galvin?" I ask, glancing at Alana and then Mickie.

Searching each other's faces, they stare at the door.

"He was right behind us a second ago," Mickie states, her lips tightening. She searches Alana's face. Alana shrugs.

Slowly, the door opens, and Galvin makes a grand entrance, hiding behind a massive arrangement of orchids, lilies, and other plants. His face glows, his tender smile telling me more than words ever could. Galvin clears off a spot on the small table for the gigantic arrangement, leaving a tiny corner for ice chips and other essential items.

Making his way to the bed, he squeezes me gently and kisses me softly on the cheek, slipping in an unseen nuzzle to my ear with his nose—our secret signal, meaning *I'm always 'ear' for you.*

"I had to get the queen's approval to bring the flowers in," he giggles, nodding at Polly sitting just outside the door like a watchdog. "She's very nice. She even invited me out for dinner. Said she can't wait to get me alone." Galvin winks, a grin on his face.

The three of us laugh, knowing Galvin's joking. Our laughter draws a scowl from Nurse Polly and a "shush" to calm us down. Galvin mimics her when she turns around. He's just a big kid in many ways. Even though it's only been a few days since I've seen my friends, it seems like so much longer. I've missed them.

Everyone gathers around, finding a place to sit on the bed. After the hugs and tears, Alana tells me how sorry she is for letting me get kidnapped.

"You didn't let me get kidnapped, Alana! That's ridiculous.

There was nothing you could have done to stop it. It's not your fault, and I never want you to say that again."

"But I was the one that was supposed to be watching out for you," she whimpers. Her bottom lip pokes out, and her head droops as she apologizes. Her eyes glisten, the light reflecting off the tears puddling in them.

"No, that's not true," I clarify. "You were supposed to be staying with me because I had a concussion. You weren't my guard dog, Alana. You were my friend and still are."

She hugs me. "I love you, Ivy," she murmurs, sniffling as she brushes the tears away.

"I love you, too, Alana," I whisper back.

Mickie changes the conversation to a more upbeat note. "We've taken care of Apela for you," she says. Her face beams, and I sense she will have difficulty letting him go, just as I did when Detective Benson took him from me in the barn.

The mere mention of Apela causes my eyes to widen—most noticeably, the one eye not covered with a bandage. I'm suddenly bubbling with energy.

"Where is he? I've missed him so much! Is he okay? I know he was hurt." I can't control my stream of questions. "Thank you for taking care of him. When can I see him?"

Galvin laughs. "I see you miss him as much as he's missed you. Mickie kept him most of the time. Her kids love him. I think there may be a dog in their future after Apela leaves." He dons an amused smile and glances at Mickie.

"Most definitely," Mickie says. "He's such a good little boy. Detective Benson was keeping him when they first found you. He's the one who got Apela to the vet and took care of him the first few days. He didn't want to let us keep him, but he knew it would be best for Apela with the care he needed and him working so much."

"I like Detective Benson. He's been more than good to me. I

knew he'd find me. I never lost hope," I say, my voice breaking. Alana hands me another tissue. "Tell me about Apela. What kind of injuries did he have?" I ask, dabbing my eye.

"Well, his injuries were not as bad as yours," Galvin begins. "He has a fractured hip and a fractured leg. The vet said it would take about eight weeks for both to heal."

Mickie adds, "He's in a cast and looks pitiful, but he gets around well. He's a very resilient little thing, a real fighter, just like you." She tenderly squeezes my hand. "No wonder the two of you bonded so well!" She chuckles, rocking backward on the bed.

Galvin grabs her to keep her from falling, and we all laugh to the point of uncomfortable silence. I can feel my heart running rampant in my chest, my anxiety building. Polly rushes in to check on me when my heartbeat rises to 115 beats per minute on the monitor. She injects a mild sedative into the IV line and gives notice that it's time to wrap up our visit.

I know visiting with my friends is not the culprit making my heart beat fast—it's the silence. I remember the sound of silence, the isolation of darkness, the fear of helplessness. I don't like silence anymore.

"Doctor Ellis said you could bring Apela to see me. He said he'd work it out," I say, trying to dissolve the uneasiness in the air.

"I'll be sure to talk to him about it, and we'll get the little guy up here," Galvin replies.

Alana tips my chin toward her. "You need to rest, Ivy. We'll be back to see you. A thousand guards couldn't keep us away! But right now, you need rest to heal." She leans over and kisses me on the forehead, then stands.

Galvin jumps in, attempting to lighten the now solemn mood. "I think our time's up, anyway. Your nurse is signaling us to get the heck out of here." He smiles and then imitates Polly, pointing to her watch, exaggerating the stern look on her face.

We all laugh, and they leave, giving hugs, kisses, and loving goodbyes before they go.

As soon as they're out the door, I feel exhausted. It's probably the sedative Polly gave me, along with all the stout pain medicine I'm taking, making me so tired. But not an inch of my body hurts, so I'm not complaining.

Closing my eyes, thoughts of Detective Benson fill my mind, how kind he's been, how I knew he'd never stop searching for me, and how he cared for Apela. Slowly, I drift into a peaceful sleep. For the first time, as far back as I can remember, I dream sweet dreams of being safe, warm, and happy.

CHAPTER 43

Saturday 8:12 p.m.

Opening my eyes, I see the enormous neon clock on the wall. Saturday, December 10, 2022, 8:12 p.m. Just outside my door, a different nurse is sitting at the desk. The dim light still shines above my bed. I notice movement to my left and glance in that direction.

Detective Benson is leaning sideways in a chair, his elbow propped on the arm, his chin resting on his closed hand. I caught him resting like this once before. The dark, puffy circles under his eyes are a tell-tell sign that it's been days since he slept well. A soft snore reveals his fatigue.

His lips stretch into a smile, and his eyes open. "I could feel you watching me," he says as he moves to sit on the edge of the bed.

Still groggy from the medication, I can't think clearly, and my speech is sluggish. "I could have sworn you were snoring." Attempting to conceal how thrilled I am to see the detective, I fight the rise of my cheeks by forcing the corners of my mouth down.

The detective wipes a hand across his face and licks his dry lips. "Nah, I was faking," he grins. "How are you feeling?"

"I'm okay," I state matter-of-factly. "I knew you'd find me. I knew you wouldn't give up." Reaching up, I tenderly touch his cheek, then push a strand of hair off his face.

His eyes moisten with tears as he takes my hand, caresses it to his mouth, and tenderly kisses it. The tears trickle softly down his cheeks. He leans over, wraps his arms around me, and lifts me gently into his arms. I snuggle my face into his shoulder, thankful to be with him again. Neither of us is in any hurry to let go.

After talking for a few minutes, I then ask him to explain how he found me.

"Mark and I had already identified the suspect in the Crestview kidnapping as Justin Clairy before he took you," the detective begins. "We thought he might be the missing link to the kidnapping and death of a college girl, Hannah Bellstone, five years ago."

He pauses, leans his head to the side, and shifts his sitting position. Looking into my one visible eye, he asks, "Remember the lipstick we found at the crime scene when you and I were there on Wednesday?"

I shake my head. "No, my memory's fragmented. I can't remember a lot about this past week." I choke on my words and look down at the detective's hand lying on mine. It's warm and comforting.

He gently squeezes my hand. "You're okay now, Ivy. What you don't remember isn't important anymore. Trust me. Some things are best forgotten."

I press my lips tight to keep my emotions at bay and nod.

"Hannah's DNA was a match to the tube of lipstick found in the alley. We never caught her killer." He sighs and stares at the wall. "I remember the case well now. Marc and I worked on it."

Closing his eyes, he pinches the bridge of his nose as though he's removing the images from his mind, then faces me. "We ruled out Clairy as the kidnapper of Hannah when his rap sheet confirmed he was in Omaha at that time, robbing a grocery store."

Detective Benson stands, collects ice chips in the cup, and places a few in my mouth. "After Clairy kidnapped you, we discovered that Hannah Bellstone was the sister of Abigail Stephens. The DNA on the lipstick matches both sisters since they were identical twins. And Abigail perfectly matched your sketch of the kidnapped victim at Crestview."

Pausing, the detective rubs his beard, once well-trimmed and neat, now scraggly and overgrown. He hasn't taken care of himself since I went missing.

He takes a deep breath, runs a hand through his hair, and releases the breath through circled lips. "Abigail became severely depressed after her sister's death. She was in and out of mental institutions almost continually from Hannah's disappearance until recently, when she dropped out of sight. The discovery of her sister's body six months after Hannah was kidnapped flipped Abigail over the edge. According to her husband, there was no hope for her after that.

"Abigail believed, being twins, she should have been experiencing just what Hannah felt when she was kidnapped and murdered." Detective Benson sighs and shakes his head. "It's so sad really. She must have been devastated by the loss of her sister to do what she did."

The detective stands and paces the floor. "Her husband said that, over the past year, Abigail told several of her psychiatrists she wanted to suffer like her sister had. She said it was her *right* to feel exactly how Hannah felt when held captive."

Stopping dead in his tracks, the detective fixes his eyes on mine, scrunching his brows. "She was seriously disturbed, Ivy. You have to understand that—*seriously* disturbed. There was nothing you could have ever done to save her—*ever*." His brows rise; his face softens. "You understand what I'm saying?"

The detective's voice is calm but firm. Even though I don't fully understand, I nod, hoping my understanding improves as he tells me more.

Noticing the tension in Detective Benson's voice, the nurse walks to the door and peers in. "Is everything okay?" she asks. "Can I get you some coffee, detective?"

Moving toward the nurse, the detective smiles, his tone softer. "That'd be great, thanks. Black coffee, please."

She nods and adds, "I'll bring you some juice, Ivy. Any preference?"

I shake my head. "Any kind is fine, thanks." She turns and leaves.

Detective Benson runs his hands over his face and stretches his arms out. "I'd sure like a lager about now," he half laughs.

"This is a pretty stiff place, but I'll try to order you one," I snicker as I push my call light, attempting to lighten the mood.

The detective's mouth falls open, and he rushes to the bed, playfully struggling with me for the call button.

A female voice answers. "Yes, Miss Preston? How can I help you?"

"Yes, could I please get two of your finest lagers?"

"No, no, that's okay, she's just kidding," the detective stammers as we tug for control of the call light.

We can hear giggling from the other end. "I'm glad you're feeling better, Miss Preston. However, alcohol is not allowed in the ICU. Is there anything else you'd like?"

"Perhaps, some sherry? Medicinal purposes, you know," I ask in my politest voice just before Detective Benson gains control over the device.

"She's kidding," the detective says, silently admonishing me for my bad behavior with looks and gestures. "I think Miss Preston is feeling much better. Perhaps too much pain medicine has gone to her head," he laughs. "I'll see if I can get her under control. Goodbye now." He drops the control on the bed like a hot potato.

When the night nurse brings the coffee for the detective and some juice for me, the three of us joke about the lager and sherry. After she leaves and the detective has taken a few sips of the coffee, I ask him to continue with the details of the case and how he found me. Detective Benson pulls his chair close to the bed, sits his coffee on the side table, props his elbows on his knees, and resumes where he left off.

"We received a phone call from a man at a gas station on a rural road off I-90 about an hour and a half after Clairy took you. He said he heard a woman screaming from the trunk of a blue Plymouth and had struggled with the driver. The driver, Clairy, had gotten away, but the man gave us good information on the car's direction. That helped us narrow the search area."

Retrieving his coffee, Detective Benson walks across the room, gazing out the window. He pulls the curtain, turns to me, and continues. "Like I said, I worked the Bellstone case." He stares down at his coffee. "It was… one of the worst cases I've ever worked. It was months before we found her body."

His jaw clenched and shoulders straightened, the detective paces the floor, sipping the coffee. He continues the back-and-forth pacing, occasionally stopping to move the curtain and stare out the window. Watching his movements and mannerisms, it's evident that he's distraught by the memory. Detective Benson finishes his coffee, crushes the cup, and tosses it into the trash can near the door. He walks to the bed, sits on the edge of it, takes my hand, and cradles it in his.

"I remembered the location of the barn where the kidnapper took Hannah and held her hostage. It was about 45 minutes from the gas station where the man said he had the run-in with Clairy. I had a gut feeling that's where you were."

The detective drops his head, focusing his eyes on our hands. He takes a deep breath and slowly blows it out, trying to control his emotions.

"I didn't know if you'd be alive or dead when we found you," he mumbles practically to himself.

Cupping his face between my hands, I force him to look at me. "It's only because of you that I *am* alive," I tell him softly, my eyes filling with emotion.

Wrapping my arms around him, I pull his head gently to my shoulder and hold him tightly. He begins to sob. And I, crying quietly, cling to the only man who ever truly cared about me.

Once we're both all cried out and calm, we touch foreheads and smile before the detective sits back. He remains by my side on the bed, grabs a box of tissues from the table, and nervously jerks out a handful. He tosses me a couple of tissues and takes a few for himself, then clumsily pats my face. He's obviously feeling awkward, but he doesn't apologize for his behavior.

I've never found crying in a man to be a sign of weakness, but more a character of a compassionate, caring person. I pull his face to me and gently kiss his forehead. Looking tenderly into his eyes, I whisper, "I'm okay, it's all okay now. Everything's going to be okay."

The detective nods, and his nervousness diminishes.

"There's more you need to know, Ivy. Some things you may not know, and some we've discovered since we found you."

"Okaaay." Confused, I drag my word and tip my head slightly. What more could there be, I wonder.

Clearing his throat, Detective Benson begins. "Abigail married a wealthy oil guy in Houston, so she had lots of money. It seems after Hannah died, Abigail bought the property where Hannah's kidnapper took her and killed her. It's the same place Clairy took you, the same barn. Abigail visited it every year around the same date Hannah disappeared. She didn't stay in the cabin but had a standing reservation at the Shadyside Inn. That's where she met Clairy's girlfriend, Henlie Brickendale when she came up this year. Brickendale was a part of the cleaning staff. And this is where it gets weird," he warns.

"It seems another employee overheard Abigail and Brickendale talking about some job Abigail would pay Brickendale and her boyfriend, Clairy, to do for her. Would pay them a hefty amount, like a hundred thousand dollars."

My eyes widen as memories surface. "I found some pieces of paper in the Plymouth when I got out of the trunk. One was like a part of a contract agreeing to pay one hundred thousand dollars to 'Ju,' but somebody had torn off the rest. The other was a newspaper article describing the kidnapping of Hannah Bellstone and that her sister Abigail Stephens was on suicide watch. And there was a yellow sticky note with the hotel name you mentioned written on it."

The detective nods and states factually, "We found the papers in the pocket of your robe." His face forms a half smile, one side of his lip rising and the eye on the same side squinching. "You're amazing, Ivy. I wondered how you could have gotten ahold of all the items you had: the papers, a couple of lighters, and a wrench of all things. How did you get those?"

Sensing the detective is impressed by my feats, I tell him about being trapped in the trunk, finding my way through the backseat into the front of the car, and using the tire iron to fight Justin when he opened the car trunk the first time.

"I thought I was doing okay until that crazy psycho Henlie caught me getting out of the car and beat the crap out of me." I giggle softly, but there's nothing funny about any of it, and my face goes from smiling to a blank stare as I relive the event in my mind.

"I know," Detective Benson whispers. "You'll have tons of different emotions over the next few months, but I'll be here to help you through it if you let me."

Nodding, I want to know what he learned about Justin and Henlie. He agrees to tell me, but only if I will get him another coffee and if I will eat something. I push the call button and put in the request.

He begins again. "So, it seems Abigail paid Henlie and Clairy to kidnap and torture her in similar ways to her sister. Abigail had confided to one of her psychiatrists that she wanted to experience, both physically and mentally, what her sister did when she was kidnapped and held captive. Abigail gave Clairy and Henlie the money upfront. So, it didn't matter to them if she lived or died. And, if she died, there would be no witnesses to accuse them of anything.

That's where what Clairy told you in the alley came in. That's the meaning of his words to you—'*It's not what you think,*' and '*She made me.*' Looking at the facts, we think he said, '*She paid me,* not '*She made me.*'

"You're right about Henlie, too, when you said a minute ago she was a psycho," he confirms. "Henlie did have a mental health diagnosis, paranoid schizophrenia. She had been in and out of several institutions and had a history of not taking her meds correctly. One of her psychiatrists described her as having an extremely violent tendency and an antisocial personality disorder. Sometimes, she would act out, especially when she didn't take her medicine. Henlie's primary psychiatrist reported that Henlie often had to be restrained and sedated to keep her under control."

"I thought as much," I acknowledge. "I could tell Henlie was hallucinating at times, and she could be very violent. I know all people with schizophrenia are not like her. It's tough for them and hard for many to get good mental health care."

Detective Benson nods in agreement as the nurse delivers a wonderfully aromatic bowl of what you might, by some stretch of the imagination, call chicken soup, some saltines, and my ever-so favorite, lime Jello. Even the detective's nose turns up when he sees it.

"I'll get you a burger tomorrow," he says, stealing one of my crackers. "Eat up!"

"So, tell me more," I insist, sipping the soup.

"I don't think Clairy wanted to go along with the kidnapping. We think he and Henlie had some kind of argument, and she shot him multiple times before she came after you. We found him lying on the kitchen floor, shot in the back. He didn't even see it coming."

My mouth drops to my chest, and my eyes pop wide. I'm stunned, and my words stumble out of my mouth. "What? What are you talking about?" I practically scream, pushing my food away. "I don't understand. You mean Justin wasn't the person I fought with in the barn before you found me? I'm confused."

This can't be true. I'm stunned that Henlie killed Justin, but I can't wrap my mind around the fact I was fighting Henlie.

I shake my head at the detective in disbelief. "I don't remember a lot about what happened before I woke up here in the hospital… I remember fighting, fighting for my life."

My hands tremble, and my insides feel like the lime Jello on my plate. My chest grows tighter and tighter. Feeling like I'm having a panic attack, I peel the cover off, searching for air.

The detective rushes to me, trying to calm me. He pushes the call light for the nurse, and she hurries in.

"I'll get her something." She hurries out and quickly returns with a syringe, plunging it into the port on my IV.

"Apela got hurt," I mumble, the sedative taking effect. "I knew I was fighting Justin. The person was so strong." Tears rush down my face like a mountain stream.

Using my hands to demonstrate my actions, I subconsciously scowl, recalling the last fight. "I remember taking the broken bottle and jamming it into my attacker's neck, then twisting it, and I remember the blood falling like a heavy rain onto my chest. The whole time, I thought it was Justin."

The detective holds me. "Shh, it's okay, Ivy. I thought you knew it was Henlie. It'll be okay." Cradling me in his arms, he rocks me back and forth until the sedative takes full effect.

CHAPTER 44

Saturday November 25, 2023
2:15 p.m.

A light rain falls gently from the cloudy Boston sky. I expect the temperature will drop soon, and we'll have snow. I've always loved the sound of rain and the beauty of crystal-white snow. It's hard to believe it's December again.

Opening the door to my brownstone feels strange after staying with my parents for the past year. It feels good to be home, able to care for myself again. I place Apela inside the front door, and he hurries around, checking out every room.

Hanging my coat in the foyer, I look around and realize everything's the same as before I left. I've missed this place. Walking through my home, I light some of the candles I brought, then build a fire in the fireplace. After pouring myself a glass of wine, I sit on the sofa beside Apela. As I watch the fire flicker, I reflect on the past year and how much has happened and changed.

Leaving Boston after being kidnapped was hard, but I had no choice. I couldn't take care of myself. Even though my friends and even Detective Benson offered to care for me, I knew I couldn't impose on them like that, so I moved to Jacksonville with Mom and Dad. All my family has been great. They want me to leave Boston and move closer to them. I'm still undecided.

My injuries were much more severe than I first thought. The bruises and swelling disappeared slowly, and I have a few small scars from the cuts. The worst one is on my back, where the nail ripped the muscle. I can only see it with a mirror, so I don't look at it much. But when I do, I try hard to replace the memories of the horror associated with it with those of triumph and survival.

The fractured ribs were very painful and seemed like they would never mend. My right pelvic bone was extremely painful and took quite a while to heal. The bone in my right leg healed well with no complications. I was bedridden for months. That was awful. I didn't like depending on my parents and family to help me, but I had no choice. I couldn't even turn myself without help. I'm more than thankful for my family. I can't imagine not having them.

I had two surgeries for multiple head injuries and a concussion, but thankfully, there's no long-term damage. The beatings and fights messed up my face pretty badly. I had a broken nose and jaw, and it took several surgeries to repair all the damage. I've lost some of the vision in my eye from damage to the retina, but it's stable now. Glasses don't help, but I can manage well enough.

The headaches and dizziness are gone now, but I still have some gaps in my memory. On the positive side, my hair is growing back. It's not as long as it was, but I think the style is cute.

For me, the worst injuries are the psychological ones, the post-traumatic stress disorder and nyctophobia, commonly known as an extreme fear of darkness. When I got kidnapped last year, all the bad things that happened occurred after the lights would flash on and off, and it would be dark again. I'm getting better, though. I only have a problem with it when the lights go out suddenly, such as a power failure.

In the beginning, I feared just being in the dark. There had to be a light on, or I would panic. It got much worse, and I started having episodes in public places. The worst one happened in a shopping mall. The lights went out during a storm, and I froze, dropped to the floor, and crawled under some clothing racks to hide. I stayed there, perfectly still, for two hours, the entire time the lights were off. The manager had to call an ambulance for me. That's when my parents realized I had a severe problem, and I started seeing a therapist. I'm much better, but I keep candles lit while I'm up at night, sleep with a light on and always have a flashlight. I can't seem to move past the fear—not yet.

I'm unsure if I will stay in Boston or move. My home and practice are here, but I don't know if that's enough to make me want to stay. I may move to Georgia near Emily. I lived there years ago, near the beach, and it was a super friendly place, but Detective Benson wouldn't be there, so I'm torn.

I've gotten to know him well. He calls regularly, and we video chat each other. He even flew to Jacksonville last summer on his vacation. I would miss him terribly if I didn't see him in person often. We're going to have dinner tonight. He's turned into a great friend.

Then there's Alana, Mickie, and Galvin. I haven't got to see them at all since I left, except on video chats. We've all stayed in touch, but long-distance friendships are not the same as spending time with someone and doing things with them. That's what happened with Nick. The long-distance relationship just didn't work for us.

I've got to make some decisions over the next couple of weeks. I could rent my house out or sell it. Or I could move back here. There are many things to decide, but I have other things to do before dealing with that.

Lighting some more candles, I prepare Apela his favorite dog food and get dressed for my dinner with Detective Benson. He's coming to pick me up in a few hours. I can't wait to see him. I even bought a new dress to wear. I want to feel pretty, like a woman again.

CHAPTER 45

Saturday 5:58 p.m.

Right on time as always, I open the door, and the detective's holding a small bouquet of red roses. He wraps his muscular arms around me and swings me through the air like a princess.

"Guess you can tell I'm excited to see you," he beams. "These are for you." He smiles, handing me the roses. "Welcome home, Ivy." He kisses me lightly on the cheek. Standing back to get a full view of me, he exclaims, "You look beautiful!" I blush.

"Where's that little furry boy? Apela!" he yells, easing past me. Apela skids around the corner and leaps into the receptive arms of the detective, licking his face like a pork chop.

"Atta boy," Detective Benson laughs, "I think you missed me!" He coos and ahhs over Apela until the fuzzy little fellow finally calms down. "Look what I got you," he tells the tiny dog, pulling out a small stuffed dog toy shaped like a frog. Apela grabs the toy and takes off for his spot on the sofa. He snuggles in, laying his paws over the little frog as though he's protecting it.

The detective's face is cheerful. "Tell you what," he begins. "Let's snuff these candles out and get going. We'll leave a couple of lights on, and," he pats his pocket, "I've always got my trusty flashlight in case of emergencies." He grins, holding my hand.

"I knew you'd be prepared," I say, pulling my flashlight from my purse. "If yours doesn't work, I have a spare!"

* * *

Arriving at the restaurant, we sit at the reserved table for two in a secluded area near a window. It's perfect. The rain has turned to snow for the moment, and the view of the city is gorgeous. Pulling out my chair, as he always does, he sits across from me, the candle on the table reflecting softly in his eyes, lighting up his smile. He's so handsome. He would be easy to fall in love with.

The waitress comes, and the detective orders a bottle of chardonnay in addition to our meals.

"You remembered my favorite wine!"

"Tonight's a special night," he announces. "You've come home."

Feeling guilty, I open the conversation about my reason for being here. "I'm just not sure if I'm staying in Boston. There are many reasons to stay, but I don't know if I want to live here anymore."

He shifts his position and leans forward, his arms resting on the table. "Remember when we built the snowman in the park with the kids?" he smiles, bringing up good memories.

"Yes, I remember. It was so much fun." A huge smile spreads over my face.

The detective becomes more solemn. "Remember when we sat under the gazebo, and you asked me whether I had been in a similar situation, witnessing a crime?"

Becoming nervous, he fumbles with the eating utensils on the table. I reach over and hold his hands. I nod. "Yes, I remember. I didn't press you about it. I knew you'd talk to me when you were ready. You can tell me anything. I hope you know that."

Nodding his head, he gazes at the candle. "My dad died from cancer when I was three. My mom dated a few guys here and there, but not much. I was her main focus. She was a beautician, and she worked hard to support us. When I was seven, I witnessed a kidnapping. I don't ever talk about it because it's too hard. It's something I've tried to forget." The detective pauses and takes a sip of wine.

"I understand what you mean," I empathize. "I don't like to talk about my experience either."

The detective nods, pressing his lips together, then continues. "My mom and I were in a grocery store. When we came out, it was dark." He stares out the window. "It was a cold, rainy night. One of the guys she had dated a time or two pulled up beside us. He insisted that she get in the car, but she refused. He pushed me down, but I got back up and tried to protect my mom. He punched me, practically knocking me out. The rest was blurry, but I know my mom was screaming, and I saw him punch her in the face, throw her in the car, and drive off."

Detective Benson looks down, and he squeezes my hands. Finally, he looks up, his eyes piercing deep into mine. "I'm telling you this, Ivy, because even if you leave Boston, it won't matter. Wherever you go, your memories are always with you. You must learn to deal with them, not try to escape them. I know firsthand."

My eyes fill with tears, and my chin quivers. I try to keep from crying. I know the detective is right, but I'm still unsure what to do.

I've known there was something Detective Benson kept hidden deep inside, but who would have thought it would be anything like this? Losing a parent when you're young is bad enough, but witnessing your mom kidnapped at age seven is unfathomable. I wish I could help him, but nothing could ever take away his pain or the memory of something so horrible.

"Did the police find your mom?" I ask, still suppressing the tears.

"No, she was never found. Not her or the kidnapper. There were no good leads, so the case went cold. Occasionally, I'll pull it out to see if I can find something the investigation team overlooked, but there's just nothing there."

The detective shrugs his shoulders, his eyes glossy from the mistiness collecting in them. Adjusting his posture and suppressing the tears, he sips more wine as the waitress brings our food.

Changing the subject, I comment on the lobster and my hunger. Laying our mood-stealing memories to the side for a while, we chat about this and that as we enjoy our meal, the wine, and each other's company. His eyes brighten, and he's laughing and joking. Since we've talked regularly over the past year and spent time together this summer, we've gotten to know each other well. In a way, I'm surprised that he hasn't told me about his mom before now.

My mind floats back to our conversation about Detective Benson's mother and what he went through. I understand now what he meant when he said, *It doesn't matter where you go; your memories go with you,* but I'm not sure I'll ever know how to deal with them.

Reminding him of what he said, I can't help but ask the one specific question I need an answer to. "How did you deal with it, detective?"

Having finished his last bite of lobster, he dabs his mouth with his napkin and takes another sip of wine. "After my mom got kidnapped, I lived with my grandmother. That's when I met Marc. He's been like a brother to me ever since. His family became my family. His dad was a police officer and a detective who worked on homicide cases. I dealt with it by becoming who I am now—a detective who works on kidnappings and homicide cases. I want to find every kidnapped victim that I can. I don't want anyone feeling the way I do, not knowing what happened to the person they cared about. That's the worst part—not knowing."

"I admire how brave you are. My experience pales in comparison to yours. I can't imagine the horror you experienced and for you to take that experience and use it to help others… I just can't tell you how much respect I have for you. Honestly."

The detective turns a light shade of red. "Thank you, kid. That's sweet of you to say." He reaches across the table, takes my hand, and gently strokes it with his thumb. He lifts his head and gazes deeply into my eyes. "No two experiences can be compared when both are equally traumatic. Don't short-change yourself, Ivy," he states affectionately. "Most people would not have survived all that you went through. I'm thankful we found you alive."

We complete our meal on a happier note, sipping the wine and talking.

Leaving the restaurant, we hear a street band playing in the park nearby. The valet brings us the detective's car, and we drive to the park to check it out.

We park a short distance away and walk toward a group gathered under a large canopy. The detective and I stand near the edge of the tent, enjoying the four-person band playing smooth jazz music: the snow, now rain, substitutes for the drums as it rhythmically beats on the tarp.

About an hour later, the rain slacks up, and we head to the car before we get drenched by the next major downpour. We walk silently, the music playing in the distance. Just before we get to the Charger, the sprinkle of rain becomes showers of tiny snowflakes. The detective looks up at the snow, reflecting on his life.

"I'm forty-six," he begins, "divorced once, a long time ago." He stops walking and turns to face me. "Never had any kids," he says slowly, thoughtfully.

There's sadness in his eyes, an emptiness. I can see who Tomas Benson is now with everything he's revealed to me tonight. Now I know just how vulnerable he can be when his Superman-Detective armor comes off.

I'm afraid of my feelings. I want to wrap my arms around him, hold him close, and be held by him. I've got to keep my emotions under control. I don't want to be hurt again like with Nick. But then, I knew that relationship wasn't working long before the final breakup. At least we parted as friends, even though my heart still ached at the loss of all we had once meant to each other. It wasn't real love. Not the kind a woman wants.

I try to think of a way to pull Detective Benson back from his thoughts and me from mine. "Hm," I say coyly. "I thought you were a lot older than that." I grin, pushing a strand of hair back from his forehead.

His eyes crinkle as he smiles. "Never judge a book by its cover," he laughs and scoots closer to me, placing his arm around my waist.

"Do you not like my book cover?" the detective quizzes, still grinning.

My face feels hot, and I feel funny inside, all fluttery. Silly. Kind of like a teenager. I decide to be flirty. "Oh, I really like your cover," I say teasingly. "I can't wait to read the book!"

I can't believe I'm so bold. I've been attracted to Detective Benson since we first met, but I never thought it would turn into anything, especially with our age difference. I know he's not quite as old as I had thought, but still, it's a significant age gap.

"I think you'll like the content if I get you past the first chapter." His voice is low and sultry, suggesting he has more than a friendship interest in me. "I'm drawn to your cover, too," he continues, clearly indicating his meaning. "I hope to read every line of your book, word by word."

Wow. Even standing in the cold with snow falling on me, I'm getting hotter by the minute, and I don't think it's from the wine! If I don't get my emotions under control, I might fall totally in love with this man.

Somehow, I find my words. "Maybe someday we can dive deeper into those chapters." I grin. "For now, I think I should go home and get some rest. It's been a very long day, and I'm exhausted."

I don't want tonight to end, but I know I should go home—before I don't.

"It has been a long day for you, the flight and all." He looks at the snow collecting on the car, then gives me a soft puppy dog look.

I can tell he doesn't want our conversation to end. I can feel his interest in taking our relationship beyond simply friendship. Even though I wish that too, now is not the time.

Despite my hesitation, I ask Detective Benson to come in for a nightcap when we arrive at my brownstone. We relax on the sofa, sipping wine and petting Apela.

"You've never told me to call you Tomas. Why not?" I ask.

"Good question." His chin lifts as he presses his lips together. "I felt I had to maintain some sense of a professional relationship while we were working the kidnapping since you were involved in it as a witness. My main focus was finding the victim. I could keep you at a distance by keeping us off a first-name basis. I know I referred to you as Ivy, but I often do that with certain individuals involved in a case. It comforts them knowing I see them as a person, not just a witness or victim." He shifts his position to face me fully. "It would be wrong for me to do otherwise. A personal relationship with a witness could have jeopardized the case when it went to court, and I couldn't take that chance."

Understanding what he means, I nod.

Detective Benson continues, speaking softly, almost in a whisper. "But we don't have that problem now." He leans closer to my face, gently lifting my chin. I stop breathing for a second as his lips draw near to mine. My heart beats rapidly, in a rhythm I'm sure he can hear.

He softly whispers the words that, until now, I could only hope to hear.

"One thing you should know, Ivy. I don't think age should dictate who you love."

And Tomas kisses me.

CHAPTER 46

Sunday December 3
10:47 a.m.

Holding Apela in my arms, I get out of the car and walk up the small hill. It's been a year today since Justin took me from my backyard. I've tried to move past it, and in some ways, I have. But the memory of all that happened is still there, lurking in the shadows of my mind. It surfaces in the absence of light—during the day when the power goes off and there are no windows to light the room, at night when the lights are off and I close my eyes to sleep, or whenever it's dark and I'm alone. I hope I can move past it after today.

The gray barn is still standing, broken and battered by the beating it took from the storm last year. The giant oak tree rests on what remains of the back wall. The shed sits next to it, just as I remember, but the lock dangles, the door open. Tomas told me the investigation team had removed some of the items. The cold and uninviting cabin sits to my right, the roof covered in a thin sheet of snow. There's no smoke swirling from the chimney the way it did when I first saw it.

"That's where Henlie killed Justin," I tell Apela. "I know you liked Justin," I whisper, holding the little furry dog in my arms. "He was good to you."

Apela looks up at me, and as I look deep into his big brown eyes, I picture the sadness and terror he felt last winter when he saw Henlie shoot Justin and the pain he suffered when she threw him against the wall. I still remember his heart-retching cry and the whimpers that followed. It took twelve weeks for the fractures in his hip and leg to heal. I rub his neck under his chin, tears pooling in my eyes.

Not wanting to go in the cabin, I look back at the barn and

approach the door. Putting Apela on the ground, I swing the double doors wide to allow as much daylight to shine in as possible and slowly inch my way inside, glancing in every direction. The barn doesn't look nearly as ominous as I remember, but I still half expect someone to jump out at me. Even though some light illuminates the barn, I turn on the large flashlight I brought. Although though my fear of the dark has improved, I'm not taking any chances of being alone, lost in the blackness of this barn again.

I go to the stall where I last saw Abby, where she told me she wanted to live. I didn't ask how her sister died or realize how depressed she was. Tomas told me Abby had confessed to one of her therapists that she wanted to experience her sister's suffering, pain, and horror. And she found a way to do just that. Abby may have discovered her desire to live toward the end, but it was too late. She died at the hands of a killer, just as her sister had. The tears I've held back trickle down my face. I wish I had asked more questions. I wish I could have saved her.

The stall is eerily empty. Looking around with my flashlight, I notice that the rope that tied her to the wall is gone, taken by the investigation team. Only the bullring remains, still nailed to the wall. I don't know why they confiscated everything. There's no one left to prosecute, no victim alive except me. No evidence will do any good at this point.

Doing what I came here to do, I turn and slowly walk from the empty stall, sliding my hand across the planks as I go, feeling the grain of the wood and the age of the barn in the grayed, cracked boards. Something moves quickly over my hand, and I jump back, startled. A giant rat scurries across the wood and leaps to the floor, running away. Taking a breath of relief, I chuckle at how silly I am to be startled by a rat after all I've been through.

Entering the stable next to Abby's, the one I occupied, my stomach churns. Drops of cold sweat form on my forehead and upper lip. My head is light, swirling like the snow falling through the open roof, and, for a moment, I think I'm going to faint. Sinking to one knee, I hold on to the stall door for support. I drop my head down low to the ground and take a few deep breaths. Apela moves closer to me and licks my hand.

Several minutes pass before I feel the color return to my face. The nausea subsides, and my heart stops swishing in my ears.

"That was close, boy," I tell Apela, rubbing his head tenderly.

Pulling myself up, using the gate as support, I shine the flashlight across the stall and immediately spot large dark spots on the hay, remnants of the blood shed by Henlie and me during our fatal battle. The blankets that once warmed me lay piled on the ground in what I once called *my spot*. The broken bottle is now evidence sitting in a bag somewhere. I notice remnants of the bottle, tiny pieces of broken glass embedded in the ground near the blood. The memory of all that happened here is fragmented and surreal; however, the horror of that day still haunts me.

Shining the flashlight at the tree that fell onto the barn, crushing the back wall and opening a gaping hole in the roof, I feel thankful. Had the tree not crashed down at just the right moment and landed on Henlie, and the tin from the top of the barn not penetrated her leg, I might not have made it through the fight alive.

Henlie might not have been weak enough for me to land the fatal blow with the glass bottle to her neck, severing her carotid artery. I remember twisting the bottle after I plunged it in. Forensic reports indicated the twisting motion caused it to penetrate deep enough to reach the carotid. The final cause of death—massive blood loss.

I don't remember any of that. There's a lot I still don't recall, and I pray I never do.

I still see Justin as a victim, too. Henlie pressured him into kidnapping Abby, and what he said to me in the alley, *'She made me,'* was accurate.

Picking up the down comforter, the one Justin kindly gave me to keep me from freezing, I finish my task and exit the stall. Walking back to the center of the barn, I take one more look around, sweeping the light I hold into every nook and cranny to be sure the barn is empty. Any critter that's in here can easily escape.

Looking down at the can of mineral spirits next to my feet, I kick it over, and it flows into the hay scattered over the barn floor. Pulling the box of matches from my pocket, I carefully remove one and strike it. Without a second thought, I toss it into the hay. The fire flares up slowly, methodically, as a sea of flames spreads over the barn floor and creeps up the walls. The smell of the burning wood is sweet, giving me a sense of comfort. The sound of the crackling wood is soothing to my soul.

Apela and I walk from the barn, no longer afraid. When we're far enough away, I turn and watch the barn blaze. The flickering red and yellow flames reach the sky, kissing the crisp white snowflakes falling around them. The storm is over.

Glancing down, Apela sits at my feet, his eyes on the burning barn. He turns and looks at the cabin, then back at the barn. I wonder what memories he has. I lean down and lift him into my arms.

Comforting him, I whisper, "Come on, boy," nuzzling his face with mine. He responds with a flurry of licks.

Walking to the cabin, I have no desire to enter it or see the blood stains on the kitchen floor. Tomas said Justin didn't see the bullet coming toward him and probably had no idea Henlie would shoot him. I wonder if that's true.

I pour another can of mineral spirits outside the cabin, then set it ablaze.

No murderous kidnapper will ever occupy the rundown old shack again.

The crackling and popping sound of the flames consuming the barn and cabin follow us as we walk to the car, the sound becoming more distant the further we move away. Eventually it fades completely.

The barn will never again steal another precious minute from any innocent person's life. Never again will it hold a prisoner captive. Even though the barn is gone, the memories of it and the terror I experienced will never go away. I will try to push them into the deepest recesses of my mind and lock them there forever.

I refuse to let them rob me of another precious minute of my life.

"Let's go home," I say softly to Apela, clutching him to my chest. "We have new memories to make."

The End

ABOUT THE AUTHOR

J.D. Guice is a retired registered nurse living in her small hometown in northwest Georgia. She lives with her husband, four cats, a dog, and a horse.

Guice found her creative love of writing after dabbling in painting and drawing. Having a passion for reading mystery, suspense thrillers, murder, and romance novels, she gets her writing inspiration from her life-long beloved genre.

She continues to write with her cozy and imaginative spirit and has plans for more books.